THE
AMULET
OF
POWER

By Mike Resnick
Published by Ballantine Books

KIRINYAGA
LARA CROFT: TOMB RAIDER: THE AMULET
   OF POWER

THE
AMULET
OF
POWER

MIKE RESNICK

BALLANTINE BOOKS • NEW YORK

Lara Croft: Tomb Raider: The Amulet of Power is a work of fiction. Names, places, and incidents either are a product of the author's imagination or are used fictitiously.

A Del Rey® Book
Published by The Random House Publishing Group
Copyright © 2003 by Core Design Limited

All rights reserved under International and Pan-American Copyright Conventions. Published in the United States by The Random House Publishing Group, a division of Random House, Inc., New York, and simultaneously in Canada by Random House of Canada Limited, Toronto.

Del Rey is a registered trademark and the Del Rey colophon is a trademark of Random House, Inc.

www.delreydigital.com

ISBN 0-345-46171-1

Manufactured in the United States of America

First Edition: December 2003

OPM   10   9   8   7   6   5   4   3   2   1

To Carol, as always

And to Kristine Kathryn Rusch
and Dean Wesley Smith
fine writers
fine editors
finer friends

PROLOGUE

She awoke to a dull throbbing at the base of her skull. She tried to touch it gingerly with her fingers, but found that she couldn't move her left hand.

What's happened? she wondered hazily. And then: *Why can't I breathe?*

Her mouth was filled with dust, and some instinct made her turn her head slightly before she inhaled through her nostrils.

Where am I?

Then, very slowly, it came back to her. She almost wished it hadn't. She was buried in the rubble of a tomb beneath the Temple of Horus in the Egyptian town of Edfu. Something was pinning her left arm to the ground, something bigger than a rock, smaller than a boulder.

Were her legs pinned, too? She didn't know. She couldn't feel them.

She tried to open her eyes to see if there was any light in the tomb. Her left eye opened. It was pitch black. Her right was stuck shut; a tear had mixed with the dust to form a layer of mud that glued her eyelashes together.

All right. Don't panic. Can I move my right arm?

She tried. It worked.

Okay, I can't free the left arm. Is it broken? Do the fingers work?

The fingers moved.

What am I doing here?

Slowly it came back to her. Set, the evil Egyptian god she had inadvertently set free, the battle, and finally his capture.

And then, in her moment of triumph, the collapse of the temple.

How about the rest of me? Can I roll over, sit up, move one way or another?

She tensed, ready to try, and the pain in her skull became so great that she passed out again.

She dreamed that she was stuck to a gigantic spiderweb. The more she tried to pull free, the more she was held motionless.

"Is someone there?"

Oh my God, she thought, still in her dream, *the spider is talking to me!*

She squirmed, trying to free herself, but she couldn't move her left arm or her legs.

"If you're there, call out!"

Call out and let the spider know where I am? How foolish does it think I am?

"Hang on! I'm almost there!"

It's almost here! I've got to get loose!

She twisted desperately, but the web held her tight.

She heard noises, rocks scraping against rocks, and the air was filled with clouds of dust again. Then a beam of light fell upon her.

Her skull began throbbing once more. The fingers of her right hand gathered up a handful of dust.

This isn't an ant or a fly you're coming after, spider. This is Lara Croft, and I don't plan to die without a fight!

She forced her left eye open, and saw a hand reaching for her. It was puzzling. She could have sworn spiders didn't have hands.

It had to be a trick, a way to get her to trust it. She waited until the spider's hand was inches away, then threw the dust where she knew its eyes would be.

"Damn it!" snapped the spider in perfect English. "What did you do that for?"

She tried to rasp out the words, "Get away from me or I'll kill you!" but her mouth was still filled with dust, and she could only cough weakly.

Two hands began moving the rubble off her.

That's very strange behavior for a spider.

Suddenly the spider's face was very near her own. It looked exactly like a human being, a rather handsome one at that.

"You're safe now," it said as it began lifting her up.

She was trying to remember whether spiders could lie when she passed out again.

PART I

——— · ———

EGYPT

1

This time she was able to open both eyes, and was almost blinded by the brilliant whiteness of her surroundings. She wondered if her left arm was working yet. She was able to move it slightly, but it felt strange. She looked at it and saw a pair of tubes going into it. That meant something, but she couldn't quite think of what.

Her head still hurt, and her eyes had trouble staying focused. She tried to wiggle her toes. It *felt* like they were moving. She looked to make sure, and found that she couldn't see them.

"My feet!" she rasped. "Where are my feet?"

She heard a deep masculine chuckle, and then a hand pulled away what she only then recognized as a bedsheet, revealing her bare feet.

"They were hiding from you," said an amused voice with a cultivated British accent.

She stared at the owner of the voice. It was the same face she'd seen in the tomb. He was a tall man, a bit on the lean side, tanned from long exposure to the sun. His hair had probably been sandy at one point, but it had been bleached almost white by the sun. She'd been right, back in the tomb: He *was* handsome, though at the moment he needed a shave and a change of clothes.

"Welcome back to the world. I thought we were going to lose you for a while there. It was quite a trip; I drove you all the way here from Edfu."

"Where is here?"

"You're in the Cairo Hospital."

She stared at him without speaking.

"Where are my manners?" he said. "Allow me to introduce myself. I am Kevin Mason." He paused. "And you are . . . ?"

"Lara Croft."

"Lara Croft," repeated Mason. "I've heard of you."

She continued staring at him, trying to get her brain to function. "Kevin Mason," she repeated.

"That's right."

She frowned. "You can't be Kevin Mason, the archaeologist. I know him."

"I'm his son—Kevin Mason Junior." He smiled. "Just Kevin to my friends."

"I've read all your father's books," said Lara. "He's one of my heroes."

"He's one of mine, too," said Mason. "That's why I followed in his footsteps. I'm an archaeologist, too."

She tried to clear the cobwebs from her mind. "You saved my life."

"Just a stroke of luck. I heard—well, *felt* is probably the proper word—I felt the tomb collapse. And I had to assume that if it hadn't collapsed in over two thousand years, there had to be a reason, so I had my men help me open it up." He stared at her. "You were in a bad way. I don't think you could have survived another hour trapped in there. I carried you to my car and drove to the Edfu infirmary, but they were having one of their periodic power outages, so I brought you here, to Cairo. You've been in hospital for almost five hours now."

"And when can I get out of here?" asked Lara.

Mason shrugged. "You've been banged up pretty thoroughly, and you've suffered a severe concussion, but they don't think anything's broken. Probably a day or two of bed rest and you'll be as good as new—though they need to make sure you haven't done any lasting damage to your lungs by breathing in all that dust." He smiled.

"Can you find me a mirror?"

"Trust me," said Mason. "You don't want to look at yourself. Not right now."

"Please," she insisted.

"As you wish," he said, walking to the bathroom and returning with a mirror that had hung on the wall. "But remember: You've been warned."

Lara took the mirror and studied the face that stared out at her. Both eyes were blackened and almost swollen shut. A roll of cotton had been inserted in her right nostril to keep it from collapsing. Her lips were dry and cracked and covered with crusted blood, her jaw was badly swollen, and her hair was still caked with dust.

"Could be worse," she muttered, handing the mirror back to him.

"Well, I'll be damned!" said Mason. "Most women would burst into tears if they looked like that."

"I'm not most women."

A nurse entered just then, walked silently to the bed, took Lara's pulse and temperature, scribbled her readings on a chart, and left.

Lara tried to sit up to better see and converse with the man who had saved her, but the effort produced blinding pains in her skull, and she fell back onto the bed.

"Hey, take it easy," said Mason. "I told you—you've had a major concussion." He pulled a chair up to the bed. "Here," he said, sitting down. "Now you don't have to move to see me."

"I read your father's paper on ancient Sudanese artifacts just last month," said Lara as the pain began to subside. "It was brilliant."

"On his behalf, I thank you. The Sudan's become my field of study, too."

"Then what were you doing here in Egypt at the Temple of Horus?"

"The Sudan is my specialty, but my field of study encompasses all of North Africa. I felt it was time for a change, so I came to Egypt." He smiled again—a very handsome smile, she noted. "It's a damned lucky thing I did. The temple is off-limits to tourists while they're restoring some of the hieroglyphs. It was all but empty when the tomb collapsed."

"Lucky is an understatement," she said.

"Maybe it wasn't all due to luck," he amended. "You keep yourself in remarkable condition. Most people wouldn't have survived."

"I've survived worse," she said.

He raised an eyebrow. "I believe you, Ms. Croft."

"I think you've earned the right to call me Lara, Dr. Mason."

"Kevin," he said.

"Tell me, Kevin. What were you looking for at the Temple of Horus?"

"Oh, nothing in particular," he answered with a shrug.

Nobody digs for "nothing in particular," she thought, studying his expression. *Oh, well, there's no reason why you should share any information with me. I'm certainly not going to grill you. You saved my life; that's more than enough.*

As if reading her thoughts, he said, "One never knows what rare and beautiful artifacts might turn up in these old temples. They're always worth a visit. After all, I found you, didn't I?" He smiled again, and continued, "I'll stick around Cairo for a day or two to make sure you're all right, and then I'll go back to work."

"I'm fine," she said. "There's no reason you have to stay."

"I've never settled for half-measures as an archaeologist, and I won't settle for them as a hero," he said wryly. "As long as I'm responsible for your life, I'm going to make sure it's properly restored to you."

"I appreciate it, Kevin, but . . ."

He held a hand up. "It's settled."

She was going to protest again, but the pain returned, and she just lay still, waiting for it to subside.

"I know why *I* was at the Temple," Mason said after a moment, staring at her intently, "but I've no idea what *you* were doing there."

"You wouldn't believe me if I told you," she said, remembering how Set had screamed in rage when she'd returned the evil god to his prison.

"I won't ask what you were searching for—that's your business. But if you left something behind in the wreckage, Lara, I'd be happy to look for it. It would remain your discovery, of course," he added hastily.

"I appreciate that, Kevin, but there was nothing, really."

"That was quite a bump on the noggin you received. If

anything should come back to you, I assure you I don't steal artifacts or credit from my peers."

"I'm sure you don't."

He got to his feet. "They have this ridiculous policy at this place of only feeding patients, so if you'll excuse me, I'm going to go out for dinner. I'll be back in a few hours to see how you're doing."

"You've done enough already."

He smiled. "Don't make me lecture you again."

"All right." Then, "You have a very nice smile."

He looked embarrassed. "So do you. I think. Perhaps someday I'll actually get to see it."

She tried to smile, but her dry lips started to split, and she groaned instead.

"No hurry," said Mason. "Let's not rush anything—not even a smile."

Then he was gone.

2

Lara drifted in and out of sleep. She kept dreaming of spiders that turned into Kevin Mason—or perhaps it was Kevin Mason turning into a spider. As if that wasn't bad enough, the slightest movement sent pain shooting up and down her arm. Soon her head was aching again, and sleep was impossible. She made an effort to sit up despite the pain, but the IV tubes in her arm made movement difficult.

With a sigh she gave up the struggle and lay back on the soft pillow. There was so much noise outside the door, so many people walking up and down the hospital corridor. Didn't they know there were sick people here, people who were trying to sleep?

She began listening to the footsteps, making a game of identifying them in the semidarkness of her room. This was the heavy-footed intern. That was the idiot nurse who'd worn high heels to work and *click-click-click*ed up and down the tiled corridor. This other one was a doctor with his entourage of students, lecturing as he walked to the operating theater.

And then there was the thud.

A *thud*? Finally she figured it out. Some orderly must have dropped a pile of laundry while he went into the next room to strip the bed.

Suddenly the light from the corridor shone across her darkened room.

Why was the orderly coming in here? Didn't he know this bed was occupied?

Then she saw that it wasn't one orderly, it was two. And they weren't dressed like orderlies. They wore the robes of

Arab tribesmen from the desert—and one of them had a knife in his hand.

Lara tried to roll off the bed, but the IVs held her in place.

"Who are you?" she demanded, ignoring the pain in her arm. "What do you want?"

Neither man said a word. They were tall, over six feet in height, and carried themselves like warriors. The one with the knife approached her and raised the blade high above his head, ready to plunge it down into her.

"You've got the wrong person!" she rasped hoarsely. "I've never seen either of you in my life!"

The two men exchanged glances, and then the knife came down.

Lara twisted at the last second. The knife barely missed her, burying itself deep in the hospital bed. She pulled the tubes from her arm—it hurt like hell, and blood began leaking from the wounds she had created—but an instant later she was on her feet, confronting her attackers, trying to ignore the blinding pain in her head. She opened her mouth to scream for help, but one of the men, the one without a knife, gestured with his hand, and suddenly her voice was gone, silenced.

Instinctively, she reached for her pistols, but all she had on was a hospital gown. She tried to focus her eyes as the two men silently closed in on her, but a wave of dizziness and nausea swept over her.

The man with the knife approached her and held out his hand as if he expected her to give him something.

I'll give you something, all right!

She landed a kick in his groin. He grunted and hit her across the face with a backhand blow that sent her careening into the trolley that held the dangling IV tubes.

The man with the knife grinned at her and charged. Lara grabbed a tube, ducked under his extended arm, sidestepped, and quickly wrapped the tube around his neck, yanking with all her strength. The man collapsed, gasping for breath, his knife clattering noisily to the floor as he clawed at his throat.

The second man was on her before she could turn to face him. She tried to twist loose, but she was too weak. Blood was still flowing from her arm, and her head felt like it was about to explode.

One bitter thought raced through her mind as she grappled with her attacker: *After all the things I've survived, I'm going to be murdered by men I've never seen before, and I don't even know why!*

She forced herself to remain conscious, to fight off the pain long enough to sell her life as dearly as possible. Maybe she was too weak to stand, maybe her weapons were buried beneath the Temple of Horus, but she still had teeth and fingernails. They wouldn't do much harm, but at least she'd die fighting, however futilely.

And then, through a haze of pain and nausea, she became aware of a third man in the room. Like her opponents, he remained silent, but she soon heard the sound of bones crunching, and suddenly she wasn't being held any longer. She fell to the floor, then rolled against a wall to avoid the battle.

And some battle it was. The man who had just entered the room landed a haymaker. It would have decked any normal man, but the big Arab just grunted, shook his head, and hurled himself at the newcomer—and now she could see that the intruder was Kevin Mason.

Mason sidestepped the charge, picked up a bottle—she had no idea what was in it, and probably he didn't either—and hurled it into the man's face. The man's mouth opened in a soundless scream, and he ran toward the door, covering his eyes. He missed, ran headfirst into a wall, and fell to the floor in a senseless heap.

Meanwhile the knife-wielding Arab was back on his feet again. He charged at Mason without a word. Mason's left hand shot out and grabbed the man's wrist, holding the knife away. With his right hand he landed two quick blows to the Arab's belly, then took a left to the jaw and staggered back.

Don't trade punches with him! Use your brain, not your muscles.

The Arab charged again at Mason, his knife raised above his head. Mason ducked and stepped forward, and the larger man, caught by surprise, spun over Mason and landed on his back. Mason kicked the knife out of his hand, then knelt down and began pummeling him, again and again, right, left, right, left. Teeth flew out of the Arab's mouth, blood poured out of his nose, and finally he lost consciousness. Mason got to his feet. "Are you all right, Lara?"

"That's twice you've saved me," she replied weakly. As suddenly as it had disappeared, her voice was back.

"This could become a habit," remarked Mason. He turned on the light, then began looking through shelves and cabinets.

"What are you doing?"

"You may not be aware of it," he replied, "but you're bleeding rather badly. We've got to get you bandaged up. Ah, here it is!"

He pulled out a roll of tape and a tube of antiseptic ointment. Then, kneeling down next to her, he swabbed away most of the blood with a towel, rubbed on the ointment as best he could, and began taping her arm.

"I'm afraid that will have to do," he announced when he had finished.

"It's not a very good job," she noted.

"I'm not a very good doctor—and I need the rest of the tape for *them*."

He knelt down and bound the two men's hands behind their backs with tape, then taped their feet together as well. By the time he was done, both had regained consciousness.

"All right," said Mason. "Are you alone or did you come with others?"

They stared at him sullenly.

"I'm only going to ask you one more time," he said. "Are you alone?"

No answer.

He picked up the knife that had nearly killed Lara. "If you won't talk, then you won't need your tongues. . . ."

At this threat, the men merely smiled. Their grins spread grotesquely wide. Empty.

"Ugh," said Lara. "Looks like someone beat you to it."

Before Mason could reply, both men began gasping for breath. A moment later they were dead.

"What the hell?" Mason frowned. "I was just bluffing with the knife. . . ."

"Afraid you scared them to death? Not those two. I've read of assassins trained from infancy, their tongues cut out to make them creatures of silence. I never believed those tales—until now." She paused. "Let's get a doctor up here to determine what killed them."

"We haven't got time," said Mason, wiping his fingerprints from the knife and dropping it. "They obviously know you're here, and if the hospital discovers the bodies, we'll both be held for questioning."

"*Who* obviously knows I'm here?" she demanded.

"The people the assassins worked for. We've got to get you to someplace where you'll be safe." He looked directly into her eyes. "I'm going to ask you one more time: Did you find anything in the Temple?"

"I told you I didn't," she answered. "What's going on here?"

"I'll tell you when we have a little time. But those two aren't the only ones they'll be sending after you."

"That *who* will be sending after me?" she insisted. "Why did two men I never saw before want to kill me?"

"Later." He helped her to her feet. "Are you strong enough to walk by yourself?"

"I don't know."

Mason frowned. "If you collapse in front of anyone, I'll never get you out of here." He paused. "I'll get a wheelchair and bring it back." He looked around, picked up a white laundry bag, and handed it to her. "These are your clothes. The hospital washed them. I know you're groggy, but try to get into them while I'm gone."

"Why?" she asked, fighting off another wave of dizziness.

"Because once we get out of here, I can't take a beautiful woman through a Moslem country with her backside peeking out of her hospital gown."

"I should have thought of that," said Lara.

"If you didn't have a lump the size of a baseball on the back of your head, I'm sure you would have. Now hurry up."

Then he was gone, and Lara took off her gown and climbed slowly, painfully, into her clothes. Her holsters were there, but her pistols were gone. Back in the tomb, probably. Which meant they were as good as gone. She felt a pang. She was going to miss those guns.

Mason came back about half a minute after she'd finished, wearing a doctor's white lab coat and pushing a wheelchair.

"In case you're wondering," said Mason, "your pistols are in my car. If you'd still been wearing them when I brought you in here, they'd be locked away in some hospital safe now."

"That's another one I owe you." She sat in the wheelchair while he walked over to the bed, pulled off a pair of lightweight blankets, and covered her with them.

"You're not exactly wearing hospital garb," he said as he tucked them around her. "No sense advertising it."

Then they were out in the corridor, and he wheeled her past the nurse's station to an elevator. The door closed and the elevator began descending.

"So far so good," said Mason.

The elevator stopped at the main floor, and the door slid open. Mason quickly surveyed the lobby. There were half a dozen doctors milling about, a trio of nurse's stations, a registration desk, and two uniformed policemen standing by the door.

"Now what?" Lara asked in a whisper.

"Hopefully this white coat I'm wearing will make them think I'm a doctor. Better cross your fingers under those blankets, Lara—here we go." He took a deep breath and wheeled her to the main entrance.

One of the guards stared at him curiously, but Mason simply smiled and continued walking, and the guard stepped aside and allowed him to wheel Lara out of the hospital and over to a late-model Land Rover.

"That was either very brave or very stupid," Lara said. "I'm not sure which."

"I read in a spy novel once that the best way to deflect suspicion is to act like you've got nothing to hide." He opened the passenger door and carefully helped her to her feet. "Can you climb in by yourself?"

"Of course I can," said Lara. She tried to pull herself onto the seat. Suddenly another wave of dizziness overcame her, and she fell back into Mason's arms. "Well, I *thought* I could."

He helped her into the Land Rover, then walked around and took his place in the driver's seat.

"Where are we going?" asked Lara.

"Away from here," said Mason. "If I step on it, we can be out of Cairo in half an hour."

"Where are my pistols?"

"The glove compartment."

She opened it, found her passport and billfold, which she pocketed, and her pistols, which she slipped lovingly into their holsters.

"Those are very unusual guns," said Mason. "I don't think I've ever seen anything quite like them."

She pulled a pistol out. "This is the Wilkes and Hawkins Black Demon .32."

"Custom job?"

"Modified to my specifications," she answered. "Fifteen shots to the clip, and it's just this side of a hair trigger. Sculpted to fit my hand, and weighted exactly as I directed—and it's got a chip that reads my palm print. No one else can fire it." She slid the pistol back into its holster. "There's not a more accurate pistol around."

"Interesting," said Mason, pulling onto a main thoroughfare.

"Are you ready to tell me what this is all about?" asked Lara.

Mason's reply was to swerve the car into a narrow alley and floor the gas pedal. "We've got company," he said, looking into the rearview mirror as three cars entered the alley behind them.

He veered onto a side street, then another, and finally hit another main drag.

"I'm going to ask you one more time," said Mason, trying to keep the urgency from his voice. "Did you find *anything*, no matter how trivial or unimportant, in the Temple?"

"I already told you," said Lara irritably. "No." She paused, trying to order her thoughts. "The men in my hospital room, and these men who are chasing us—how did they know I'd been to the Temple of Horus, anyway?"

"They—or the ones they work for—were keeping a watch on it."

The back window shattered as a bullet crashed through.

"Keep your head down," warned Mason.

"But why did they come after me?" demanded Lara, ducking. "Why didn't they simply steal what they wanted from the Temple of Horus?"

"Because they couldn't find it," said Mason. He swerved sharply as another bullet took away his side mirror.

Just what have I stumbled into? Lara wondered as the Land Rover sped south along the Nile.

3

"Damn!" muttered Mason as they raced out of the city and into the desert.

"What now?" asked Lara.

"I can't outrun them." He glanced at the rearview mirror again. "They're not gaining on us, but I'm not putting any more distance between us . . . and I have to. There's nothing between here and Luxor, and I don't have enough petrol to get us there."

"Where are the police?"

"Maybe they've been bribed. Maybe they stop at the city limits. Maybe they just don't expect people to be racing down the highway at three in the morning. Whatever the reason, I haven't seen one since we left the hospital."

"Then we'll have to make a fight of it."

He grimaced. "There are six or seven men in those cars, maybe more—and you're in no condition to fight."

"You worry about the driving," said Lara. "I'll worry about the fighting."

"Lara . . ." he began.

"Just drive," she said. She turned in her seat, steadied her hand against the headrest, aimed her Black Demon out the gaping hole where the back window had been, and heard a *click* as the hammer fell on an empty chamber. She pulled the trigger twice more. Two more *clicks*.

"Kevin?"

"Yes, Lara?"

"Where are my bullets?"

"That's what I was trying to tell you." He reached into a

pocket and tossed a handful of sleek narrow clips to her. "I emptied them for your own good," he explained. "I knew I might have to take you out of hospital tonight, and I knew you would want your guns, but I didn't want you firing them. In your condition, you're as likely to shoot me or yourself as an enemy."

"Let *me* worry about my condition," she said furiously, ignoring the pain in her head and loading the clips into the weapons. "And don't ever mess with my pistols again."

He was about to answer when a bullet smacked into the dash between them. Mason cursed and resumed swerving as the speedometer crept up to 110 miles an hour.

Lara tried to focus her eyes on the pursuing vehicles. It seemed to get blurrier and darker, and the next thing she knew, Mason's hand was on her shoulder and he was shaking her awake.

"Are you all right?" he asked. "You passed out."

"We've stopped!" she exclaimed.

"For the moment."

She began blinking her eyes furiously. "How long have I been out?"

"Perhaps an hour, perhaps a little more."

She looked around. "Where are the bad guys?"

"Probably hunting for us in Luxor by now. At least, I hope so."

"I don't understand."

"We're in a village of sorts. I suppose it has a name, but it's not on any map I've ever seen. Most of these small villages aren't. The road began twisting and turning for a few miles, and once I was out of their line of sight I pulled in behind a couple of buildings. They went past and never gave us a look."

"What now?"

"I've only got about two gallons of petrol, if that much. I can't get us to Luxor and I can't go back to Cairo—and I've been up and down this road often enough to know that there aren't any petrol stations within fifty miles."

"Then I repeat: What now?"

"A few of the locals stopped by to see who we were, and I've made an arrangement with them," said Mason. "We'll take a small dhow to Luxor and then hop one of the bigger cruise boats going south."

"That could take hours," said Lara. "Why not drive toward Luxor until we're out of petrol and *then* go the rest of the way on the Nile?"

"You're still not thinking clearly," said Mason.

"See how well *you* think after a temple falls down on you!"

"Point taken," said Mason. "I'm assuming our friends are searching for us in Luxor—but there's always a chance they'll figure out they passed us, and I'd prefer not to meet them head-on as they come back looking for us."

"Let's get on with it before I start passing out again," she said. "How far do we have to go?"

"The river's only about forty yards away, and the dhow's right there. Do you think you can make it?"

She was about to nod her head, but some instinct told her not to. Instead she merely grunted a "Yes," climbed out of the Land Rover, and began walking, Mason at her side. Once they reached the river, he helped her into the boat, fixed the sail, pushed off from shore, and jumped in.

"Nice dhow," he said.

"It's called a *felluca* on the Nile," she corrected him absently.

"Whatever," said Mason with a shrug. "The fellow who rented me the dhow—er, *felluca*—has a ham radio. He was able to find out what tour boats are in Luxor now."

"Is there one in particular that you want?"

"The least popular, of course," answered Mason. "There's a grubby little boat, only twenty cabins, called the *Amenhotep*, privately owned, and it's due to leave an hour after sunrise. The owner is the captain, and there's no office. He picks up any passengers who happen to be handy and takes off, so if we can get there in time to board it, there'll be no way to trace us." He smiled. "If we don't die of food poisoning, I think we'll be safe."

"For how long?" asked Lara.

"For as long as it takes."

She was getting tired of half-answers. "As long as *what*

takes?" she demanded angrily—and the anger and tension sent bolts of pain shooting through her skull again.

"Careful!" said Mason, reaching over and steadying her by the shoulder. "I know the Nile's not very deep, but we don't want you falling overboard anyway."

She tried to answer him, found she couldn't speak, and lay back, allowing consciousness to float away on the warm Egyptian breeze.

4

Lara was lying on a lumpy mattress with her head resting on a torn pillow. Mason was sitting on a wooden stool right next to her.

"What happened?" she asked.

He smiled. "You caught up on your sleep."

"How long this time?"

"Damned near twenty-four hours," said Mason. "How do you feel?"

She ran a mental survey of her various aches and pains. "Better," she said. "Much better."

"Good. I'm sorry I had to rush you out of hospital, but it really couldn't be avoided."

Lara looked around the tiny, decrepit room. "Where are we?"

"Aboard the *Amenhotep*," answered Mason. "We made it before sunrise, and this is the kind of boat where no one saw anything unusual about picking up two British passengers from a beat-up *felluca*, even though one of them was unconscious." He paused. "Are you hungry? I don't think you've eaten since I found you in the Temple of Horus."

"They fed me a light dinner at hospital," she replied. "But I *am* famished."

"I'll get you something." He walked to the door. "I'll be back soon."

"I think I'm up to coming with you," she said, swinging her feet to the floor.

"Bad idea."

"Look, Kevin. I'm grateful that you saved me, but I don't like being patronized," said Lara. "If you explain *why* it's a bad idea, I'll listen; if you just state it, talk to the wall—it will be a more receptive audience than I will."

Mason looked annoyed, but acquiesced to her demand. "Only two or three people saw us come aboard, and it was too dark for them to see that you're a beautiful woman with a pair of black eyes. Whoever's looking for us is looking for a couple, and they know that the woman was pretty badly banged up. Let's not make it too easy for them."

"I thought you told me that this was a tiny boat and no one would find us here," said Lara.

"I said they wouldn't think to *look* for us here," responded Mason. "But that doesn't mean the word isn't out that they *are* looking for us. Why give the crew or the passengers any information to sell?"

"All right," she said, putting her feet back up. "But when you get back, we're going to have a long talk about exactly what's going on."

"I promise," he said as he walked out onto the deck and closed the door behind him.

Lara ran her hands down her hips and realized that her holsters were missing. She sat up abruptly—there was some pain, but nothing like the day before—and then relaxed as she saw the holsters, pistols still in them, sitting on a crooked wooden table. She checked: The Black Demon .32s were loaded, ready to spit death at whoever was after her.

She stood up, expecting to experience horrible stabbing pains in her head and being pleasantly surprised when they didn't occur, then entered the bathroom. There was a sour taste in her mouth, and she wanted to rinse it out. She turned on the tap and a very thin stream of brownish water trickled out. She decided to live with the taste.

She took a thorough inventory of her various wounds, bruises, and abrasions. She picked up the only towel, which was ragged and had three small holes in it, and wiped off the filthy mirror over the sink. The swelling was down on her left eye, still pretty big there on her right—and both eyes would stay black for at least a few more days.

She gently pulled the bloodstained wad of cotton out of her

nostril and took a breath. No obstructions, and her nose didn't look or feel broken, so she decided not to reinsert it.

Her lips were still cracked and dry. She toyed with rubbing some of the brown water on them, then decided against it. Whatever drink Mason brought her—juice, bottled water, tea, coffee—would serve the same purpose and probably wasn't filled with dysentery germs and bilharzia mites.

She tried raising and lowering her left arm. No problem. Then she bent it—and winced. Whatever had pinned her back in the tomb had evidently fallen onto her elbow. It didn't look swollen, and she was pretty sure it wasn't broken, but it was still very sore.

Still, she could live with all the cuts and bruises, as long as the pain in her head subsided and she stopped losing her balance and passing out every fifteen minutes or so. She turned and took a few tentative steps around the tiny room, secure in the knowledge that if she did fall, she would almost certainly land on the bed. Her knees hurt, her ankles were stiff, and there was a momentary wave of dizziness, but it was so much better than she'd felt in the hospital or the car or the *felluca* that she mentally pronounced herself Ready and Able.

Now, as soon as Mason returned, she was determined to find out exactly what she was Ready and Able *for*.

He entered the room almost as the thought crossed her mind, and set a tray down at the foot of the bed.

"I'm afraid the food isn't much better than the accommodations," he apologized, and then pointed to the various things on the tray. "Mango juice, melon of some sort, tea. I tried to get some eggs, but they don't have any. Ditto for coffee, in case you prefer it to tea."

"This will be fine," she said, taking a sip of the juice. It burned the cuts on her lips, but at least they didn't feel quite so dry once she had finished. Mason walked to the wooden stool and seated himself, and she turned to him. "It's time for answers, Kevin. Who are these people, and why are they trying to kill me?"

"What do you know about the Amulet of Mareish?" asked Mason.

"Just that it's supposed to be about four thousand years old and that it was created by a Sudanese sorcerer named Mareish. It is said to give its possessor certain extraordinary powers, two of which are great physical strength and invulnerability, and a third is immortality. It is said that he who owns it will possess irresistible charisma and be an absolute ruler of men. Supposedly, once Mareish realized just how powerful it was, he didn't trust his king or anyone else with it, and he took it with him to his grave. Most people think that it's a myth."

"And what do you think?"

"I have no opinion. Why?"

"Because it's not a myth," said Mason. "It is very real, and quite possibly the most powerful artifact in the world."

Lara shook her head. "If it existed, and did all that the legends say, someone would be wearing it right now, ruling the world and living forever. Or are you going to tell me it's still buried in Mareish's tomb?"

"No," he said. "It is not in Mareish's tomb. I've looked there."

"Well, this is all very interesting, whether true or a fairy tale, but it doesn't explain why people are trying to kill me."

"Hear me out," said Mason. "They're after you because they think you've got the Amulet."

"That doesn't make any sense!" Lara protested. "It's a Sudanese artifact. Why in the world would they think that it's here in Egypt?"

"Because Chinese Gordon was smarter than anyone gave him credit for."

"Chinese Gordon?" she repeated. There was something familiar about that name. . . . Then she had it. "Are you talking about General Charles Gordon?"

"You *are* feeling better," said Mason with a smile. "Gordon made his reputation by winning a series of absolutely brilliant battles in China in 1863 and 1864, and got his nickname there, too. Chinese Gordon, the Englishman who was the equivalent of any ten Chinese generals—or so they liked to say."

"I've read about him," said Lara. "He was one of the great Victorian heroes. After China they sent him to the Sudan, and he single-handedly ended slavery there. He was probably more popular than anyone in England except Queen Victoria herself."

"With people who didn't know him, anyway," said Mason. "He was a hardheaded, totally undisciplined sort, always ignoring his orders. The only reason he wasn't mustered out was because he succeeded spectacularly every time he disobeyed his superiors." He paused. "They even made a motion picture about him. Huge budget. Of course they hired an American, Charlton Heston, to portray him, but then what can you expect from Hollywood?"

"Okay, we're talking about the same General Gordon, the one who died at the fall of Khartoum," said Lara. "That was in 1885, well over a century ago. What does it have to do with me?"

"I'm coming to that," said Mason. "Eat your melon and be patient."

"I'm not much better at taking orders than Gordon was," she shot back. "I'll eat when I'm ready to."

"I thought you were starving."

"Just keep talking."

He shrugged. "Where was I?"

"The fall of Khartoum."

"No," he corrected her. "Earlier than that. There was a Sudanese warrior, a holy man known as the Mahdi—the Expected One. I think Sir Laurence Olivier played him in the movie. Typical Hollywood, eh? Anyway, we sent an army against him, and he led them deeper and deeper into the desert and eventually destroyed them, down to the very last man. It was one of the worst defeats in our history."

"I know. That's when the government decided to send Gordon back to the Sudan."

"Well, yes and no. We were putting down uprisings in South Africa and all over the world, and the government didn't want yet another war. But they couldn't just wash their hands of it, not with an entire army dead in the desert and the public demanding action. So they hit upon sending their greatest hero—Gordon, of course—to the Sudan. But because they didn't want a war, they sent him with just a couple officers and nothing else: no army, no money, no artillery. He was to go there, putter around for a while, and come home, and then the government could mollify the people by saying, in essence, 'Well, if Gordon couldn't solve the situation, then it obviously can't be solved.' "

She nodded. "But it didn't work out that way."

Mason smiled. "Gordon disobeyed his orders, as always. Even though the Mahdi commanded an army of more than a million men, Gordon put together a battalion of ragtag desert warriors, paid them out of his own personal fortune, and actually defeated the Mahdi at Omdurman."

"I know about the fall of Khartoum—every British student learns about it," said Lara. "But I never heard of Omdurman."

"Most people haven't," replied Mason. "Omdurman is just across the Nile from Khartoum. Outnumbered twenty to one, Gordon managed to wrest a victory from the jaws of almost certain defeat. Military scholars think it was a brilliant job of soldiering." He paused for a long moment. "The truth was much stranger."

"In what way?"

"The Mahdi was not the simple illiterate most people think. He left many writings behind. Most have been lost or destroyed, but a few scraps still exist. According to them—and mind you, this was written in his own hand—he received his charismatic power, the ability he had to draw huge numbers of fanatical followers to his cause, even his supposed invulnerability in battle, from a mystic charm that he wore around his neck."

"The Amulet of Mareish?" asked Lara.

"Right," said Mason. "One day he was just an obscure peasant. Then he somehow stumbled onto Mareish's tomb and appropriated the Amulet—he may not even have known what it was at the time. But two years later he controlled half of North Africa, with millions of men from Morocco to Abyssinia believing that he was truly the Expected One. His men swore that as long as he wore the Amulet, swords broke when they hit him and bullets bounced off him, just like a comic-book superhero."

"It's still a fairy tale," said Lara.

"Why do you think so?"

"You just told me Gordon beat him at Omdurman, and I know that Gordon held him off for almost half a year during the Siege of Khartoum. How could he do either of those things if the Amulet was as powerful as you say?"

"Because Gordon or one of his lieutenants found out about the powers inherent in the Amulet and stole it just before the battle of Omdurman!" said Mason with an air of triumph.

"I'm not buying it," responded Lara. "Why would a modern, educated, sophisticated Englishman believe in the Amulet of Mareish?"

"The answer is that Gordon was as much of a religious fanatic as the Mahdi."

"They were different religions," noted Lara.

"True," he agreed. "But they had the same devout belief in the supernatural."

She stared at him thoughtfully. "Go on," she said after a moment.

"All right," said Mason. "After Omdurman, the Mahdi called a sixty-day halt to his war on the unbelievers while he went into the desert alone to commune with Allah and plan his next move—and Gordon used that time to hide the Amulet."

"I don't remember hearing or reading that Gordon ever returned to Egypt after he was sent to stop the Mahdi," protested Lara.

"He didn't," answered Mason. "But he sent his most trusted aide, Colonel J. D. H. Stewart, to Egypt. Stewart spent only a single day there before returning to Khartoum."

"How do you know that?"

"He was seen out of uniform in Edfu, entering the Temple of Horus, by a local journalist."

"If you know it, why didn't the Mahdi know it—and if he knew it, why didn't he come after the Amulet?"

"The newsman never published what he saw," explained Mason. "He was British, and since he didn't know why Stewart was there, he didn't want to endanger his mission by publicizing it—but his diary turned up a few months ago, and he described the incident in some detail."

"So that's the real reason you were there," said Lara.

"Yes," said Mason. "And that's what I assumed you were hunting for, too."

"You were mistaken. I had bigger fish to fry." *And an evil god to capture.*

"There are no bigger fish." He frowned. "The problem is that we'll never convince *them* of it."

"Who *are* they?"

"Fanatical fundamentalists."

"There seem to be a lot of them around these days," commented Lara with a grimace.

"Not like these," said Mason. "These are Mahdists—absolute believers in the power of the Mahdi. The Mahdi died only five months after Gordon, and they've been waiting for more than a century for someone to pick up his mantle and lead them in a *jihad* against the infidels."

"I should think they've had their choice of leaders over the years," said Lara.

Mason shook his head. "They know that the true successor to the Mahdi will possess the Amulet of Mareish—and the Mahdists believe in the power of the Amulet. 'Belief' is almost too weak a word. They worship it like a god. They think that if they can just gain possession of it, it will somehow call forth a new Mahdi, an indestructible man who can purify the world by slaughtering every last infidel."

"And they're what's been chasing us?"

He nodded. "That's right."

"Well, then they should know I don't have it! I mean, I'm obviously not invulnerable. So why do they keep attacking?"

"It's not that simple, Lara."

"Somehow it never is."

"The Mahdists believe that for the Amulet to function at its most powerful—at full throttle, if you will—the possessor must believe in it totally. If you are a Jew, or a Christian, or even a traditional Moslem, you believe in other things, in God or Jesus or Mohammed, and to the extent that you believe in them, the power of the Amulet is weakened and you *can* be killed. That's why Gordon couldn't use it to defeat the Mahdi. He must have been tempted—after all, it would have worked to *some* extent—but he knew it was ultimately evil, and he was devout enough to turn his back on it and hide it where no one could use it."

She considered what she had heard for a moment, then looked directly at him. "Do you believe in it?"

"I believe it exists. I believe that the Mahdi accomplished things that seem almost like magic. And I believe he was never the same after he lost possession of it."

"Why should you say that?" asked Lara curiously. "He took Khartoum and killed Gordon, didn't he?"

"Yes, he killed Gordon and overran Khartoum—but he outnumbered Gordon's forces twenty-to-one, and even so, Gordon held him at bay for almost half a year. And don't forget—he himself died just months after defeating Gordon." He sighed wearily. "So maybe there's something to it. But what I believe doesn't matter. What matters is that the *Mahdists* believe in it, and there are thousands, maybe tens of thousands, of them."

"And they're all coming after us," said Lara grimly.

Mason shook his head. "The fact of the matter is, they're all coming after *you*. After all, you should have died under that rubble, and you didn't. You may not be invulnerable, but they figure you are a lot harder to kill than a normal person. That's proof enough to them that you have the Amulet. As for me, they assume I'm simply under your charismatic spell." He smiled. "Which isn't far wrong."

"What if I just tell them I don't have it?"

"They won't believe you. You're an infidel, and they believe it's the nature of infidels to lie. Besides, you're not totally unknown in this part of the world, Lara. They'll assume you've got it, and that you plan to sell it or use it yourself."

"You know," she said, "a while back I found myself wondering just what I'd gotten myself into." She grimaced again. "Of all the possibilities that occurred to me, none of them were remotely like this."

"Well, like they say, truth is stranger than fiction," Mason observed.

"It's certainly deadlier," she said.

5

It was late morning when Lara felt strong enough to emerge from her cabin. Mason argued against it for the reasons he had given her earlier, but she refused to stay in her cramped quarters any longer.

"If you're afraid someone will spot us," she said as she walked to the door, "you can stay here. After all, they're looking for a couple."

"They're looking for a girl whose face looks like it's been used for a punching bag," answered Mason. "Whether you're alone or with me, you're not going to be able to hide those bruises."

"Then I'll just have to take my chances," she said sharply. "I've been buried in a tomb, attacked in a hospital, shot at in a car, and now I'm in a room about the size of a broom closet. I've *got* to get some fresh air. I appreciate all your help, but I'm used to taking care of myself. I have a feeling you wouldn't be half this solicitous if I were a man."

"I resent that."

"Resent it all you like," she said. "Just don't deny it. I want you to stop giving me orders and stop treating me as if I was a piece of rare china that might break at any instant."

"All right," he said unhappily. "But at least leave your guns here. They'll stand out even more than your face."

"I wasn't wearing them when you took me to hospital, or when we escaped from it," replied Lara. "Why should my guns identify me?"

"If for no other reason, they're what I'd call an attention-getting device." He stared at her, then shrugged. "What the hell. You're probably the only Western woman on the boat, and you really are quite eye-catching. I don't suppose the guns can make you stand out any more."

She strapped her holsters on, spun the Black Demons into them, and opened the door.

"You're sure you don't want to come with me?"

"I've *seen* the boat," said Mason, making a face. "It's not worth a second look." He stepped out on deck behind her. "I think I'm going to take a nap. Wake me when you've had enough fresh air—which, I might add, is well over one hundred degrees Fahrenheit and getting hotter." He grimaced. "We're a lot safer here, but at least an upscale cruise boat would have been air-conditioned."

She walked out onto the deck, closed the door behind her, and set out to explore the *Amenhotep*. One glance told her that it wasn't going to take very long.

There were ten doors facing the port side. Most of them had obvious mold and mildew damage. A couple had been riddled by termites. The wooden deck was warped and in need of repair. Beyond the rooms was a restaurant that would have had trouble passing a health inspection anywhere in the world. There was a small open area at the back of the boat—she couldn't bring herself to think of it as a ship—that held three rickety wooden chairs and two broken chaise lounges.

She looked over the edge of the rusted railing. The boat was riding too high to have much of a cargo hold. Her first thought had been that it was carrying contraband material, but she quickly concluded that it couldn't be anything heavier than drugs, and in an impoverished country like Egypt there simply wasn't much profit in dealing drugs anywhere south of Cairo. Of course, they could be hauling some stolen antiquities if they were small enough and lightweight enough. . . . But she would never trust any valuable artifact to this dilapidated boat, and she was pretty sure that no one else would either.

Probably, she concluded, looking at three robed men sitting on the wooden chairs, the only cargo was human beings. What kind? She considered the possibilities. They could be felons on the run, men who had paid to be transported from

Luxor to Aswan or even farther south. Perhaps they could even be terrorists. Or, she concluded with a shrug, perhaps the most likely answer was the correct one—that they were passengers who simply couldn't afford any better transportation than the *Amenhotep*.

She looked ashore and tried to get her bearings. If they'd passed Luxor, they'd be coming to Esna and Edfu before long, and Kom Ombo and finally Aswan. The major tour boats plied their trade only between Luxor and Aswan, but she had a feeling that this one was going to follow the Nile a lot farther south. After all, if there were thousands of Mahdists looking for them, it didn't make much sense for Mason to put them on a boat whose route terminated at a major city like Aswan, and it made even less sense to go back to Luxor.

She walked to the front of the boat, nodded pleasantly to the captain, who smiled back at her from the ancient controls inside a wood-and-glass cabin, then crossed to the starboard side. There were ten more rooms, almost identical to the port side, except that one door was missing entirely, and the iron railing was, if anything, even rustier.

As she had on the port side of the boat, she stared across the Nile at the arid landscape beyond, trying to spot some landmark so she would know exactly where they were. They passed by a small village where a dozen children were playing soccer up and down the single dirt street, and then the village ended as abruptly as it had begun and the land was cultivated for the next mile.

It's amazing, she thought. *Here along the Nile, it's like good British farmland—green, rich, fertile. But go just half a mile inland from the river in either direction and it's almost indistinguishable from the Sahara or the Gobi deserts.*

She waved to a *felluca* that carried a quartet of local fishermen. They waved back. One of the men stood up unsteadily, gained his balance, pointed to her pistols, and mimicked a fast draw. She laughed, aimed her finger at him, and pretended to shoot. He grabbed his chest and fell theatrically into the Nile, which seemed to amuse his companions no end.

They finally pulled him out just as the *Amenhotep* passed by, and its wake almost capsized the little fishing boat.

The fishing must have been good, she concluded, because they began passing a number of boats carrying fishermen. She stayed at the railing, still searching for landmarks, returning the waves and smiles of the fishermen, reveling in just being strong enough to remain on her feet and feel the gentle breeze on her swollen face.

She was aware that a number of robed Arabic men had come and gone from the restaurant, and that each had stared at her, some with open hostility, some with semi-open lust, a couple with simple curiosity. None of them approached her, and she felt no urge to initiate contact. For all she knew, any one of them would betray her to the Mahdists. They might even *be* Mahdists. So she remained alone, content merely to stand by the rail and watch the Egyptian landscape pass by.

Another *felluca* approached, this one carrying two fishermen, one wearing a robe, the other in just a loincloth. Both wore turbans. The one in the loincloth called out a greeting in broken English.

"Hi, Missy!" he said, waving his hand at her. "You are most beautiful lady I see all month!"

"Thank you," said Lara.

"You are English, yes?"

"Yes."

"I have been to London," said the man proudly. "London Bridge. Buckingham Palace. Piccadilly Circus."

"And I have been to Cairo," replied Lara. "The pyramids. The sphinx. The Mosque of Ibn Tulun."

The man laughed. "You are good traveler, Missy."

"A frequent traveler, anyway."

"What happen to your face?" asked the man. "Your husband, he find you with another man?"

"I bumped into a door."

The *felluca* drifted closer. "Very hard door," said the man, peering at her blackened eyes. Suddenly he noticed her pistols. "Why you wear guns, Missy?" he asked. "You shoot Egyptian man if he get fresh?"

She smiled. "Get fresh and you'll find out."

"You are inviting me to get fresh?" he said, and broke into a little dance that almost cost him his balance.

She laughed in amusement. Then, out of the corner of her eye, she became aware of a flurry of motion at the other end of the *felluca*. While the man in the loincloth had been holding her attention, the one in the robe had withdrawn a gun and was aiming it at her.

She threw herself to the deck, drawing her Black Demons, and as his bullet bounced off the rusted rail, she snapped off five quick shots. The man clutched at his chest, then screamed once and fell overboard.

Lara turned back to the man in the loincloth. He had a dagger in his hand and was about to throw it when her bullet tore it from his grasp. He looked at his empty hand in disbelief, then turned to Lara.

"Come closer," she said, both pistols trained on him. "I have some questions for you."

The man opened his mouth as if to reply, but then Lara saw that he was gasping for breath, his eyes bulging, his face turning red, his tongue protruding as though ghostly fingers were squeezing his throat. *Just like the men in the hospital,* she thought as her assailant collapsed in the boat without a sound.

She got to her feet and turned around, wondering what kind of attention she'd attracted, but to her surprise, no one was approaching or threatening her. A number of robed men had emerged from the restaurant or their rooms and were looking at her curiously, some sullenly, but no one came toward her. They had their own business to tend to, probably illegal, and if hers required her to kill a couple of fishermen, that was no concern of theirs.

Mason was at her side a moment later.

"What the hell happened?" he asked, looking first at the *felluca* and then glaring at the few men at the back of the boat who were still watching Lara.

"Somebody knows we're here," she said as the men looked away uncomfortably. "They tried to kill me."

"They?" he repeated. "There's just one man in the boat."

"The other's in the river."

He frowned. "Damn! I could have sworn no one saw us get on the *Amenhotep*."

"Probably no one did," said Lara. "I get the feeling that they were checking out each boat as it passed by."

"You should have stayed in the cabin like I told you," said Mason sternly.

"And I told you to stop giving me orders," replied Lara. "Besides, those were just two men. If there are hundreds or thousands of them searching up and down the Nile, we couldn't have remained hidden for long anyway. I think it's reasonable to assume they'll have men boarding or at least inspecting each boat as it stops. There are locks at Edfu, and we'll have to let passengers out at Aswan, so that gives them at least two more cracks at us." She stared at him. "Perhaps you'd better tell me exactly where this boat is going."

"South."

"How far south?"

"It depends."

"On what?"

"On how much more I pay the captain," said Mason. "I gave him enough to take us halfway through the Sudan. I suppose he'll take us all the way to Uganda if I give him enough money."

"At the rate this boat travels, that's weeks off," said Lara. "I think I'd better tend to a more immediate problem."

She leaned over the railing and put another half-dozen shots into the floor of the *felluca*. Water began rushing in, and the little fishing boat began sinking, along with its human cargo.

"That's that," she announced, staring at a pair of bearded faces that appeared at the back of the boat until they vanished back into the restaurant, then spinning the pistols back into their holsters.

"They won't stay hidden forever," said Mason. "Sooner or later those bodies are going to turn up."

"They won't be the first dead bodies to show up in the Nile," said Lara. "Or the thousandth, or probably even the millionth. By the time they're found and identified, either we'll have this business solved, or . . ." She let the sentence linger, unfinished.

"Or what?"

"Or we'll have joined them," answered Lara.

6

"How long before we reach Aswan?" asked Lara as the late-afternoon sun cast long shadows on the deck.

"My guess is that it'll be two or three in the morning," answered Mason.

She nodded. "That gives us plenty of time to get off."

"Get off?" he repeated incredulously. "I paid our fare into the Sudan! We'll never make it there on foot."

"Oh, we'll take the *Amenhotep* to the Sudan," said Lara. "But we won't be on it when it reaches Aswan. Too many probing eyes."

"If you have some plan in mind, I wish you'd share it with me."

"I saw a pair of lifeboats hanging over the side, just before the stern. We'll borrow one after dark, row past the High Dam south of Aswan, and come back aboard tomorrow morning when the *Amenhotep* has gone through one of those channels to the west of the dam and emerged onto Lake Nasser."

Mason considered it. "It might work," he admitted. "It all depends on you."

"On me?"

"We'll be paddling upriver, against the current. Forty-eight hours ago I didn't even know if you'd still be alive today. Are you up to it?"

"If inspectors or police come aboard at Aswan, what are our chances of hiding from them?" she asked.

"Zero."

"Then what choice do we have?"

"None," he admitted.

She looked up at the sky. "The sun doesn't just set in Africa," she noted. "It plummets. I'd say it'll be dark in ninety minutes."

"All right," replied Mason. "I'll meet you here in, shall we say, two hours?"

She shook her head. "You will meet me here in, shall we say, seven hours."

It was his turn to frown. "Seven? Are you sure?"

"Well, you can show up in two hours if you want, but we won't lower the lifeboat for seven."

"Why not?"

"Why row for miles if we don't have to?" said Lara. "We'll be passing Elephantine Island a couple of miles before the Old Dam at Aswan. When we see it, we'll know it's time to get into the lifeboat."

"It makes sense at that," he admitted.

"It may even afford us an easier way of getting past Aswan," she continued. "Elephantine Island is a tourist attraction that houses a beautifully kept botanical garden. There just might be a motorboat or two parked there that we can borrow."

"There might also be an armed guard or three," suggested Mason.

"There might—but it will be dark, and the lifeboat will be silent. They won't know we're there until we're well away from the island, and even if they know it then, how are they going to follow us?"

"In another motorboat."

"At three in the morning?" she said. "I think they'd rather report the theft and claim the insurance."

"You can't be sure of that."

"The only thing I'm sure of is that we're going over the side in seven hours," said Lara. "We'll play it by ear from that point on."

"You're taking a lot of the decision-making upon yourself," he said, trying not to sound petulant.

"Why not?" she shot back. "I'm the one they're after."

He was about to reply, then changed his mind. "What the hell," he said. "When you're right, you're right." He checked his watch. "It's almost five o'clock. I'll see you at midnight."

"Don't oversleep."

"I'm not recovering from a concussion," he said with a smile. "Don't *you* oversleep."

"I've had enough sleep the past two days," Lara assured him. "I won't be sleeping at all."

"I'll see you then," he said, walking off to the cabin next to hers. He pushed the door open, entered, and closed the door behind him.

Lara decided she was getting hungry again, and walked over to the small restaurant. There were six tables. Three of them were occupied by eight men, all wearing robes of varying types. They stared at her silently as she entered and approached the farthest table. There were half a dozen insects fighting over some crumbs that were left over from lunchtime, and she quickly chose a different table.

A small man with a drooping black mustache emerged from the kitchen and crossed over to her.

"What have you got?" she asked him.

"We do not serve unescorted ladies," said the man.

An instant later he found himself staring down the barrels of her Black Demon .32s.

"Allow me to introduce my escorts," said Lara.

"Those are fine escorts," he said quickly as his knees started to shake.

"I repeat: What's on the menu?"

"Lamb."

"What else?"

"The rest of the lamb."

"That being the case, I'll have lamb," said Lara. "What's to drink?"

"Water."

"Bring me some water."

"Yes, ma'am," said the waiter, turning to leave.

"Just a moment," she said sharply. He froze in his tracks, then turned to her. "I know better than to drink from the Nile if there's any alternative. I want you to boil the water, then pour some in a cup and put a tea bag in it."

"We don't have any tea bags."

She cocked the pistol. "You'll find one."

He gulped. "I will find one."

"How very thoughtful of you," she said, twirling the gun and replacing it in her holsters.

The waiter scurried off to the kitchen, and Lara turned to look at the men who had been observing the little scene. Six of them glared at her with undisguised contempt. The two at the table nearest the door, a pair of big burly men, seemed amused. "How's the lamb?" she asked.

"The best that can be said for it is that it is dead," replied one of the burly men.

"Probably," added the other.

"It's probably dead, or that's probably the best that can be said for it?" she asked with a smile.

"Yes," he said, returning her smile.

She laughed, and then the waiter returned with an unappetizing piece of meat on a dirty plate.

"I'm glad to see you didn't risk getting burned," she said dryly.

"I do not understand," said the waiter.

"I like my meat cooked," she said. "Take it back and cook it properly."

"It *is* cooked."

"Are we going to go through all this again?" she said with a weary sigh. Suddenly he was facing her pistols again. "Take it back and cook it."

"I will take it back and cook it!" he shouted, practically running back into the kitchen.

One of the bearded men uttered an offended curse, got up, and stalked out of the restaurant.

"Pay no attention," said the larger of the two men who had spoken to her. "He was finished anyway."

"Then I guess I won't have to suffer from the guilt after all," she replied. This time neither man laughed, and she assumed that their English and her wry humor didn't quite mesh.

The waiter returned and laid the plate before her. She inspected the meat, and nodded her approval.

"Don't forget the tea," she said as he began retreating.

The tea arrived just as she was chewing her first mouthful of lamb, which she had already decided was going to be her last mouthful of lamb. She'd encountered strange diets in her travels, eaten foods that would have revolted most of her countrymen, but she couldn't for the life of her figure out how anyone survived on the cuisine of the *Amenhotep*.

She drank her weak tea, then stood up.

"You are finished?" asked the waiter, who had been watching her from the kitchen door, and now gingerly approached her table again.

"I am finished," she said. "I would throw the lamb into the Nile, but why kill innocent fish?"

This time the two large men chuckled, but the waiter stared at her uncomprehendingly. She considered going into the kitchen and grabbing a piece of the melon she'd had earlier in the day, but she didn't relish the thought of having shared it with every insect on the boat, so she simply pushed her chair back and walked out onto the deck.

The sun was low in the sky, but it wasn't appreciably cooler. Once night came it would drop a quick thirty degrees or more, but it would stay warm for at least another hour.

She couldn't bear the thought of returning to her tiny, airless room, so she walked to the back of the boat. All three chairs were taken, and she received another round of surly glares. Then it occurred to her that she could kill two birds with one stone: get a little breeze and prepare anyone who might be wandering the deck after midnight for the fact that there was nothing unusual about seeing the crazy English-woman in one of the lifeboats.

She went to the less unseaworthy of the lifeboats and made quite a production of slinging a leg over the railing and climbing into it. She made enough noise that all three men seated on the chairs noticed her, and so did a fourth man who was emerging from his cabin.

Lara lay back on the lifeboat and closed her eyes. She hadn't planned to sleep, but when she opened them again it was because she had suddenly become quite chilly. She sat up, looked at the brilliant full moon, and estimated from its position that it was close to eleven o'clock.

She looked out across the Nile, but couldn't make out anything large enough to be Elephantine Island.

Oh, well. She shrugged and stretched. *We'll be up and traveling all night. At least now I won't get sleepy. I hope.*

She sat in the lifeboat, adjusting to the cold night breeze, for almost an hour. Then she heard Mason's voice.

"Lara," he whispered. "Are you on deck?"

"Over here," she said softly.

"Over where?"

"In the lifeboat."

Then he was leaning over the rail, looking at her. "Am I late?"

"No. I was a little early."

"Did anyone see you?" he asked.

"No," she said. It was easier than explaining it to him.

He climbed over the rail and into the boat, then began working the pulley that held it in place. A moment later the boat touched down gently in the Nile, and he cut the ropes loose.

He began rowing, then looked back at the *Amenhotep*.

"Oh, crap!" he muttered.

Lara turned to see what had distressed him. It was the waiter from the restaurant, staring curiously at them.

"The disadvantages of a full moon," said Lara.

"I suppose we could go into a romantic clinch and make him think we just wanted to be alone," suggested Mason.

"We have our cabins if we wanted a tryst," she said. "You keep rowing. I'll take care of this."

She pulled out a pistol and pointed it at the waiter. With her other hand, she held a forefinger to her lips.

He understood immediately, and mimicked her gesture, then placed his hand to his heart to show his sincerity.

"That's it?" asked Mason dubiously. "Can you trust the little bugger?"

"For ten or fifteen minutes," answered Lara. "Until he knows we're not coming back."

"Then what?"

"That ought to be enough time. You've already paid our way to the Sudan. Do you really think the captain is going to divert the *Amenhotep* simply to recover a broken-down lifeboat?"

Mason uttered a self-deprecating laugh. "I'm sorry," he said. "I'm an archaeologist. I'm all right in a fight, I suppose, but I'm not very good at doping out this hugger-mugger, cloak-and-dagger stuff."

"You were good enough at it to save my life," she said. "That's more than sufficient for me."

They came to Elephantine Island half an hour later, and pulled the boat onto the shore.

"Thank goodness!" said Mason. "I'm going to be pulling slivers out of my hands for the next week."

"Maybe longer," said Lara. "It all depends on whether we can find a speedboat."

He looked up and down the shore. "Where do you suppose we're likely to find one?"

She put her hands on her hips and peered into the darkness. "See that building about five hundred yards away, with the single light in the window?"

"Yes."

"If there's a light on, it means there's someone there. Maybe a guard, maybe some other employee. It stands to reason if he's got a boat he wouldn't leave it too far away. Besides," she added, "the island's only a little more than a mile long. If we just walk in that direction along the shore, we're bound to come to a boat sooner or later. Let's just hope that it's not a rowboat or a *felluca*."

They walked along the damp shore that was half sand and half mud, and after a quarter mile Mason felt Lara's hand reach out and squeeze his arm.

"There it is!" she whispered.

He looked where she was pointing and saw a small boat, floating in the water and tethered to a palm tree.

"I don't see a mast or any oars!" he whispered excitedly. "I think we've hit paydirt!"

They raced up to the boat and saw the moonlight glint off the outboard motor.

"Let's hope it has petrol," said Mason.

"Of course it does," said Lara. "There isn't any fueling station on the island. Whoever owns the boat plans to get home, so its tanks won't be empty."

She began working on the rope, untying the knot that held the boat to the tree in a matter of seconds, then looked around for a long stick. She found one and stuck it into the sand right next to the boat.

"What are you doing?" asked Mason.

"Thanking our benefactor," she whispered, pulling out some British pounds and impaling them on the spear. "Now climb in."

Mason waded out a few feet, then clambered into the boat and sat by the motor.

"Get in yourself," he said, "and I'll start the engine."

"No!" she said quickly. "We'll drift downstream and *then* start it. Why let whoever's in the building know we're stealing his boat?"

"He'll hear it when we go past the island."

"Boats go past the island all night," said Lara. "We just don't want him to hear us starting the motor right here."

"I'm sorry," said Mason, looking embarrassed, "As I told you, I'm not used to thinking along these lines."

"Stop apologizing."

"I'm . . ." He caught himself. "Right."

They floated downstream in silence for almost a mile. Then she nodded, he started the engine, and soon they were speeding past the island. In another five minutes they reached Aswan.

"We'll reach the First Cataract any minute now," said Lara, "and even if we get past it, we still have to negotiate those channels west of the Old Dam and behind the High Dam."

"I don't like it," said Mason. "There are too many people near the dams. We'll have Mahdists looking for you, and if the guy back on the island didn't want to sell, or thinks you didn't leave enough cash, we'll also have officials, and maybe even the military, looking for the boat."

"I agree. That means we'll have to portage."

"We can't carry the damned boat," protested Mason, looking at her like she was crazy. "The motor alone weighs one hundred and fifty pounds, and the dams are four miles apart."

"I know that," said Lara. She paused. "It's about twelve-thirty A.M. That gives us six hours to find someone with a truck who wants to make some money and isn't too fussy about the finer points of the law."

"I suppose that's really the only viable alternative," agreed Mason. "Which shore do you prefer?"

"Most of the city's off to the east. Let's land on the star-board side."

He steered the boat to the right, spotted a large all-night gas station, and pulled the boat onto the shore a few hundred yards north of it.

"Well, if we're going to find what we need, that's the place to look," said Mason, heading off.

"I'll go," said Lara. "You make sure no one steals the boat."

"*I'll* go. You stay here." She seemed about to object, and he held up a hand to silence her. "If you walk into that station with your pistols in the middle of the night, they'll shoot you or call the police. And this is Egypt, not England: If a lone woman walks in there without any weapons, she'll probably never be seen again."

"I'm tougher than you think."

"Don't be so sure," said Mason. "I already think you're plenty tough. But this isn't about who's toughest. And I'm not patronizing you. It simply makes more sense for you to stay here and protect the boat while I go arrange our transportation."

She saw the logic of his argument and agreed to remain with the boat. He spent almost half an hour in the station, chatting with the attendant, feeling out the various truckers who had stopped for gas. Finally he found one he thought he could trust, made him an offer, haggled for another ten min-utes, and returned to Lara.

"Did you get what we needed?" she asked.

"It's perfect," replied Mason. "He's hauling a tractor on a flatbed. He'll pull it off, leave it at the station, and come get us. With a little luck, we'll be back on the Nile, south of the High Dam, in less than an hour."

When the truck pulled up, it took all three of them to load the boat onto the flatbed. Then they climbed into the truck's cab, and true to Mason's prediction, they were back in the water, eight miles to the south of Aswan on the man-made Lake Nasser, an hour later.

"Well, we made it," said Mason with a sigh of relief.

"So far," replied Lara. "Now all we have to do is spot the *Amenhotep* before the Mahdists spot *us*."

7

Lara peered into the darkness as a cloud passed in front of the moon.

"What time is it?" she asked.

Mason squinted at the phosphorescent hands on his watch. "About half past three. The *Amenhotep* should be arriving any minute."

She frowned. "It had better be. I feel very exposed in this dinky little boat."

"They could be awhile," cautioned Mason. "They're not just letting criminals off; they're probably taking some new ones on, as well. And the captain may have to slip some money to the local officials." He looked north through the darkness. "Ah! Here it comes already."

"That's not the *Amenhotep*," said Lara. "The lights are too low."

The craft slowly approached them, and soon they could make out its outline.

"That's one hell of a cabin cruiser," said Mason admiringly. "I wish I had the money someone shelled out for it. It was probably built for an oil-rich sheikh."

"What's it doing here?" said Lara. "Ninety-eight percent of all the boat traffic is north of the High Dam."

"Maybe the fishing's better," suggested Mason. "Or maybe he lives here. There are worse sights to wake up to each morning than Lake Nasser."

"Maybe," she said dubiously.

The cabin cruiser came closer still, and suddenly its spotlight hit the small motorboat.

"Duck!" cried Lara, instinctively hurling herself to the

floor of the boat as a hail of bullets thudded into the side of the boat and splashed into the water around them.

"Damn!" muttered Mason.

"Are you hit?"

"No," he said. "I cracked my head against the side of the boat."

"Let's hope that'll be the extent of your injuries," she said, pulling out her pistols.

"I don't know how you can see anyone to shoot at," said Mason, peeking over the edge of the boat. "That light is blinding!"

"Let's even the odds," she said, blinking her eyes and waiting for her vision to return. Then she took aim and fired a single shot. The spotlight seemed to explode, and the men aboard the cabin cruiser began firing again.

"Give me one of your guns," said Mason.

"I told you—they read my palm print. They won't fire for anyone else." She peered into the darkness. "How many can you make out?"

"Three, I think," he said, squinting at the cabin cruiser.

"I agree. One by the burnt-out light, one to his right, and one near the controls."

They exchanged another burst of fire with no discernible effect.

"So what do we do now?" asked Mason. "They're higher out of the water than we are, and that damned solid railing's protecting them."

She stared at the cabin cruiser, which was only about fifty feet distant now, then at Mason.

"Dive into the water," she whispered.

"Are you crazy?" he shot back. "I'll be a sitting duck!"

"Their spotlight's gone. They'll have to lean over the railing to see where you are, and then I'll have a clear shot at them in the moonlight."

He looked doubtful. "How good a shot are you with that thing?"

"I hit what I aim at."

"I hope you're right."

He crawled to the front of the boat, then crouched low, ready to dive over the edge.

"Don't miss!" he said, and then he was in the water.

All three men on the cabin cruiser heard the splash, and as she had expected, they raced to the side of their vessel and leaned over, searching for a sign of him, their silhouettes clear in the moonlight. Before they could spot Mason and riddle him with their bullets, Lara fired half a dozen quick shots. Each man screamed in turn and plunged into Lake Nasser.

"Kevin, get back here!" she yelled.

Mason reached the boat a few seconds later. "Are they dead?" he asked as he pulled himself out of the water.

"Wounded, I think." Cries of pain and fury came to their ears. "Wounded, definitely."

"Then let's get the hell out of here!" said Mason. "We can meet the *Amenhotep* twenty miles upstream!"

"In a minute," she said, firing a few shots just above the water.

"What was that about?"

"Watch," said Lara, pointing. All three men began racing to shore as fast as they could force their wounded bodies to swim. She turned back to him. "Now start the motor and get us next to the cabin cruiser."

"We can't take their boat!" protested Mason. "The second they get to shore they're going to tell whoever they report to that we're on it!"

"We're not taking it," replied Lara. "Just do what I tell you."

He started the motor, and a moment later they were next to the cabin cruiser.

"I'll be back in a minute," she said, climbing out of the motorboat and onto the larger vessel.

"What are you going to do?"

"Empty its fuel tanks," answered Lara. "Why make it easy for their confederates to follow us?"

She walked to the back of the boat, found the tanks, opened them, and jettisoned their precious mixture into the water. She was walking back to where she'd climbed on when a body raced out of the darkness and hurled itself at her.

Even as she fell she was pummeling her attacker, trying every trick she knew to disable him quickly: a thumb in the eye, a heel in the groin, the flat of her hand pushing up against his nose. Nothing seemed to work. He flinched, but he wouldn't let go of her, and now she saw that he had a knife in his right hand.

As it plunged down toward her, she rolled away from it. It missed her throat by inches, and was delivered with such force that it stuck in the wooden deck. As her opponent tried to pull it out, she got to her feet.

"Who are you?" she asked—or tried to. But when she opened her mouth, no sound came out.

The man gave another yank, and the blade came free. He stood up to face her, and approached silently. He smiled, his mouth opening grotesquely wide, and she saw that his tongue was gone.

She pulled her guns.

The man's hand moved in a blur, releasing the knife toward her heart.

Lara's pistols fired in unison. One bullet deflected the dagger. The other struck the man between the eyes.

A moment later, she was back in the motorboat.

"I heard your guns," said Kevin. "What happened?"

"Another one of our silent friends," she said grimly. As before, her voice had returned with the death of the silent assassin. "Let's go a few miles upstream. There's no sense being stationary targets."

Mason turned the motorboat around, heading to the south. "By the way," he said, "I saw all three men make it to shore."

"You sound disapproving."

"You should have killed them."

"Why?"

"What do you mean, why?" he responded. "They were trying to kill *us*!"

"I don't like killing, Kevin. It's my least-preferred solution. Those men won't bother us again, and besides, it's not as if killing them would have solved my problems." She took a deep breath and released it slowly. "I wonder if there's anyone in this whole country who's not out to kill me."

"Probably that ugly little waiter on the *Amenhotep*," he laughed.

"He'll likely be the one to do it, too," she replied. Suddenly she became serious again. "Still, it would be nice if *someone* would convince the Mahdists that I don't have the Amulet."

"They'll never believe it, especially since you've proven so adept at eluding them and protecting yourself," said Mason with absolute conviction. "And since you're an infidel, they'll assume the Amulet won't make you totally invulnerable."

"You certainly know how to cheer a girl up."

He stared at her for a long moment, as if making up his mind about something. Finally he spoke.

"I feel responsible to some degree for your situation," he began.

"Don't be silly, Kevin. If you hadn't dug me out of that tomb and taken me to the Cairo hospital, I'd be dead by now."

"Hear me out," he said. "I knew people have been looking for the Amulet of Mareish for more than a century. Hell, I was looking for it myself. I knew the dangers involved—but I was so anxious to get you taken care of that I didn't make any attempt to hide your identity when I brought you to hospital." He shook his head self-deprecatingly. "I wasn't thinking, and now you're paying the price."

"I repeat," said Lara firmly, "if it hadn't been for you, I'd be dead. I have no problems with what you did."

"Well, *I* have a problem with it," said Kevin. "So I propose an alliance."

"An alliance?"

"I think we both know that the only way to end these attacks is to actually *find* the Amulet. If it wasn't in the Temple of Horus, then the journalist was wrong all those years ago—either the man he saw wasn't Colonel Stewart, or it was Stewart but General Gordon had sent him to Egypt for some other reason." He paused. "And if the Amulet wasn't in Egypt, then it's still in the Sudan."

"How can you be sure it's not in the Temple of Horus?" asked Lara. "*I* wasn't looking for it."

"The Mahdists have turned that place inside out for months, and I'm not the only archaeologist to hunt for it there," answered Mason. "No, I'm convinced that if it was hidden there, it would have been found already. I was within a day of giving up when I found you."

"All right," said Lara. "Let's say it's still in the Sudan. So what?"

"So two experts are twice as likely to find it as one," continued Mason. "All my other work can wait. I'll come to the Sudan with you and stay there until we either find the Amulet or become convinced that it no longer exists—or at least that it's no longer there."

"Think about what you're saying, Kevin," replied Lara. "They're not after *you*. You can say good-bye to me when I board the *Amenhotep* in a few minutes and nobody will be trying to kill you tomorrow."

"It's not that simple. Right now they think you've got it—but once they know you don't, they'll decide that you gave it to me sometime in the past forty-eight hours—or perhaps even that I found it when I was rescuing you from the tomb." He grimaced. "In truth, I'm probably not a hell of a lot safer than you are."

"Then why did you go out of your way to convince me you were?" demanded Lara.

He spent a little too long trying to formulate an answer.

"Get it through your head that I'm not a frail flower," she said, trying to hide her annoyance. "If you withhold any information from me, it just makes it that much harder to solve the problem—and this problem's hard enough without some additional if well-meaning sexism."

"You're right," he admitted. "It won't happen again."

"See to it," said Lara. "It's not enough that we merely search for the Amulet. We're actually in a race; we've got to find it before they find us. Or, as the old pulp magazines would say, we're in a race against death."

"Maybe not," said Mason. "As long as we're running *from* them in Egypt, they're going to assume one of us has the Amulet. But once we show up in the Sudan, rather than going to England, they'll know we're still looking for it."

"Why?" asked Lara. "Maybe they'll think I found it and plan to rule the Sudan as the new Mahdi."

"It doesn't work that way," said Kevin. "You have to be a true believer to be the Expected One, and you and I are both infidels. They know neither of us can become the Mahdi, and that means they know neither of us will be invulnerable even if we've got possession of the Amulet. That being the case, we'd have to be idiots to go to the Mahdist's stronghold if we had the Amulet. No, the only reason for us to go to the Sudan is because we *don't* have it. Because we are still searching for it. That's the truth, and more important, the Mahdists will accept it as the truth." He paused. "Oh, a few of them may think our going to Khartoum is a ruse and keep trying to kill us, but I think most of them will be content to watch us and let us find the Amulet for them."

"How will they know we've found it . . . assuming we do?"

He shrugged. "I'm sure they have their methods."

"They think I've got it now, and I don't, so they must not have very reliable methods."

He shrugged again.

"And what do we do with it if we *do* find it?" Lara continued. "If everyone knows why we're there, the government won't want us to take it out of the country, and I don't know that I trust any government enough to hand that kind of power over to them, even if there's no magic to it at all, but only the power of fanatical belief."

"I haven't thought that far ahead," admitted Mason. "I suppose we'll try to hunt up a truly worthy man, and give it to him."

"There you go again," said Lara. "Aren't there any truly worthy *women* in the world?"

"Point taken," he said sheepishly.

"And what if—assuming it's a man, after all—he's a Lincoln rather than a Sadat?"

"I don't follow you."

"What if the best person we can find, the one truly worthy person, is an unbeliever, an infidel?"

"Then he or she won't be invulnerable or immortal," answered Mason. "But they'll still possess a source of enormous power. Unlike pulp magazine heroes, they won't have the power to cloud men's minds, but they'll certainly have the power to influence them for good."

"I don't know," she said dubiously.

"What's the problem?"

"If absolute power corrupts absolutely, then almost-absolute power corrupts *almost* absolutely."

"Let's assume whoever we find will be able to resist the corruption."

"Gordon was a devout man, and he knew better," Lara pointed out. "How do you destroy the thing, anyway?"

"Destroy the Amulet of Mareish?" he repeated, shocked at the thought. "I've spent half my life looking for it!"

"If it's half what you say it is, it'd be better if no one ever found it—but since I don't seem to be able to walk away without getting shot at anyway, I'd like to know how to rid the world of it once I find it."

"I won't even consider it," said Mason. "We'll simply give it to the best person we can find."

"What if we can't find someone we trust?"

"That's a very cynical thing to suggest," remarked Mason. "Surely you've met trustworthy people before."

"Not many."

"Then we'll keep it under lock and key until the day we *can* find one."

"I've spent my whole life taking things that were under lock and key—and worse," said Lara.

"Let's worry about that when we come to it," said Mason. "The main thing is that by the mere act of openly searching for the Amulet in the Sudan, we'll put an end to most of these crazed attacks. Besides," he added, "as an archaeologist, I think it's the most exciting challenge of my career." He stared at her for a moment. "Do we have a deal?"

"I think you're risking your life rather foolishly," she said. "But if you want to come to the Sudan, I can't stop you."

"Then we're partners," said Mason.

8

---·---

"There it is!" said Mason as the *Amenhotep* finally appeared out of the darkness. He stood up in the stern of the motorboat and waved his arms.

"I've been thinking," said Lara. "Why should they stop for us? After all, you've already paid the captain for our passage all the way to the Sudan."

"I paid him half," replied Mason. "He gets the other half when we reach our destination." He shot her a disarming smile. "I may not know hugger-mugger, but I know how to bargain in the Third World!"

The *Amenhotep* slowed down as it approached them, and the captain leaned over the side.

"I thought you were still on the boat," he said.

"My wife was waiting for me at Aswan," lied Mason smoothly. "I decided it was best to avoid her."

The captain uttered a knowing chuckle. "Just a moment, and we'll lower a rope ladder for you." A crew member came up and whispered something to him, and he leaned over the side again. "I have just been informed that one of our lifeboats is missing. Would you happen to know anything about it?"

"You don't need it," said Lara. "Ever since they built the High Dam, the Nile's only five or six feet deep in most places. If your ship springs a leak or capsizes, the passengers can walk to shore."

"That isn't the point," said the captain. "It is ours, and we want it back."

"I don't have it any longer," said Mason. "How would you like to have this boat as a replacement?"

The captain's eyes narrowed greedily as he computed how much he could sell it for. "Is the motor included?"

"Certainly," said Mason. "What would I do with a motor and no boat?"

"It's a deal," said the captain. He turned to the crewman. "Lower the ladder."

A minute later Lara and Mason were on deck, and a minute after that the *Amenhotep* was once again heading upstream, towing the motorboat behind it.

"Four o'clock," announced Mason, looking at his watch when the two of them were alone again. "It's been a long night. I think I'm going to bed."

"I slept before we went to Elephantine Island," replied Lara. "I'm going to stay on deck for an hour or two. I hate that little cabin. It smells bad and makes me feel claustrophobic."

"Claustrophobic?" queried Mason in disbelief. "Lara Croft, who's wiggled her way into places even smaller . . . and smellier, for that matter?"

Lara grimaced. "The last place I wiggled my way into, as you put it, collapsed on top of me and nearly killed me. I guess I haven't gotten over it yet."

"Give yourself some time," said Mason, walking off. "It's only been a few days. I'll see you in the morning."

Lara walked to the area at the stern that housed the three wooden chairs. She pulled one of them to within a foot of the railing, and adjusted another just in front of it. Finally she sat down, leaned back until the chair was balancing against the railing on two of its four legs, and used the other chair as a footstool.

The clouds had vanished, and she stared up at the stars, trying to assimilate everything that she'd undergone since being trapped in the tomb. Most of it still seemed like a dream to her: the unleashing of the evil deity Set, his efforts to plunge the world into total darkness, the battle, even her eventual triumph. The only thing that seemed truly real to her was being trapped, barely able to breathe or move, in the rubble of the tomb.

Finally, refusing to let the memory of her ordeal master

her, she began making plans. The logical place to start looking for the Amulet was Khartoum. It had been Gordon's home for the last year of his life. If he or one of his men actually stole the Amulet from the Mahdi, it made sense that it was brought back to Khartoum. After all, that was the only city under Gordon's control, the only place that was safe, even temporarily, from the Mahdi's forces.

But most of the Mahdi's men were Sudanese. Why hadn't they just walked in, posing as citizens of Khartoum, and kept an eye on him once they knew the Amulet was gone—and they had to know it after Gordon defeated the Mahdi at Omdurman.

You're not thinking clearly, Lara, she told herself. Gordon or his men stole it *before* Omdurman or he wouldn't have defeated the Mahdi there, and it made sense that possibly excepting the Mahdi, no one knew it until the battle was over. So that was why they couldn't watch to see where he hid it.

Still, *someone* had to know where it was. Surely Gordon knew. Perhaps Stewart, too, or one of the locals, maybe more than one. Why didn't the Mahdi just send his spies into Khartoum and try to find out where it was?

And then she remembered all the books she had read about Gordon, in school and on her own. The Mahdi *couldn't* send anyone into Khartoum, not so much as a single spy. Khartoum lay at the juncture of the White and Blue Niles, and Gordon had flooded a channel around the city, literally turning Khartoum into an island. That was how he'd held off a far superior army for months. The city only fell when the water level dropped during the dry season and the Mahdi's army could finally march and ride across it.

Brilliant man, that Gordon, she concluded. Who else would have thought of flooding the plains around the city? It didn't help in the long run—a British relief column, fully capable of standing up to the Mahdi's forces, arrived days after the city had fallen and Gordon was dead—but still, she had to admire his creativity.

And *that*, of course, made her task all the more difficult. To find an artifact that was hidden more than a century ago in a relatively primitive country was hard enough—but to find one that had been hidden by a man of Gordon's intellect . . . that was going to take hard work and intensive study. She'd have to read everything the man had written, everything that had ever been written about him, until she knew exactly how his mind worked. And even then, she'd need more than work and study—she'd need *luck*. Lots of it.

"It is time that we spoke, Lara Croft."

Surprised, Lara righted her chair and stood up. She found herself in the company of the two burly Arabs who had been friendly to her in the restaurant. They didn't look so friendly now. In fact, one of them, the smaller of the two, was pointing a Luger straight at her. The other held a dagger.

More Mahdists, she thought. Her hand snaked down toward a pistol.

"I do not wish to shoot you," the man with the Luger said. "Raise your hands slowly."

She complied. "Who are you?"

"My name is Hassam," he said. "And this is Gaafar."

Gaafar stared at her intently. "Have you found it?"

"Have I found what?" she asked innocently.

"Please don't pretend to be stupid," said Gaafar, whose English was somewhat better than Hassam's. "It is unbecoming. Did you find the Amulet?"

"No."

"Truly?"

"Truly," said Lara. "So you see, there's no reason for you to kill me."

Both men looked at her as if she were crazy.

"Do you know who we are?" asked Gaafar.

"I know from your accents that you're Sudanese," she said. "I assumed you were Mahdists, but now . . ."

"We are Sudanese," affirmed Gaafar. "And we don't want the Sudan, and eventually the world, to be awash in blood. We *oppose* the Mahdists."

"I don't understand," said Lara. "Didn't you just ask me about the Amulet?"

"Yes."

"Then you *do* want to find it."

"Only to *destroy* it," answered Gaafar. "The world can never have another Mahdi! The next one might be even worse!"

She stared at them, trying to decide if they were telling the truth.

"If you want the Amulet destroyed," she said at last, "you're the first."

"There are more of us," Gaafar assured her. "Ever since we have been aware that Colonel Stewart visited the temple at Edfu, it has been our duty to keep watch over it. It had been fully explored and measured and charted over the years, so we knew that if someone of your reputation went there, it was almost certainly to find the Amulet of Mareish."

"I'm sorry to disappoint you, but that's not why I was there. I didn't even know it existed, and I never saw anything resembling an amulet."

Gaafar stared at her for an uncomfortably long moment. "I believe you," he said at last.

It was Hassam's turn to stare at her. Finally he said, "Dare we ask her?"

Gaafar seemed to consider the question, and then nodded his assent. "We might as well," he said. "We need her help every bit as much as she needs our protection."

"What are you talking about?" she said.

"Lara Croft," began Hassam formally, "you have a history of finding that which everyone says cannot be found. Will you help us find the Amulet of Mareish?"

"You're joking, right?"

The two men glanced at each other, puzzled.

Lara gestured. "You're asking me to help you . . . at gunpoint?"

Puzzlement changed to embarrassment. "A thousand pardons, Lara Croft!" cried Gaafar.

Hassam, meanwhile, handed the Luger to her butt first. "Here, take it."

She did. And pointed it at Gaafar. "That knife of yours is still making me nervous."

Gaafar slid the offending blade back into his robes. "Now

we stand before you empty-handed," he said. "We ask you humbly: Will you help us find the Amulet and destroy it?"

"Why should I trust you?"

"You hold our lives in your hand. We have given you this power. Does this not prove our sincerity?"

Lara considered for a moment. Whatever they were up to, killing her wasn't a part of it, or she'd be dead already. She decided to play along for now. If they were trustworthy, fine. If not, she'd make them wish they *had* killed her. She returned the Luger to Hassam, again butt first. "All right, I'll help you find it," she said. "But I can't promise to destroy it."

"But you must!" said Hassam. "Its power is too great, too dangerous. . . ."

"You'll just have to trust me to do the right thing when the time comes. I trusted you, didn't I?"

The two men looked at each other, then back at Lara, and nodded.

"Good," she said. "Let me go wake up my friend. He'll want to help as well."

"No," said Gaafar. "We know of Lara Croft's reputation. We know nothing of your friend." He paused. "You are in danger as long as you remain on the *Amenhotep*. Too many people know you are here. Soon we will leave the boat and be met by our confederates. You will come with us, and we will travel across the desert to Khartoum. Your friend will stay here on the boat."

"You're making a big mistake," said Lara. "My friend is Kevin Mason Junior, the son of an archaeologist who is more famous than I'll ever be. He's not only followed his father's footsteps, but he can probably draw upon his father's knowledge and wisdom."

"No!" repeated Gaafar harshly. "There will be many hardships and dangers ahead. *You* may be up to them; we don't know that *he* will be."

"He saved my life and has shared all the dangers with me," protested Lara adamantly. "He is my friend. How can I leave him behind?"

"If you care for him at all, let him remain on the *Amenhotep*. Surely you agree that he will be in far less danger if he is not at your side. You can meet him once we reach Khartoum, where we can provide better security."

"All right," she said. "I'll go with you, but I must at least be allowed to leave a note telling Kevin that I left willingly, that I haven't been abducted, and letting him know where I'll meet him in Khartoum."

"That is acceptable."

"When do we leave?" she asked.

Gaafar briefly studied the shore. "In another ten miles," he said. "Hopefully it will be before sunrise."

"We must leave the boat before it reaches the Temple of Abu Simbel," added Hassam. "We have information that a group of Mahdists have gathered there. They will of course assume that you are aboard the *Amenhotep*."

"All right," said Lara. "I'll go write that note to Kevin now." She paused thoughtfully. "I'll tell him to meet me at the Khartoum Hilton."

Gaafar shook his head. "No. That is the first place they will be watching."

"The only other hotel I know is the Aeropole," suggested Lara. "How about that?"

"Our leader says no," said Gaafar. "There are too many English there. When you do not show up at the Hilton, the Mahdists will look at the Aeropole next."

"Okay, I give up," said Lara. "You choose one."

"I will ask our leader," said Gaafar.

"He's aboard the *Amenhotep*?"

"Yes. I will get him."

Gaafar walked down the deck and returned a moment later. "He suggests that you meet your friend at the Bortai Hotel. We can provide security for you there."

"All right," she said. Then, curiously: "Have I seen your leader?"

"Oh, yes," Gaafar assured her. "Omar has been on the *Amenhotep* as long as we have."

"Omar," she repeated, trying to remember all the passengers' faces. "What does he look like?"

"I've been traveling incognito," said a voice behind her, and she spun around to confront the leader of the anti-Mahdists.

Her eyes widened in surprise. *Things are getting very interesting indeed,* she thought.

"I'm pleased to meet you too," replied Omar the waiter with an amused smile.

9

It was still half an hour before sunrise when they set foot upon dry land, pulling the lifeboat ashore behind them. Two robed men were waiting for them, each holding three camels by the lead shanks attached to their halters.

"You have found her!" enthused one of the men. "You have found Lara Croft!"

"Yes," answered Omar. "She does not have the Amulet, as we had hoped, but she has agreed to help us find it. Now we must reach Khartoum before the Mahdists find *us*."

"We are ready," said the man.

Omar shook his head. "You will not be coming with us—at least, not immediately."

The men's expressions registered disappointment.

"There is an Englishman onboard," continued Omar. "His name is . . ." He turned to Lara.

"Kevin Mason," she said promptly.

"His name is Kevin Mason," repeated Omar. "He is a friend of Lara Croft's, the son of a great scholar, and a worthy scholar in his own right. He may prove useful in our search for the Amulet. I want you to make sure that no harm comes to him on his journey to Khartoum."

"If Lara Croft is not on the boat, why should any harm befall him?" asked the other man.

"The Mahdists may have spies aboard the boat right now. They will surely send more when it stops at Abu Simbel. He is the only Englishman aboard, and it is known that Lara Croft escaped Cairo in the company of an Englishman. If they capture him, they will surely torture him to find out where she is. If he tells them, they will be waiting for us when we arrive at the Bortai Hotel. If he does not tell them, they will almost certainly kill him. It is your job to make sure this does not happen. You will protect his life with your own."

The men's disappointed expressions were replaced by looks of fierce anticipation at the thought of fighting their enemies aboard the *Amenhotep*.

Omar uttered a low command, and the camels dropped to their knees. He walked over and mounted the smallest of them. Hassam followed suit. Gaafar handed a leather crop to Lara and climbed onto his own camel.

"Have you ever ridden a camel before, Lara Croft?" asked Omar.

"I still have the saddle sores," she replied with a self-deprecating laugh.

"Just hook your left leg around what you would call the pommel of the saddle," said Gaafar. "Lock your right leg over it, hold the reins in your left hand, and if you wish him to run, hit him with the leather whip, and yell 'Hut! Hut! Hut!' "

"Until such time as someone actually starts shooting at us," answered Lara, "I plan to hold the reins in my left hand, tuck the whip in my belt, and tell my camel to walk slowly and gently."

"We will walk until it becomes necessary to run," agreed Omar. He turned to one of the men who had been waiting on the shore. "Leave the saddles on the other two camels. Gaafar, lead them by the reins until we are well away from the river and any dwellings."

"Then what?" asked Lara.

"Then we will turn them loose. They're herd animals; they will follow us."

"Rather like a spare tire," she suggested.

"Exactly," said Omar. "We hope we won't need them, but if we do, you'll be very glad that we have them."

"And if any small group should stumble across our tracks, this may cause them to think that we're six instead of four," added Gaafar. "It might cause them to think twice about attacking us."

"I assume you have your route planned?" asked Lara,

looking at the seemingly endless desert that began half a mile inland from the river.

"Certainly," replied Omar. "The Nile goes all the way to Khartoum. We will ride inland, but parallel to it. There will be oases along the way, and once we are well into the Sudan, there will be friendly villages as well."

"How long will the trip take?"

"That depends on how long it takes the Mahdists to figure out where we are."

"Inshallah," said Hassam.

"Inshallah," agreed Omar and Gaafar.

"You remain silent, Lara Croft," observed Omar. "You do not know what *Inshallah* means?"

"I know," answered Lara. "I'm just not buying it."

"I do not understand."

"It means, 'if God wills it.' I'm afraid that's too fatalistic for me." She stared at Omar. "No offense, but I believe in making my own fate. You can say *Inshallah*, Omar. As for me, I say: Let the enemy beware."

A smile crossed Omar's homely face. "I like you, Lara Croft. Even if I didn't, I would still risk my life for you, because of what you have promised us. But it is rare to find a beautiful woman who has the heart of a warrior."

"Is it?" asked Lara. "Perhaps almost as rare as finding a waiter with a warrior's heart."

Her three companions laughed at that, and then, at Omar's signal, they urged their camels to their feet and began heading away from Lake Nasser. The two men who had brought the camels now climbed into the battered little lifeboat and rowed out to the *Amenhotep*.

"Just out of curiosity, how did you know I'd be on the *Amenhotep* and not some other boat?" asked Lara, steering her camel next to Omar's.

"I didn't," answered Omar. "I have been on that horrible boat for almost three weeks."

"Why?"

"We knew that sooner or later *someone* would visit the Temple of Horus in search of the Amulet of Mareish. That is why we arranged to have it closed to the public—so that we would know that whoever entered it was no tourist, but was almost certainly looking for the Amulet." Omar paused and slapped at a fly that had landed on his cheek, then flicked it away. "We didn't know who it would be, but we knew that the Mahdists would surely try to kill him—or as it turned out, *her*. Of course, we couldn't know that part of the temple would collapse on you, or that you'd be taken to a Cairo hospital before the Mahdists could react . . . but we knew if you survived, eventually you would make your way to the Sudan."

"Why should you think so?"

"To return the Amulet if you found it," said Omar, "and to search for it in the Sudan if you failed to find it in the Temple of Horus."

"Why are you so sure I would take the Amulet to the Sudan if I found it?" interrupted Lara.

"Even if you do not believe in its power, you know that it is an historically important and valuable artifact, and that it is easily identified," explained Omar. "Even if you stole it and managed to smuggle it out of the country, where could you sell it without having to answer some very troublesome questions? Whereas if you returned it to the Sudanese government, there would be a sizable reward."

"Makes sense," agreed Lara.

"That is the sensible answer," he agreed. "The true answer is that the Amulet possesses powers whether you believe it or not, and those powers were made to be exercised in the Sudan. It will draw its owner there, possibly even against his or her will. Its power is released in proportion to the character of he who controls it. It is easier for an immoral man to tap into its reservoirs of strength, but a moral man—or woman—can utilize more of its powers. . . . And from all that we have been able to ascertain, you are a moral woman.

"Anyway," Omar continued, "we knew whoever found it would eventually try to make his—excuse me: *her*—way to the Sudan, and sooner rather than later. The Mahdists are watching all the airports, the train only runs sporadically— once every two or three weeks, which is not very helpful when people are hunting for you—and almost all the major cruise ships ply their trade only between Luxor and Aswan. There are only two reasonable escape routes, and both are along the Nile: either north past Cairo and eventually Alexandria to the Mediterranean, or south to the Sudan. There are only one or two boats that go all the way to Sudan, and only a handful go all the way north to Alexandria and the sea. It wasn't difficult to pick the one most likely to appeal to someone who was running for her life."

"What if I'd gone north?" she asked.

"Then my brother would be enjoying the pleasure of your company rather than my humble self," answered Omar. Suddenly he made a face. "I sincerely hope his ship's kitchen was cleaner than mine."

"So you deduced that I'd eventually make my way to the *Amenhotep* or its sister ship."

"If you were smart enough to elude the Mahdists, then you were smart enough to choose the right ship. And we couldn't help you until you did. We are badly outnumbered in Egypt." He grimaced. "Actually, we are badly outnumbered everywhere."

"How encouraging," remarked Lara dryly.

"We will prevail," concluded Omar. *"Inshallah."* He glanced at her, a mischievous glint in his eye. "No offense, Lara Croft."

She laughed. "If Allah would like to lend a hand, that will be all right with me."

Omar smiled. "I speak to Him five times a day. I will transmit your message."

She returned his smile, then began searching through her camel's equipment.

"What are you looking for?" asked Gaafar.

"A canteen," said Lara.

"Hassam has them all."

"May I have mine, please?"

"We must make our water last," replied Gaafar. "We will not reach the first oasis for two days."

"Let her drink," said Omar. Gaafar looked at him questioningly. "Our agents have told us that she was in a hospital just two days ago. Any other woman, or even a strong man, could not do what she has done in the last two days. Most could not even get out of their hospital beds. Despite everything she has accomplished, she is in a weakened condition, and since she is our best chance of recovering the Amulet and is under our protection, she can have all the water she wants. If necessary, she can drink ours as well. We are men of the desert; we will survive until we reach the oasis."

"As you say," said Hassam. He urged his camel forward until he was next to Lara, then handed her a canteen.

She stared at it without opening it. "Now I feel guilty," she said.

"Would you rather feel guilty and thirsty or guilty and sated?" asked Omar.

"A telling argument," she said, unscrewing the cap and taking a single swallow. She carefully put the cap back on and tried to hand it back to Hassam, but he pulled his camel out of reach.

"It is yours," he said. "When it is empty, tell me and I will bring you another."

She realized that it was useless to argue, so she simply thanked him, then turned back to Omar. "How long can a man of the desert go without water?"

"Not as long as we would like you to think," he replied with a smile. "Two days, perhaps three if we protect ourselves from the sun."

"What about a camel?"

He considered the question. "It depends on the individual animal and the conditions, but I think any camel, if he is allowed to drink until he is sated, can go at least sixteen or seventeen days. I would guess that twenty-two is the outside limit of all but a tiny handful of them."

"So before the advent of the motorcar, you could never travel more than a twenty-two-day march from the Nile unless you already knew the locations of various wells and oases," said Lara.

"No *camel* could travel more than twenty-two days from the Nile," said Omar.

"Is there some animal that could?" she asked.

"Certainly."

"Which animal is that?"

"Man," said Omar.

She frowned. "Could a camel carry more than a twenty-two-day supply of water while he was carrying a rider as well?"

"Probably not."

"Then I don't understand how a man could last longer in the desert than his camel."

"The explanation is, shall we say, indelicate?"

"I've got a strong stomach, and I'm curious," said Lara.

"A camel weighs five or six times as much as a large man," began Omar. "It therefore requires considerably more water to power a camel than a man. So that after, say, twenty days in the desert, a camel may live for only two more days, but he still carries enough water within him for a man to live for a week or more. When early travelers realized that their camels were on the verge of death and that they could not reach a well in time to save them, they would take a riding crop much like you are carrying, stick it down the animal's throat, and force it to regurgitate. They would catch and save the water in their canvas saddlecloths, then kill the animal and slice off a few pounds of meat to take along with them. On more than one occasion this would make the difference between dying in the desert or living to the next well or oasis."

"I see," said Lara. "That is a fascinating piece of information."

She fell silent for a few moments.

"Are you all right?" asked Omar solicitously.

"Yes. I was just thinking."

"About what?"

"I was thinking," she replied, "that the *Amenhotep*'s restaurant wasn't so terrible after all."

"I warned you that the explanation would upset you," said Omar.

"It is not an appetizing picture," responded Lara. "But it doesn't upset me. When you are facing death, you do what you have to do."

"I *knew* I liked you!" said Omar.

"Not everyone does, you know."

"Show me someone who doesn't, and I will convince them of the error of their ways," said Omar confidently.

"They're on that hill," she said, looking over his shoulder at half a dozen mounted men who had just appeared atop a ridge half a mile away.

Suddenly a shot rang out, then two more.

"And they're going to take a lot of convincing," said Lara grimly.

10

"There are no trees, no places to hide," said Gaafar. "We'll have to make our fight right here." He turned to Lara. "Get off your camel. We'll have the beasts kneel down and use them for cover."

"Why?" demanded Lara.

"This is what we have always done."

"Well, it's stupid," she said. "If the camels are shot, how will we get out of here even if we survive?"

"What do you suggest?"

"Have you got any explosives?" she asked. "Even a hand grenade?"

Hassam pulled out a bag of grenades. "I have half a dozen, but it will do no good. By the time those men are close enough for me to use them, they will have killed us all."

"Drop the bag on the ground right now!" ordered Lara.

Hassam looked at Omar, who nodded his assent.

"Now, do we all agree I'm the only one they want?" said Lara as a bullet kicked up the sand some fifteen yards away.

"Yes."

"Then start riding off."

"We will not leave you!" insisted Omar.

"I don't want you to leave me," said Lara. "I want you to obey me! I'm going to ride about fifty yards with you, then surrender. I'll stand there with my hands raised and wait for them to approach me."

"They will shoot you," said Gaafar.

"Why? If I tell them where the Amulet is, it's easier for them than searching for it. *You're* the guys who want it to stay hidden or be destroyed; *they're* the guys who want it found."

"Surrendering isn't much of a strategy," said Gaafar disapprovingly.

"When they get within a few yards of the grenades, the best marksman among you will shoot into the bag," explained Lara. "With a little luck, it will wipe them out, and I'll be far enough away that neither the explosion nor the flying shrapnel will cause me any problem."

"You're asking us to hit the grenades at perhaps two hundred yards," said Omar. "What if we miss?"

"Then I'll try to hit them myself," answered Lara. "But it'd be better if you don't miss. The second I reach for my pistols, they're going to shoot me."

"And if we all miss it?"

"If we all miss it," she replied, "we'll sell our lives as dearly as possible—which is what we were going to do anyway. Now ride!"

Omar nodded again, and the three men rode off. Lara followed them, then pretended to lose her balance and fall off the camel, landing heavily on the sand. She didn't know how realistic it looked, but she couldn't think of any other way to dismount that wouldn't arouse their suspicions. They just might believe that the Englishwoman couldn't balance on a running camel.

They were within 150 yards of her, and closing fast. She raised her arms and yelled, "Don't shoot! I give up!" Then, for good measure, she repeated it in Egyptian, Arabic, and one of the more widespread Sudanese dialects.

The men stopped firing and approached more slowly, keeping their rifles trained on her. Now they were sixty yards from the bag of grenades, now forty, now twenty.

Shoot! she thought anxiously. *If you miss, you have time for a second shot. If you wait another four or five seconds, you don't!* The seconds seemed like hours, and then, finally, a single shot rang out—and all hell broke loose.

Camels screamed in pain and terror, men screamed even louder, as bodies and body parts were hurled in every direction. A rifle flew through the air, straight at Lara's head. She ducked at the last second and threw herself to the ground, then felt a heavy object land on the back of her left thigh. She rolled over quickly and saw that it was a camel's head, the eyes still open.

She jumped to her feet and surveyed the carnage. Four camels were dead; the other two lay on the ground, twitching feebly. Five Mahdists had been killed almost instantly. The sixth was crawling away, his white robes drenched in blood.

Another shot rang out, and the Mahdist pitched forward on his face and lay perfectly still.

Wonderful, she thought irritably. *You couldn't let him live long enough to question him. You had to be macho to impress me.*

Lara's three companions approached her, rifles at the ready in case one of the Mahdists was faking, but none of them were. Gaafar walked over to the two dying camels and put them out of their pain with a bullet to each one's head.

"Which one of you fired the shot that hit the grenades?" asked Lara.

"That was Hassam," said Omar. "He is the best shot."

"I was very nervous," admitted Hassam. "It is not like target practice, or even like hunting. If I had missed, you would surely be dead now."

"So would we all," agreed Omar. "Lara Croft may owe her life to Hassam's marksmanship, but all four of us owe our lives to her quick thinking."

"You look unhappy," Lara noted. "You just killed all the bad guys. What's the matter?"

"I am ashamed."

"Why?" she asked curiously.

"Hassam is a better shot than I am. Gaafar is far stronger. Both are much better suited for adventuring in the desert. I am the leader because I exercise the only muscle that counts"— he placed a forefinger to his head—"the one between my ears. And yet when the attack came, I did not think of what was clearly the only possible means of victory."

"I have a feeling you'll have more chances to redeem yourself," said Lara.

"Part of me almost hopes so, just so that I *can* redeem myself," answered Omar.

Lara looked at the dead men and camels. "Should we bury them?"

"No, it would take too much time."

"They have already gone to Allah," added Hassam.

"I don't mean for religious reasons," said Lara. "But to hide them, so no one will know what happened."

"When they don't report back, their superiors will know they're dead," answered Omar. "It is better that we reach the Sudan's border as quickly as possible. We have *no* allies here; at least we have *some* there."

She shrugged. "Whatever you say. Let me just climb up on Seattle Slew here, and we'll be off."

"What is a Seattle Slew?" asked Gaafar.

"The name of a very famous racehorse in America," said Omar. "I saw him once on television."

"This is an Arab camel," said Hassam. "He should have an Arab name."

"I don't know any Arab racehorses," said Lara.

"I do," said Omar. "Since he has no name, we shall name him after one of the greatest of our racehorses—El Khobar."

"El Khobar," she repeated approvingly. "The Fleet One. I like it; I just hope he can live up to it." She paused. "Do you ever have camel races?"

"For pleasure, yes. But there are no racetracks for camels. The horse is our animal of choice." Omar smiled. "Unfortunately, the desert is not our environment of choice. The Sudanese love water and trees and moderate weather, just as you do. But to borrow a phrase I have heard in the American movies, we must play the cards we are dealt, and we have been dealt both sand and camels."

"Not to denigrate horses or camels, but I think my own steed of choice would be a Land Rover," said Lara.

"Not in the deep and shifting sands of the desert," said Gaafar. "If we are attacked any time between here and Khartoum, it will be by men on camels."

Lara mounted El Khobar. "Which way?" she asked.

"Lake Nasser is about twenty miles away," answered Omar. "We'll parallel it and then the Nile until we reach Khartoum."

"And you say the first oasis is almost a two-day trek from here?"

"That is correct."

"What's to stop us from turning toward Lake Nasser at sunset, getting water to drink," suggested Lara, "and then going back inland?"

"It would add many days to the journey, and the water would probably make you ill."

"Why just me?"

"We have drunk from the Nile all our lives," said Omar. "Those of us who don't die from it—and very few do—develop a resistance to its diseases and impurities, a resistance Europeans and Americans do not possess. We will drink at the wells and the oases."

"You're the leader," she said, more to bolster his ego than to agree with his assessment of her Western frailty. "Let's get started."

Omar urged his camel on, and the others fell into line behind him. After a few minutes Omar turned to them.

"This is wrong," he announced.

They all stopped and stared at him uncomprehendingly.

"Hassam, you will ride on Lara Croft's left. Gaafar, move your camel up and ride on her right. We must not allow her to be a sharpshooter's target."

"This is ridiculous!" protested Lara. "I don't want anyone to have to take a bullet for me!"

"It is no problem," Gaafar assured her. "You saved our lives a few minutes ago, so they now belong to you until we can return the favor."

"Besides," added Omar, "if Hassam or Gaafar is killed, we may still find the Amulet before the Mahdists do. But if you are killed, we have lost our best chance."

Suddenly Lara smiled. "Now *that* sounds like a true leader's reasoning."

Omar returned her smile. "Perhaps I think better when I'm not being shot at."

Gaafar and Hassam laughed aloud, and kept laughing.

"It wasn't *that* funny," remarked Lara after a while.

"Omar has been shot at more than any man you have ever met," said Gaafar.

"And tortured," added Hassam.

"Please," said Omar uncomfortably. "Lara Croft does not wish to hear ancient history."

"I think I'd find it very interesting," she said.

"Some other time," replied Omar with an air of finality.

They rode in silence for the next three hours. Then Omar signaled a halt, and they dismounted.

"The camels need rest," he announced, "and we need food."

"We haven't abused them," commented Lara. "They should be able to walk all day at this pace."

"True."

"Then why—?"

"Because if we travel at this pace with no breaks in our journey, we will reach the oasis at midday tomorrow, and it will be much safer not to arrive until dark."

"You could have just said so."

"I did not wish to distress you."

Gaafar and Hassam broke out laughing again.

"All right," admitted Omar. "I should know by now that you are not easily distressed."

"So how long do we sit here?"

"Perhaps an hour, perhaps two." He walked over to his camel, pulled his rifle out of its sheath, and brought it back with a cloth and some oil. "While we rest, I will clean the Eye of Amen-Ra."

"I beg your pardon?" said Lara. "The Eye of Amen-Ra?"

"My rifle," said Omar.

"Mine is Anubis, the Death Bringer," added Gaafar. He pulled out a dagger. "And this is the Scalpel of Isis."

"What do you call your pistols?" asked Hassam.

"I call them my guns," said Lara.

"You have no names for them?" persisted Hassam, surprised.

"I think it's a guy thing."

"Do you carry a knife?" asked Gaafar.

"Sometimes," she replied. "Not today."

Gaafar walked to his camel and withdrew a dagger with an engraved handle from his pack. "Then I will present you with the Leopard's Tooth."

"It's beautiful," she said, testing its heft and balance. "Thank you."

"You honor me by accepting it," replied the large man. "And whenever you cut a Mahdist's throat with it, you will think of Gaafar."

"Well, let's hope I don't have to think of you too often," she said.

The four of them fell to cleaning their weapons, and after an hour had passed they got up and began riding to the south again, always staying between twenty and twenty-five miles inland from the lake.

They bedded down shortly after dark. Lara thought she'd stay awake for a few more hours, but her injuries and her exertions of the previous night caught up with her the second she lay down, and the next thing she knew Omar was gently shaking her awake and explaining that she had slept for almost twelve hours and it was time to leave.

The day passed uneventfully. About two hours before sunset Omar sent Hassam ahead to make sure the oasis was free from Mahdists. He reported back to them ninety minutes later, stating that there was absolutely no sign of life there.

"Good," said Omar. "We will reach it an hour after sunset, let the camels drink, and fill our canteens. Barring dust storms, we should only have to stop once more for water before we cross the border and enter the Sudan."

"Sounds good to me," said Lara.

They urged their camels on as a strong wind arose, and reached their goal when Omar had predicted. There was a small water hole surrounded by no more than a dozen palm trees. Lara couldn't figure out why the water didn't evaporate, and finally decided it must be fed by a ground spring.

"Gaafar," ordered Omar, as they all dismounted, "make sure the area is secure. Hassam, fill our canteens while the camels drink."

"No!" yelled Lara suddenly, and everyone froze.

"What is it?" asked Omar.

"Hassam, don't touch that water!" she said.

He looked at her curiously.

"Did you drink from it when you were here earlier?" she asked.

"No," he replied, looking offended. "I do not drink before my leader."

"But your camel did, didn't he?"

Hassam frowned. "Yes."

"What is this all about?" demanded Omar.

"Look," said Lara, pointing to Hassam's camel, which had not advanced toward the water with the others, but was hanging back.

The poor beast was swaying unsteadily on weakened legs, a stream of white foam dripping from its mouth. Hassam rushed over to it, but before he could reach it the camel collapsed. It began bleating, and then, suddenly, it stiffened its forelegs spasmodically and died.

Hassam opened the dead animal's mouth. The tongue was black and bloated.

"This is the only well for a hundred miles or more, right?" asked Lara.

"That is correct," said Omar.

"The Mahdists are obviously a well-organized force," said Lara. "They knew we weren't going to show ourselves by going alongside the Nile, and they figured that if we survived their first attack, sooner or later we'd wind up at this well, so they poisoned the water. If we'd arrived even five minutes sooner, before the camel began showing any symptoms, that would have been all our fates in another two or three hours."

"What kind of wondrous woman are we traveling with?" said Gaafar almost worshipfully. "Lara Croft, you have saved our lives for the second time!"

"I haven't done a thing," replied Lara.

"But you have," insisted Gaafar stubbornly.

"We're in the desert, we've lost a camel, the oasis is poisoned, and we're out of water," she said grimly. "Somebody had better save the saver."

11

"We'd better give this some serious thought," said Omar as the wind continued blowing sand through the air. "Obviously we can't continue on our route. For all we know, the next six or eight or ten oases and wells are poisoned."

"Why would they bother?" asked Hassam. "They will assume we died here."

"Will they still assume it when they come by to collect the Amulet in the morning and there are no bodies here and only one camel?" asked Lara sardonically.

"He's a really good shot, though," said Omar with a smile of amusement as Hassam lowered his eyes in embarrassment and shifted his weight uncomfortably.

"I think the first thing we'd better do is bury the camel and see if there's any way to hide the fact that we were here at all," suggested Lara. "If they don't know that we figured out the water was poisoned, if they think we were in a hurry and just went right past it, they may wait until we reach the next oasis or well before coming after us, whereas if they know we found out this oasis was poisoned, they'll figure out that we're smart enough not to continue going from oasis to oasis."

"All but one of us, anyway," said Hassam, still mortified.

"You're right, of course," Omar said to Lara. "We'll have to return to Lake Nasser."

"I don't like it," said Gaafar.

"We have to have water," said Lara. "And now we have some use for the spare tires," she added, indicating the two camels that had been tagging along since the journey began.

"We won't have much use for *any* of the camels," said Omar.

Lara smiled. "We're going to buy a *felluca*, right?"

"Wrong," said Omar. "We're going to steal one."

"Why take the chance?" asked Lara. "I have more than enough money."

"The Mahdists are looking for an Englishwoman who is heading south along Lake Nasser and the Nile," explained Omar. "If we purchase it, even if you do not speak, someone will figure out who you are. Even if they care nothing for the Mahdists, they have no reason to keep your identity a secret—and I assure you that the Mahdists will give them more than ample reason to reveal it to them. No, it is much better to steal it in the dead of night and let them think it was a thief from a neighboring village."

Lara turned to Hassam. "Move over," she said wryly. "You've got company."

"I do not understand," said Hassam. "Move where?"

"Never mind. It doesn't translate very well."

Suddenly Lara realized that Omar was staring intently at her in the dim moonlight.

"Is something wrong?" she asked at last.

"As I said, you don't have to utter a word to be identified as an Englishwoman. No Moslem woman wears shorts—certainly not like yours—and none would carry pistols." He walked to his saddlebags, pulled out a robe, and tossed it to her. "Put this on. I am closer to your size than Gaafar or Hassam."

She got into the robe, then stood still while Gaafar wrapped her head.

"Well?" she asked when they were done.

"It drags on the ground," observed Omar.

"What difference does that make?" asked Gaafar. "She will be sitting in a *felluca*."

"If no one gets too near," said Omar, "if they see you from the shore while we are on the boat, if no fisherman's boat comes close to ours . . ."

"It will work," said Gaafar decisively. "It hides her shape sufficiently. She can pass for a teenaged boy."

"I get the feeling Omar doesn't think so," replied Lara dubiously.

"Yes he does," said Gaafar. "But it is Omar's job to antici- pate the unexpected so that we can be prepared for any even- tuality." He looked at her again and repeated: "It will work."

"Yes, probably it will," said Omar. He glanced around the oasis. "I was mistaken," he announced. "There is no sense burying the camel or clearing the area of footprints and hoof- prints. Let's ride to Lake Nasser. With luck we can be there a few hours before dawn and be a few miles away before any- one realizes a boat is missing."

"Right," replied Lara, nodding her agreement. "And you weren't mistaken; it was *my* suggestion. I didn't think it through."

"I know I will regret asking," said Hassam. "But why are we not trying to hide the fact that we were here and that we know the water is poisoned?"

"If we spend three or four hours making the oasis pristine, we won't reach Lake Nasser until daylight," said Omar. "We want to steal a boat, not acquire one in a pitched gun battle."

"Besides," added Lara, "the wind will soon die down. It may cover the first few miles of tracks we leave, but we're more than twenty miles from the lake. Unless you know a way to cover *all* the tracks we're going to make, it won't be too long before the Mahdists figure out where we're going."

"We can talk while we ride," said Omar, "and time is of the essence. We *must* reach the lake before sunrise."

Lara took the last swallow from her canteen. "How long will it take to reach Lake Nasser?" she asked as El Khobar rose to his feet and fell into step behind Gaafar's camel, with Omar's next to hers and Hassam's bringing up the rear.

"Perhaps five hours, perhaps six," replied Omar. "With luck we'll get there four hours before dawn, which is fortu- nate because I do not know for a fact that there will be a vil- lage where we reach the lake. We may have to ride along the shore for a few miles."

Lara looked at the canteen, then shrugged and slung it over her shoulder. "Six hours. That's not too long to go without a drink."

"I warned you before," cautioned Omar. "You may be- come ill from the water."

"You informed me of the alternative," said Lara distastefully. "Let's let the camels keep the water they've already drunk."

Omar laughed. "That was done only in situations of the greatest desperation. Our situation may be desperate, but thankfully not in that way. We are being hunted by enemies. If they catch or confront us, we have rifles and pistols and can return their fire. Who do you shoot at when you are lost in the desert and there is no water?"

"Point taken," admitted Lara. "Tell me about the Mahdists."

"What do you wish to know?"

"The Mahdi's grandson, whose name eludes me. . . ." began Lara.

"Sadiq al Mahdi," provided Omar promptly.

"Sadiq al Mahdi," she repeated. "He was elected as the Sudan's prime minister back in the 1960s, wasn't he?"

"In 1965," said Omar. "But his government fell in 1967."

"But then he came back again, didn't he?"

"He was elected in 1986," answered Omar. "And he was thrown out a second time three years later."

"Then my question is simply this: Since there's still a bloodline tracing to the Mahdi, and since one of them was popular enough to be elected not once but twice, why don't the Mahdists support one of the Mahdi's descendants to run the country? Why waste all this effort trying to find the Amulet?"

"Sadiq al Mahdi was elected twice because of his bloodline, and he was removed twice because of his performance in office," answered Omar. "This served to show the Mahdists that merely having the blood of the original Mahdi is not enough. Their hoped-for leader must have the power as well, and that power resides in the Amulet."

"If they should find it before we do, will they give it to a descendant of the Mahdi?" she asked.

"Whoever possesses it will *be* the Mahdi," explained Omar. "The grandson and others took it as a family name, but the original Mahdi was actually named Muhammad Ahmad. The word *Mahdi* actually means the Expected One; in your culture, it would be the equivalent of the Messiah."

"I see," said Lara. "So the Mahdists really have no ties to the current Mahdi clan?"

"No," answered Omar. "In fact, should the Mahdists come into possession of the Amulet, I think they will probably slaughter all who bear the name as heretics, just as they will kill those of us who do not accept the possessor as the true Mahdi."

"Then shouldn't those who carry the Mahdi's blood be willing to help us?" she asked.

"The descendants of Muhammad Ahmad believe authority over the people and affairs of the Sudan should be theirs by right of birth. They oppose the Mahdists because of the Amulet, but they oppose us because we do not agree that their blood gives them the right to rule us." Omar smiled. "In this case," he concluded, "the enemy of my enemy is not my friend."

"Exactly how many Mahdists are there?"

"Who knows? A hundred thousand, a million, five million. They are spread across all of North Africa, and as far away as Istanbul. Wherever people await the Expected One, there are Mahdists."

"And how many of your anti-Mahdists are there?"

"There *are* anti-Mahdists, those who do not want the Amulet found, but we do not call ourselves anti-Mahdists," said Omar. "In fact, we do not call ourselves anything at all. We number a few thousand at most. We coalesced when we learned of Colonel Stewart's visit to the Temple of Horus. There simply wasn't anything to do before that, because no one knew where the Amulet was. Once we knew it still existed, it became our holy mission to find and destroy it."

"There was nothing in the Temple," said Lara.

"But the Mahdists don't know that."

"That fact has been forcibly impressed upon me," she said grimly.

"And that is why we must now find it, rather than simply stopping anyone else from finding it," continued Omar. "Otherwise they will kill you, and your friend Kevin Mason." He paused. "If we have any advantage at all, it is that they will soon conclude that you did not find the Amulet, and I think they will then be content to wait while you and Mason search for it in the Sudan. After all, why should they kill the two people who are most likely to find that which they so greatly desire?"

"I thought I was in big trouble when I was buried in that tomb," said Lara. She grimaced, remembering her confrontation with the hideous god Set. "Now I think that Fate was just giving me a chance to rest before *really* putting me through the wringer."

They continued riding through the night, Lara asking Omar an occasional question about the Sudan, Gaafar and Hassam constantly scanning the darkness for enemies.

Finally they came to the shore of Lake Nasser. Lara climbed off El Khobar and filled her canteen.

"Impressive, isn't it?" she said, straightening up and looking out across the lake.

"It is the largest man-made lake in the world, created when they built the High Dam," said Omar, "but it is the water of the Nile all the same. There is nothing to compare to it."

"There is one lake," replied Lara. "Lake Kariba in Zimbabwe, made when they built a dam across the Zambezi."

"I have never been there, but I have seen maps. It is nowhere as large as Lake Nasser."

"No," she agreed, "but it's much deeper. In fact, the weight of the water caused the floor of the lake to collapse. It's known as the lake that put a dent in the Earth."

"The Zambezi is not the Nile," said Omar, convinced that if they were having an argument he had just won it.

Gaafar walked up to them. "We'd better start riding," he said. "We must find a boat before sunrise."

Omar nodded, and a moment later they were going south along the lakeshore. In three miles they came to a small village, and silently lifted a *felluca* and carried it to the water.

"We will tether the camels and leave them here as payment," said Omar.

"Won't the villagers scream to the authorities?"

Omar smiled. "Five camels are worth an entire fleet of *fellucas*. They will consider themselves blessed by Allah, and they will tell no one, for fear that the government will confiscate some of the camels in lieu of taxes."

Gaafar and Hassam finished their work and moved the saddles, saddle pads, rifle sheaths, and all the other equipment the camels had been carrying into the *felluca*. Then Omar tethered the camels' forelegs, he, Lara and Hassam got into the *felluca*, and Gaafar, the largest and strongest of them, pushed the boat away from shore and jumped in.

"Good-bye, El Khobar," said Lara softly, looking back at the camels. "You'll be a lot safer without me."

El Khobar turned his head briefly at the sound of her voice and snorted once, as if in total agreement.

12

After Gaafar and Hassam had rowed against the current for an hour a wind came up, and Omar quickly attached the sail to the small mast of the *felluca*. Their speed picked up considerably, and each of the men took a drink from their canteens.

"At least we won't have to worry about water for the rest of the trip," said Omar.

"It's a comforting thought," agreed Lara. "I do have a question, though: What are we going to do for food?"

"There are fishing poles and nets on the bottom of the boat. We'll catch some fish along the way."

"Good thing I like sushi," said Lara.

Suddenly there was a ripple in the water, and Lara pointed it out. "What is that?" she asked. "It seems big for a fish."

Omar shrugged. "The Nile is a big river. It grows big fish."

"What about crocs?"

"Crocs?"

"Crocodiles. Are there any around here?"

"No," answered Omar. "The last of them was killed a very long time ago."

"That's strange," commented Lara. "I've seen huge crocs—some as long as eighteen feet—in Lake Turkana in the north of Kenya, and in Lake Tanganyika, and everyone refers to the species as Nile Crocodiles."

"Once there were tens of thousands of them here," answered Omar. "Half were killed because they were a menace to the villagers who lived on the Nile, and the other half were killed to make shoes for the delicate feet of European gentlemen and ladies."

"I am told they are still in that section of the Nile that runs through Uganda to Lake Victoria," said Gaafar.

"Yes, they are," affirmed Lara. "I've seen them there."

"You are quite a traveler, Lara Croft," remarked Omar.

"I get around."

"An understatement," said Omar with a smile.

"Perhaps." She looked across the lake. "How about hippos?" she asked. "Are they all gone, too?"

"They say a few remain, but I have never seen one," said Omar. "Once they were as plentiful in the Nile as crocodiles. They were called River Horses, though no one ever put a saddle or a bridle on one."

"I always wondered why they were given that name," said Lara. "They should have been River Pigs. They're far more closely related."

"They are awesome and noble beasts," explained Hassam. "The horse is noble, whereas the pig is unclean."

"You told me why the Egyptians and Sudanese killed off the Nile crocs, and it makes sense," said Lara. "But if you think of the hippos as noble, awesome, horselike creatures, why kill them off, too?"

"*We* didn't," answered Gaafar.

"Surely you're not suggesting European hunters killed all your hippos?"

"No, it was the climate," said Omar. "Once, centuries ago, Northern Africa was a mild and temperate land, with heavy rainfall and thick vegetation. Over time it turned into desert, until it appears the way you see it now, with ninety-five percent of the Egyptian and Sudanese populations living along the Nile, the only source of life in this arid land." He paused. "The hippopotamus spends his days in the water, because the water protects his sensitive skin from the rays of the sun. But he does not eat in the water. Each night he climbs ashore and forages inland, eating up to three hundred pounds of vegetation before returning to the water." He waved a hand toward the shore. "Look around you. Nothing grows two miles inland. Even with irrigation ditches, five miles from the Nile—or what used to be the Nile before they created Lake Nasser—all you will find is desert. With all the vegetation gone, it was only a matter of time—a very short time—before the hippos were gone, too. Some starved, some moved south . . . but none remained."

"Perhaps whoever discovers the Amulet of Mareish can turn the land green again," suggested Hassam.

"More likely, he will turn it red—with blood," replied Gaafar.

"What does the Amulet look like?" asked Lara. "If I'm to hunt for it, I have to know what I'm looking for."

"It is so big," said Omar, juxtaposing his thumbs and forefingers in a circle about three inches in diameter. "We know that it is made of bronze, and on it are engraved a scimitar, a dagger, and a representation of the sun—though no one is exactly sure of what it looks like. These words are the Mahdi's description of it, written in his own hand in his private diaries. It hung from his neck on a silver chain, but we have no idea if the chain is still attached."

"Are there any drawings of it?" she asked.

"There are many," answered Omar. "But all are drawn from descriptions of it. None are from life. No artist has ever actually seen the Amulet."

"Did General Gordon ever mention it?"

"Not to my knowledge," said Omar. "But he wrote a large number of monographs and letters, so it is possible that he mentioned or even described it and we simply have not discovered that writing yet."

"It's not going to be an easy task," said Lara. "You've got an Amulet that no living person has ever seen, that no one in the past has ever photographed or accurately drawn. It may be attached to a silver chain that is also not described, or it may not be. And it's probably hidden in a country that is larger than England and France put together with most of Spain tossed in for good measure. And some of the Mahdists will be out to kill me before I find it, and some will be trying to take it from me the moment I do." She paused. "You sure know how to make a girl feel wanted."

"You will have Kevin Mason's help," said Omar.

"Let's be honest," she replied. "You never even heard of

him. The only reason you think he'll be a help is because I told you that this is his field of expertise."

"Why would you lie to us?" asked Hassam. "We are all that stands between you and the Mahdists."

"You are just the most comforting, reassuring bunch of guys I've ever met," said Lara.

"We are?" he replied, brightening noticeably.

She sighed and decided not to explain the notion of sarcasm to him.

At noon the next day they reached the Great Temple of Ramses II at Abu Simbel, with its four sixty-five-foot-tall statues of the seated Pharaoh. Everything the ancient Egyptians had built was on a giant scale, and except for the pyramids, the Great Temple was the most gigantic and impressive of all, made even more so by the knowledge that UNESCO engineers had disassembled and moved the entire structure, as well as the nearby Temple of Hathor, the almost-as-impressive monument to Ramses' consort, Queen Nefertari, from its original site, now submerged beneath the Nile.

There were the usual few hundred tourists milling about, and Lara assumed another hundred were inside the Great Temple with their local guides. She felt very exposed, because there were no other boats of any kind in the vicinity. Tourist ships never went south of the High Dam; any groups that wanted to visit were flown in from Aswan.

"Do you see anything suspicious?" she asked, staring intently at the shore.

"It looks normal to me," said Omar.

"But I was told there would be Mahdists waiting at Abu Simbel," she continued.

"There probably are," agreed Omar. "But they're waiting for three men and a woman approaching the Great Temple on camels. They are not looking for four male fishermen floating leisurely past in a *felluca*."

"I hope you're right," said Lara, "but . . ."

"But what?"

"But I think you're making them out to be a lot dumber than they probably are."

"Look at the people on shore," said Hassam. "They are paying no attention to us."

"If I was going to shoot four people in a boat from the shore, I wouldn't do it in front of a hundred tourists," said Lara. "I'd do it from the top of one of the temples, or from behind one of those parked vans."

"We are drifting farther and farther past the temples," said Gaafar. "I think if they were going to shoot, they'd have fired already."

"Then where are they?" said Lara.

"Maybe they are not here after all," suggested Hassam.

She shook her head. "Your information has been accurate so far. Why should it be wrong this time? The Mahdists have to have known for more than a day that we didn't die at the oasis."

"I have no answers," said Omar. "I am just grateful that our information *was* wrong. In another three or four minutes we will be out of rifle range and then there will be no question that they were not waiting for us."

"Just keep your eyes open," she said, scanning the shore.

But nothing happened for the next five minutes, and finally even Lara began to relax.

"It's very puzzling," she said. "No plane lands between Aswan and Abu Simbel. I doubt that there are even any landing strips for private planes. The train won't run from Cairo to Khartoum for at least another week. They have to know that we're still alive, and they know the only two routes to Khartoum will take us past Abu Simbel, one by land, one by water. So why weren't they waiting for us?"

"They didn't want to shoot us in front of witnesses," said Gaafar.

She shook her head. "I'm not buying that for a minute."

"Why not?"

"Let's say three bearded men who are mostly covered by the same robes everyone else around here wears shoot four people in a boat and drive off ten seconds later. How many tourists will even notice what happened, let alone be able to identify them? The police or the army won't get very far searching for three bearded men in the south of Egypt."

"Then why do *you* think they let us pass?" asked Gaafar.

"Maybe they have decided that Lara Croft is their best chance of finding the Amulet, and that killing her would be, as the British say, counterproductive," said Omar.

"They just tried to kill us the night before last," replied Lara. "Not that much has changed."

"You are a very suspicious woman," said Gaafar.

"I'm also alive," said Lara. "The two go hand-in-hand."

As she spoke, she saw a ripple in the water, larger than the one she had remarked upon the day before. She stared curiously at it, and then saw three more a few yards away. And a moment later she saw something else.

"There are no more River Horses in these parts, right?" she said.

"That is right," answered Omar.

"That's what I thought."

Suddenly she drew her Black Demons and in less than two seconds had fired twenty quick shots into the water, which soon turned red with blood. Four bodies, each wearing a wet suit, an aqualung, and with a trident gun slung over one shoulder, slowly floated to the surface.

"All praises to Wilkes and Hawkins," she said. "Who else could give me .32 caliber bullets that go straight and true through five feet of water?"

"Who are they?" asked Hassam, staring at the bodies.

"River Rats," said Lara, holstering her weapons. "A suddenly-extinct species."

"But why . . . ?" began Omar.

"They weren't afraid of witnesses," said Lara. "They were afraid that they might miss us and alert us to their presence. These four were going to fire at point-blank range." She stared back at the Great Temple, which was still barely visible. "Take us out farther from shore," she said. "They can't have seen what happened. If we move far enough out so they can't spot us, they may think we're dead, and that perhaps we killed their assassins as well. That might buy us some time."

Omar adjusted the sail and the boat's bow turned slightly to the left, moving them farther and farther away from the shoreline.

"How did you know?" he asked. "They *could* have been marine biologists. Scientists are always studying the Nile. They wouldn't be the first to show up here."

"I saw one of the tridents," answered Lara. "The only things requiring that big a weapon are crocs and hippos—and men. And you yourself told me that there weren't any hippos or crocs left in these waters."

"So I did," said Omar, surprised.

"That's why we let him talk so much," said Gaafar with a chuckle. "He may bore us to tears, but every now and then he does say something that saves our lives."

"*He* didn't save our lives," Hassam corrected him. "*She* did—for the third time. You had better hope we live to be as old as the Hebrews' Methuselah, for it will take that long to pay off our debt to her."

"You're exaggerating," said Lara with a smile. "I'm sure it won't take more than a century or two."

PART II

———— • ————

SUDAN

13

They sailed south for four days, and finally came to the end of Lake Nasser, which simply became the mighty Nile once again. There was no sign of the *Amenhotep*. Lara was sure it could catch them easily if it was traveling under full steam, which led her to conclude that the captain was stopping frequently to pick up contraband materials and get rid of contraband passengers.

She found herself thinking more and more of Kevin Mason. His father's towering reputation had impressed her for years, but she'd never considered that he might be related to a handsome man who was good with his fists and made as much of a habit of saving her life as she seemed to be making of saving Omar and his companions.

Then, too, it would have been nice to have someone to talk to about the Amulet. Kevin wasn't his father, but he clearly knew his stuff when it came to the Amulet of Mareish. Not that Omar wasn't happy to discuss it, but he was no archaeologist. All he knew was that it was the source of the Mahdi's power (or so he believed), and he could recite some of the legends concerning it. His only concern was making certain that it didn't fall into the hands of any potential Mahdis.

She was pretty sure it had to be within, if not the official city limits of Khartoum, then at least that area around (and including) Khartoum that Gordon had turned into an island when he joined the Blue and White Niles. After all, it was the only piece of turf he controlled; there was simply no way he could have gone out into the desert to hide it without getting killed in the process.

She was still mulling the problem when Omar gently prodded her shoulder.

"What is it?" she asked.

"We are about to enter the Sudan."

"Oh, hell!" she said suddenly.

"What is it?"

"I don't have an exit stamp from Egypt on my passport," she said. "Not to mention the fact that I don't exactly resemble my passport photo at the moment."

"Don't worry," said Omar. He waved at a uniformed soldier, who waved back.

"One of yours?" asked Lara.

"My cousin," said Omar as the boat floated across the border.

"But what if we had gone by camel after all? How would we have passed through customs then?" asked Lara.

"One of my uncles," said Omar. "I have placed men at every station."

"But surely the Mahdists have done the same," said Lara.

"They *tried*," replied Omar with a smile that left no doubt as to the fate of those Mahdists. "As for your passport," he continued, "do not worry; as soon as we reach Khartoum, I will get all the proper stamps for it."

"It is a good thing you have a large family," said Lara.

Omar laughed aloud, then stared intently at her.

"What is it?" asked Lara.

"I am still not satisfied with your disguise. I was wondering how you would look in a beard."

"We're going to let that remain one of life's little mysteries," she answered firmly. "Not only won't I wear a false beard, but once we're in Khartoum, I don't plan to wear these robes any longer."

"Women are not so independent in our country," commented Hassam.

"Fine!" she shot back. "Get a Sudanese woman to find your Amulet."

"Please!" said Omar. "We are allies. Let us not fight among ourselves. The enemy is out there."

"I apologize," said Hassam.

"Humbly," insisted Omar.

"Humbly," repeated Hassam.

"So do I," said Lara. "Blame it on all the raw fish we've been eating."

"You've had your last meal of raw fish," announced Omar.

"Oh?"

He nodded. "We are back in our own country. We have friends here. We will go a few more miles, until we are sure no one is following us on the water or the shore, and then we will stop at a small village that will supply us with food and—"

"Let me guess," Lara interrupted him. "More camels."

"We can't drive to Khartoum," explained Omar. "There is only one road. It will be under observation, with possible ambushes awaiting us."

"Where is this village?"

"A few miles beyond Wadi Halfa."

"Wadi Halfa isn't much more than a village itself," noted Lara.

Omar seemed amused by that. "It is the largest municipality for more than two hundred miles in any direction."

"Nevertheless," said Lara.

Omar sighed. "True. But it is my country, and I am proud of it."

"There's no reason not to be proud. The world has many huge cities that I find incredibly distasteful. Size is not the measure of a man or a city."

"That is something I tell myself every day," replied the undersize Omar.

"How many people live there?"

"Five extended families," said Omar. "Perhaps one hundred and thirty people in all."

"One hundred and thirty," she repeated. "Is it on any maps?"

"I doubt it."

"Has it got a name?"

"Yes, but it is better if you remain ignorant of it."

"Why?"

He looked uncomfortable. "I have family there. Anyone

who helps us is, by definition, an enemy of the Mahdists. If you are captured and tortured, and reveal the name of the village, you will condemn them to a terrible fate."

"I wouldn't talk," replied Lara. "But I don't expect you to take my word for it. Not with the lives of your family at risk."

Omar looked relieved. "I am glad you feel that way."

They reached Wadi Halfa in four hours. Lara bent over and hid her face from view as they wended their way through dozens of fishing boats, and didn't straighten up until Omar told her that they had run the gauntlet and there were no other crafts within sight.

They went two more miles, and then, for the first time in five days, they took the *felluca* ashore. Each man removed his rifle and his personal possessions, along with the saddles and other equipment the camels had carried. Lara stood aside and waited for them.

"Where's the village?" she asked when they were done. "All I see is sand."

"South."

"How far of a walk?"

Omar looked at her uncomfortably.

"I know that expression by now," she sighed. "Out with it, Omar."

"I spoke earlier about the danger to my family if you knew the name of the village and revealed it. The same is true if you know the location. Lara Croft, I will not try to force you—indeed, I doubt even the three of us could force you to do anything you did not wish to do—but I ask, with the greatest respect, that you allow yourself to be blindfolded and led into the village."

"If anyone else asked me such a thing, I would laugh in his face," said Lara after a moment. "Or spit in it. But you have earned my trust and respect, Omar. All of you have. When you first approached me aboard the *Amenhotep*, I didn't fully believe you were telling me the truth. Now that I know you, I am almost ashamed of my doubts. You may blindfold me. I trust you."

Hassam stepped forward with a strip of rag torn into a blindfold, but Omar raised a hand to stop him.

"Lara Croft," said Omar, his eyes glistening, "it is I who am ashamed. You will not enter my village blindfolded. You will enter as Lara Croft, a trusted and honored guest."

"But Omar," Hassam began.

"She has saved our lives three times already," said Omar. "They belong to her. I say no blindfold."

"No blindfold," Hassam agreed with a nod, letting the blindfold drop to the sand as if it were unclean.

They began walking south. There was too much equipment to carry, so they left the saddles and other heavy items behind; Omar said that men from the village would fetch it all later. After about a mile, Lara glimpsed the village in the distance. It was composed of mud and brick houses, shaded by doum palms, and surrounded by narrow cultivated fields. A half-dozen domestic cattle and eight small goats grazed on some brush near them, while some twenty camels stood in a fenced enclosure at the far end of the village.

"Even in my village," said Omar, "we must remain on guard."

"Then perhaps I should stay disguised," Lara suggested.

"Your disguise will fool no one who gets within five feet of you," said Omar. "No, we will introduce you as yourself. But we must tread carefully. My people are conservative and set in their ways."

"I don't want to make anyone here uncomfortable," said Lara. "I'll follow your lead, Omar."

A few people came out of their homes and stared at the approaching party. Then more and more appeared, and finally, when they recognized Omar, a number of them began waving, and one small girl raced up and threw her arms around the small man.

Omar exchanged greetings with the village folk and began speaking to them so rapidly that Lara, whose knowledge of local Sudanese dialects was far more limited than her Arabic and more than a bit rusty, couldn't follow the gist of the conversation. At one point, hearing her name mentioned and seeing the eyes of the villagers dart toward her in curiosity, she nodded deeply but said nothing. Finally, Omar turned to her.

"We will spend the night here, and leave on camels in the

morning," he announced. He pointed to a small hut. "You will sleep there. We will dine at sunset." Suddenly he smiled. "I told them we would prefer not to have fish, cooked or otherwise."

Lara thanked her hosts in Arabic, which was spoken throughout the Sudan, then walked over to her hut, entered it, gratefully got out of her robes, and lay down. She awoke two hours later when the smell of cooking meat came to her nostrils, and she realized that she was even hungrier than she had thought. She searched the hut for a mirror, curious to see what traces of her injuries still remained, but her search yielded nothing.

There was a knock at the door.

"Are you ready for dinner?" called Omar from outside.

"One minute," she said.

While she was sleeping, her dirty robes had been taken away and replaced with clean ones. Though she hated the idea of wearing the confining garments again, which did a good job of concealing her weapons while making it difficult for her to reach them quickly, she dressed in the robes that had been provided. A bowl of water and a bar of soap and some towels had been provided, and she washed her face quickly and ran her fingers through her hair, the closest thing to a comb she had.

"They have prepared a goat in your honor," said Omar as she emerged from the hut. "We told them how you saved our lives."

"It will taste better than the finest filet at the Savoy," she replied earnestly.

The meal was served outside, now that the sun was down, and the entire village sat around a huge fire where the goat roasted on a spit. Before long the children had their fill and went off to play, and the women retired to their houses, leaving Lara as the only female present.

"It is time that we spoke of important things," said the headman of the village, in a tone markedly different from the pleasant heartiness of his previous speech welcoming Lara and thanking her for saving the lives of Omar, Hassam, and Gaafar.

"I am happy to speak to you, Abdul, my cousin," said Omar. His tone suggested that he was not happy at all. "Of what shall we speak?"

"The Amulet of Mareish, of course," said Abdul. "Do not deny that you have enlisted Lara Croft to help you find it."

"Why should I deny it?" asked Omar. "Lara Croft's reputation is known to all. She is famous throughout the world for finding objects lost to history. Why should we not take advantage of her expertise if she offers to help us?"

"I tell you now," said Abdul, glowering. "The Amulet must never be found—not by Lara Croft, not by anyone!"

Lara was having trouble not speaking up on her own behalf, but Omar shot her a glance that was half-warning, half-plea, and she bit her tongue with difficulty.

"I do not understand, Abdul," said Omar. "If Lara Croft should find the Amulet and turn it over to me to destroy, why would that displease you?"

"She will not turn it over to you! The Amulet has a life of its own, and it does not want to die! She will think she is using it, but it will use her and you! The Mahdi was an ignorant peasant, and a year after he found the Amulet he could read and write and influence millions of men. Do you think he suddenly went to the British university? It was not the Mahdi speaking and reading and writing—it was the Amulet! Lara Croft must not be allowed to find it. No one must find it. You are my cousin, Omar, but if I thought there was a chance that you could find the Amulet, I would kill you right this moment."

"Now I must speak," said Lara. She stood, ignoring the outraged looks and murmurs from the men of the village. "I have heard that among the people of the Sudan, there is no more sacred obligation than that of the host toward his guests. Yet I hear my host threaten the lives of his guests . . . among them, his own cousin, whom I know to be a brave and honorable man."

A flush spread across Abdul's cheeks as he listened. "You have heard correctly, Lara Croft," he acknowledged at last. "The obligation of hospitality is indeed most sacred, but you do not understand the power of the Amulet. You do not know, as we do, the temptation it can wield, how it can seduce even the purest heart to evil. For this reason, we have pledged to sacrifice our lives, if necessary, to make sure the Amulet stays lost."

"Nothing stays lost forever," said Lara. "Believe me, I know: It's my business. Rather than hope that no one will find the Amulet, why not find it yourselves and destroy it?"

"No one finds the Amulet unless it wishes to be found," said Abdul. "That is why the Mahdists have not found it, though they have searched for over a hundred years. But not one of them has been judged worthy to follow in the footsteps of the Mahdi. If one of us found the Amulet, it would mean that the Amulet had chosen that person as the new Mahdi, and that person, whatever his intentions, would be unable to destroy the Amulet. From the moment he touched it, it would be too late. That is why it is dangerous even to look for the Amulet."

"You are forgetting the spell," said Omar. "It gives us the power to destroy the Amulet before we can be corrupted."

Derisive murmurs erupted from the villagers at this statement. "You speak heresy, my cousin," said Abdul in a cold voice. "Everyone knows that the spell of which you speak is a lie, a fairy tale. Only fools and children believe in it. Until now, I had not realized that you were a child, Omar. Or do you fall into the other category?"

Lara's hands moved beneath her robes, drawing her Black Demons. But Omar simply smiled. "It is late, Abdul. Let us not say things that cannot be unsaid."

Abdul, who had been watching Lara's movements closely, smiled and spread his hands as if to calm his fellow villagers. "You are right, Omar. Let us not dishonor our shared blood or our shared cause. It is the Mahdists who are our true enemies."

"You speak wisely, my cousin."

"Go now and rest," Abdul said. "You have traveled far and endured much. Tomorrow, we will speed you on your way."

"It shall be as you say, Abdul," said Omar with a respectful nod.

An hour later, Lara came instantly awake as someone entered her hut. She reached for her Black Demons, sure that the Mahdists had found her again, when a familiar voice whispered from out of the shadows: "Lara Croft! Are you awake?"

"What is it, Omar?" she asked, lowering her weapons.

"My cousin," Omar replied. "He means to betray us. We must leave this place at once!"

Lara stood and strapped on her holsters. "I know you and Abdul disagree about the Amulet," she said, "but I can't believe he'd sell us out to the Mahdists!"

"Not to the Mahdists," Omar said.

"Then who?"

"I am ashamed to say, but it is to our own people."

"I don't understand . . ."

"My people have been fighting the Mahdists for over a century. In that time, a fanatical group of elite assassins has emerged. Men who believe not only that the Amulet must never be found, but that it should never even be looked for. And that those who dare to search for the Amulet must be hunted down and killed."

"And Abdul is one of them?"

"No. The members of this cult are identifiable by a single shared characteristic, which Abdul lacks. But it is clear from his words that he sympathizes with their aims."

"What is this characteristic?" asked Lara.

"They mutilate themselves," Omar said with distaste, "by cutting out their own tongues. And they carry poison, so that in case of capture, they can escape any torture that might compel them to reveal their secrets in writing. For these reasons, and others, they are called the Silent Ones."

"I've already met these Silent Ones of yours. In fact, they've already tried to kill me."

"Then you know there is no time to lose," said Omar.

"Won't the villagers try to stop us from leaving?" Lara asked as she and Omar moved toward the door of the hut and the moonlit landscape beyond.

"These men are not warriors," said Omar as he led her through the darkened village. "And Abdul, though it pains me to say so about a relative, is a coward at heart. They watch us now, from behind their doors and windows, but they will not interfere."

Gaafar and Hassam were waiting for them beyond the outskirts with what appeared to be a small herd of camels.

"Just how many camels do we need?" asked Lara.

"All of them," said Omar. "We'll turn them loose at midday, and they'll find their way back here, but why give the villagers animals to ride if they decide to pursue us?"

Then they each mounted a camel and turned toward distant Khartoum. As they rode deeper into the Sudan, Lara found herself wondering if there was anyone in the whole country besides her three companions who didn't want to kill her.

14

The midday sun beat down upon the four travelers.

Lara could almost feel the oppressive heat rising from the ground. She had donned her robes a few minutes after the sun came up, but they didn't make her feel any cooler.

Her camel was drenched with sweat, and was using so much energy just to walk that he had none left to bleat or fight her commands. The only positive thing was that as long as they walked near the Nile they didn't have to conserve their water, and she'd already emptied her canteen twice since sunrise.

"Shouldn't we be traveling by night and sleeping during the heat of the day?" she asked Omar.

"From this point on, we will travel by day *and* night," he responded. "The sooner we get to Khartoum, the better able we will be to protect you from the Mahdists and the Silent Ones." He paused, then asked solicitously, "I keep forgetting that you are not used to the heat. Will you be all right?"

"If you can make it, I can make it."

"But we have lived in the desert all our lives," Hassam pointed out.

"Let's see who quits first," said Lara. She turned back to Omar. "How safe will we be when we approach the next few villages?"

"Most have no electricity, and cell phones have not yet made their appearance in the desert. They will not know that we had to escape from the last village."

"Someone might have ridden ahead to tell them," suggested Lara. "A horse can make better time than a camel, at least for a few hours."

"I did not see any horses in the village," answered Omar. "Besides, the land is absolutely flat and covered by sand. If a rider tried to pass us and alert the villages up ahead, he'd have to be many miles inland so we wouldn't see all the sand he raises, and even a horse can't spot us that much distance, nor can he stay that far from water." He shook his head. "No, the main danger we will face from the upcoming villages is that they will come to the same conclusion as the last one: that they don't want *anyone* to find the Amulet."

"Or perhaps they'll be Mahdists," added Gaafar.

"Well, at least they won't spot me as an Englishwoman right away," said Lara, indicating her robes. "I'm back to being a teenaged boy again."

"From a distance, the disguise is good," said Omar. "But up close, it will not work so well."

"I have an idea," said Lara.

"Most of your ideas have been just fine," said Omar. "Let us hear this one."

"I suggest that when the people of the next village come out to greet us, the three of you explain to them that I'm slow-witted, that I don't speak and barely understand. Say that it's my job to tend to the camels. I'll water them and walk them to the far end of the village, where I'll wait for you. If any children wander up, I'll just smile rather stupidly and not react to anything they say."

"I knew you were exceptional from the first moment I saw you!" said Omar enthusiastically. "It will work!"

Lara's camel bleated as if in agreement. Everyone laughed, and Lara said, "I'm glad Secretariat here approves."

"Secretariat?" asked Gaafar. "Another American racehorse?"

"One of the greatest," said Omar. "But we must give your camel a good Arabian name."

"I can't call him El Khobar," she said. "We've used that one already."

"Let me think," mused Omar, idly stroking his chin as he contemplated. Then suddenly his face lit up. "I have it!" he said. "We passed one of the Aga Khan's palaces just before reaching Aswan. We will name this one Nasrullah, after the Aga Khan's greatest horse."

"I know that name," said Lara. "Wasn't he imported to America?"

"Yes," said Hassam. "He sired many champions, including Bold Ruler and Nashua. He was even in the pedigrees of your beloved Seattle Slew and Secretariat."

"Bold Ruler and Nashua," she repeated. "I've read about them. You certainly know your racehorses."

"All Arabs know horseflesh," answered Omar. "There can be no more valuable possession than a fine horse—except for the Amulet of Mareish."

15

They traveled south along the Nile for three days without incident. No one came after them—at least, no one caught up with them—and Lara, portraying a slow-witted boy, drew no attention at the next seven villages they passed through.

"Why do you keep looking behind us?" asked Omar as they continued their journey.

"I'm looking at the river," answered Lara.

"I know," said Omar. "But exactly what is it that you expect to see?"

"It's what I hope I *don't* see—the *Amenhotep*," she said. "If it passes us, Kevin will get to Khartoum before we can let him know where I'll be."

"Then he will check into the Hilton, where all the Americans and Europeans stay, and we will get word to him."

"And hope he doesn't lead our enemies directly to us," added Gaafar.

"We will see to it that he doesn't," replied Omar.

They rode a little farther, and then Lara turned back to Omar.

"I have a question," she said.

"I will answer it if I can."

"You tell me there may be more than a million Mahdists," she began.

"That is correct," said Omar. "What is your question?"

"They constitute quite an impressive force, with or without the Amulet," said Lara. "So my question is: Why has no one heard of them?"

"I have heard of them," said Omar. "You have heard of them. Your friend Mason has heard of them."

"Spare me your catalog," said Lara, holding up a hand.

"What I mean is why has almost no one beyond the immediate area of the Sudan heard of them? A movement like this should be worldwide news."

"Can one in ten Americans or Englishmen even find the Sudan on a map? Can one in twenty tell you what country Khartoum is in?" Omar smiled bitterly. "We have no oil. We are not white by the standards of white nations. We are not Christians. We cannot militarily threaten Europe or the United States." He paused. "What happens within our borders is simply not news to the rest of the world. Everyone here knows of the Mahdists—but until word came to us of the possibility that the Amulet might be in the Temple of Horus, there was no Mahdist activity beyond our borders. Why should they fight and die to gain ascendancy now, when it cannot be denied them if they possess the Amulet?"

"Furthermore, it is our sworn duty to stop the Sudan from becoming news," added Gaafar. "For if the Amulet should fall into the hands of the wrong man, of a new Mahdi, then indeed will the world learn who the Mahdists are and where we are."

"Well, you have one thing in your favor," said Lara.

"And what is that?"

"The Mahdists have been searching for it for more than a century. If they had any legitimate leads to go on, they'd have found it by now. If it's a race between us and them, I'd put my money on us. I may not know much about the Amulet, but I know an awful lot about finding lost and hidden artifacts. I think that gives me an advantage over people who may know far more about the Amulet, but who have proven over more than a century that they're not very good at finding things." She paused. "I still don't understand why, if the Amulet is so powerful, the Mahdi wasn't ruling the whole world within a year of possessing it."

"He didn't understand its full power or how to unleash it," said Omar. "Yet even in his ignorance, he controlled a million square miles as a relatively young man. Since that time the Mahdists have studied his writings and his teachings, have learned the history and secrets of the Amulet—and believe me when I tell you that they will know how to make maximum use of it."

Lara had seen enough inexplicable things in her adventures that she was willing to suspend judgment as to the magical qualities of the Amulet until it was actually found and examined. Just for a moment, she found herself wishing that Von Croy was here to exchange ideas and observations and help her sort things out. She was going to have quite a story to tell her mentor when they saw each other again. *If I survive that long,* she thought grimly.

A sudden wind blew across the bleak, barren landscape. It became stronger and stronger, and Omar climbed down from his camel. Gaafar and Hassam followed suit, and they signaled Lara to do the same.

"The wind comes from the west," said Omar. "Make your camel kneel and position yourself beyond him, so that he protects you from the sand."

"Kneel, Nasrullah," she commanded. The camel stood perfectly still, and she realized she had spoken to him in English and he only understood half a dozen words, all Arabic. She changed languages, the camel knelt, and Lara lay up against him as the sand swirled around them.

And then, suddenly, the sand seemed to coalesce and take shape. She found herself looking at a towering, humanlike but totally inhuman creature about ten feet tall. It approached to within twenty yards of her and made a vague gesture with its right arm.

"He threatens!" whispered Hassam.

"No, he beckons!" said Gaafar.

Lara pulled out one of her Black Demons and emptied the full clip into the sand monster. It paid no attention as the bullets whistled through its insubstantial body, but waved its arm again.

"What do you want?" she yelled.

But suddenly, almost magically, the storm subsided, and the creature once more joined the sand floor of the desert.

"What was that?" said Lara. "Something else from the Mahdist sorcerers?"

"No," said Omar. "I think it was the Amulet itself. It knows that you are searching for it, just as Abdul said."

"Was it urging me on or trying to frighten me away?"

Omar shrugged helplessly. "Only time will tell. *Did* it frighten you?"

"Do I look frightened?" she said angrily, inserting a fresh clip into the pistol. "I put fifteen bullets into it." She stared at the now-empty place where she had last seen it. "Maybe next time I'll try a bucket of water."

The four of them got to their feet, allowing their camels to do the same. They mounted and began riding, but after another quarter hour Lara pulled her camel to a stop and dismounted.

"I've got sand and grit in my hair, in my eyes, all over me," she complained.

"We all do," said Gaafar. "One learns to live with it when traveling in the desert."

"Why should you?" demanded Lara. "There's a great bathtub thirty yards away," she continued, pointing to the Nile. "I'm going to rinse myself off."

She removed her robes, and put her holsters and pistols in her saddle pack. Then she slipped off her boots, leaving the knife called the Leopard's Tooth in the right boot. When she looked up, she noticed that all three men had turned their camels so that their backs were to her. "It's all right," she announced. "I'm not getting out of my shorts and shirt. I just want to wash my arms and face and hair."

As the men turned their camels back and allowed them to approach the Nile and drink from it, Lara walked into the water until it was up to her shoulders, then lowered herself and completely submerged herself. She scrubbed the sand out of her hair with her fingers as best she could, then rubbed her arms and legs vigorously. When at last she felt she was finally clean—or at least as clean as she was likely to get—she turned back to shore.

That was when she discovered that she and her three companions were no longer alone.

Five men, all mounted on horseback, had ridden up while she was in the water. They all wore robes similar to Omar's and her own, and each carried a rifle in a sheath.

Lara climbed out of the water and approached them.

Well, there's no sense pretending I'm a boy. There's probably no reason to pretend I'm retarded either—but I don't know what Omar's told them, so I'd better be careful and play it by ear.

"Bashira," Omar said as she walked up, "these are men of the village of Sulikhander."

"I am honored to meet you," she said in Arabic.

"An accent," noted one of the men, who seemed to be their leader.

I'm not tanned enough to pass as a native. What do I say to that?

"I am a Circassian," she said at last, claiming membership in the one very pale-skinned race that inhabited the North African countries. "This is not my native language."

"They are going to a great gathering of the Mahdists," continued Omar quickly, eager to get out the information before she made a verbal misstep. "We have been invited to join them. I told them that of course we are Mahdists too, but we have urgent business south of Khartoum."

"This is true," affirmed Lara. "But like you, we count the days until the appearance of the Expected One."

She noticed all five men staring disapprovingly at her.

"You are a shameless woman," announced the leader, "to appear thus in front of grown men."

"I did not know you would be joining us," answered Lara. "And they are my family."

She walked to her camel and began donning her robe, which she had left slung over the saddle. Next came the boots, with the Leopard's Tooth still hidden inside the right one.

"How can they be your family if you are a Circassian?" demanded the leader suspiciously.

"They are my family by marriage," answered Lara. She pointed to Omar. "He is my husband." Then to Gaafar and Hassam. "And they are his brothers."

"Something is not right here," said the man. "He did not say you were his wife. . . ."

"You didn't ask me," interjected Omar.

"You claim to be Circassian, but no Circassian woman wears such shameful clothing even under a robe."

"How many Circassian women have you seen without their robes?" asked Lara.

"And you are impudent," continued the leader.

"You are wasting our time," said Gaafar. "We have important business elsewhere."

The leader frowned. "There is nothing more important than paving the way for the Expected One. What kind of Mahdists are you?"

"Late ones," said Omar. "And our business has to do with the Mahdi."

"What is it?"

"I am not at liberty to discuss it," said Omar. "But be assured that were we not devout Mahdists who have the trust of our leaders, this duty would not have fallen to us."

"Your answers are almost *too* facile," said the leader. He looked from Omar to Lara and back again, then sighed. "Still, I could be wrong."

"Then we have your permission to leave?" asked Omar.

"Yes. Go in peace."

Lara grabbed her camel's reins. "Kneel, Nasrullah."

"What did you call him?" asked the leader sharply.

"Nasrullah," said Lara. Then, contemptuously: "Have you never heard of him?"

Suddenly five rifles were out of their sheaths and pointing at Lara and her party.

"In answer to your question," said the leader, "every Arab knows Nasrullah. He was the Aga Khan's greatest stallion."

"Then what—?"

"The Aga Khan made war against the Mahdists," explained the leader with a nasty smile. "No Mahdist would ever give a horse or a camel that name. And if you are not a Mahdist," he continued, "you are almost certainly not a Circassian. And if you are not a Circassian, then your name is not Bashira. But *I* know what your name must be." He paused. "I think you and your companions are coming to our gathering after all, Lara Croft."

16

They rode slowly across the desert, inland from the Nile. The leader, who informed them that his name was Rahman, rode alongside Lara.

"You could save yourself a great deal of pain if you would simply tell me where the Amulet is," he said.

"If I had it, do you think you could have captured us?" she shot back.

"I did not say you had it," he replied. "But you are Lara Croft, whose fame has reached even the Sudan. If you do not have it, you at least know where it is."

"I know you're not going to believe this," said Lara, "but I not only don't know where it is, I don't even know what it looks like."

"If you keep lying, it will go hard with you," he said seriously. "Very hard indeed."

"You've already told me you're going to kill me if I don't tell you what you want to know," she said. "How much harder can it go?"

"Harder than I hope you can imagine, Lara Croft," answered Rahman.

"I must say that you are certainly encouraging me to find it."

"Just tell me where it is and I will retrieve it."

"I have no idea where it is, but once I find it, you in particular are going to wish I hadn't."

He laughed humorlessly. "After we kill you and these three false believers who have accompanied you, we will force Kevin Mason to deliver the Amulet to us, so you see that you cannot keep it from us. Why do you persist in defying me?"

"I don't like your beard," said Lara.

"My beard?" he repeated, surprised.

"Or your face, or your breath, or your manners, or your threats."

He laughed again, this time in genuine amusement. "I admire your spirit, Lara Croft. I say this in all sincerity. It is almost a shame that it will so soon be separated from your broken, shattered body."

"You talk too much."

"And you do not talk enough," replied Rahman. "I will ask you one last time: Where is the Amulet?"

"Good," said Lara.

He looked confused. "What is good?"

"The fact that you have asked me for the last time."

"Perhaps you have *too* much spirit," said Rahman. "Why are you so uncooperative? We have your weapons. You know that you cannot escape. We can kill you whenever we want."

"No you can't," answered Lara. "Whoever's giving you your orders wants us alive."

"He wants *you* alive," responded Rahman. "He has no interest in your companions, living or dead." He paused thoughtfully. "Possibly you would feel more talkative if I began killing each one in turn."

"They mean nothing to me," she said with an unconcerned shrug. "They're just hired guides."

"Where are they taking you?"

"It's no secret that I'm going to Khartoum."

"So the Amulet is in Khartoum?"

"You're welcome to think so."

"Why else would you go there?" demanded Rahman.

"To outfit an expedition."

"To where?"

She smiled. "To find the Amulet, of course."

He cursed at her and then fell silent.

Well, I took your mind off killing my friends. But I'd better think of something more, before we get to wherever it is you're taking us.

They'd gone another mile as Lara considered various possibilities, each more suicidal than the last. Then, finally, she remembered Omar's warning about the dangers of drinking directly from the Nile.

"Are we getting close?" she asked.

"You will know when we get there," said Rahman.

"Is it soon?" she asked desperately.

He frowned. "Why?"

"I swallowed a bunch of water when I was swimming," she said, hunching her body over. "I feel . . . I don't know . . ."

"That is what happens when Europeans drink from the Nile," laughed Rahman.

"It's not funny!" snapped Lara weakly. "I'm sick!"

"If the Nile can do this to you, I am afraid you are not going to provide us very much amusement when we extract the secret of the Amulet's location from you."

Don't do this too fast, Lara, she told herself. *You're only going to get one shot at it.*

"Go to hell!" she snapped, and acted as if she had decided to stoically bear her pain. She rode in silence for the next quarter mile, grimacing as if in agony, but not uttering a word, which added to the reality of her performance.

Finally she began groaning aloud.

"What is it now?" demanded Rahman in bored tones.

"Stomach cramps," she muttered, doubling over—and as she did so, her right hand snaked down, withdrew the Leopard's Tooth from her boot, and tucked it in the sleeve of her robe.

"English!" he muttered contemptuously.

"I think . . ." began Lara, rolling her eyes.

"You think what?"

"I think I'm going to . . ." She went limp and fell onto the ground.

"Lara!" cried Omar, jumping off his own camel and running up to her. "Are you all right?"

"Get back, son of a pig!" said Rahman harshly. "*I* will tend to the prisoner."

She heard the rustling of his robe as he approached. Then he was turning her over roughly. Suddenly she reached out, spun him around, and in an instant she was behind him, the sharp edge of the Leopard's Tooth pressed against his neck.

His men instantly had their guns out, but Lara had Rahman positioned between them and herself. She backed up until she and Rahman were next to her camel.

"Drop your weapons or he's a dead man!" she demanded.

"He is nothing!" said one of Rahman's companions, taking aim. "The Amulet is everything!"

A shot rang out and thudded into Rahman's body. Lara felt him go limp, but she continued to prop him up as a shield with one hand while she reached into her saddle bag with the other and pulled out a Black Demon. She fired off ten quick rounds and suddenly three of Rahman's men lay dead on the ground. The fourth fired off a quick shot that struck Rahman's body with such force that the dead man and Lara fell to the ground. A second hurried shot, aimed at Lara where she fell, hit the Leopard's Tooth instead, destroying the blade.

The horseman realized that all four of his companions were dead, panicked, and began racing off across the sand. Hassam ran to one of the corpses, picked up a rifle, and took careful aim. It seemed to Lara that he would never pull the trigger, that soon the rider would be out of range, but finally he fired a single shot. An instant later the horse collapsed, and the rider went flying through the air, landing heavily about forty feet away. The horse tried futilely to rise, but it was obvious that the shot had shattered one of its legs.

Hassam, tears streaming down his face, ran up to the horse, placed the muzzle of the rifle in its ear, and fired again. The animal died without a sound.

"You!" bellowed Hassam, walking over to the writhing man. "You made me kill a horse, Allah's most perfect creature! Know that after I kill you I will bury you facing away from Mecca!"

The man began crying and begging, but Hassam was deaf to his entreaties. He fired his rifle again, and a moment later he was scraping out a shallow grave.

"That was very quick thinking," said Omar, retrieving his weapons and walking up to Lara.

"It was my own fault we were in this mess," she replied, examining the Leopard's Tooth and finally tossing the ruined weapon onto the sand. "From now on, the only name for any camel I ride will be Camel."

"Don't blame yourself. How could you have known?"

"Maybe you're right," she admitted. "But we've *all* got to be more careful."

"We can start by riding back to the Nile and turning south," said Omar. "The longer we take to reach Khartoum, the greater the likelihood that we'll run into more Mahdists, and the more frequently we meet them, the more chance that we'll say or do something that will give away your identity."

She walked to her camel, had it kneel, and climbed into the saddle. Gaafar had dismounted long enough to pick up his rifle, and he and Omar were soon astride their own camels.

"I'd rather ride the horses," he said, "but they're too easily identified."

"I agree," said Lara. "Reluctantly."

"Shall we proceed?" asked Omar.

"What about Hassam?" asked Lara.

"He is burying the horse."

"He's digging a grave for the horse?" she said incredulously.

"No," said Gaafar. "But he has moved the horse and now he is covering it with sand."

"Moved it?" she repeated, frowning. "It's right where it fell."

"He has turned it so that it faces Mecca," explained Gaafar. "Hassam believes that horses as well as men have souls. All righteous Moslems wish to be buried facing Mecca. Hassam is punishing this one's soul by facing the body away from Mecca, but he sees no reason to punish the horse as well, or to leave it out for the vultures."

"Isn't that carrying his love of horses a little bit too far?" asked Lara.

"Did the man try to kill you?" asked Gaafar.

"Yes."

"Did the horse?"

"All right," replied Lara. "You have a point."

"He will bury the other four men and then catch up with us," said Omar.

"Facing away from Mecca?" she asked.

"They were not honorable men," said Omar disapprovingly. "But Hassam is a good Moslem, and he will not cause their souls to wander for eternity. He will point them toward Mecca."

"So obviously he thinks causing him to kill a horse is a worse sin than making him kill a man?"

"The men were enemies, and they meant to kill us. The horse was not to blame." Omar sighed. "Horses are born innocent. Only men are capable of blame."

Hassam trudged back through the sand. Her last sight of him as they headed back to the Nile was of his facing each corpse toward Mecca before scraping out shallow graves for them with his bare hands.

"Will he be able to find us?" she asked.

"I know it seems like only our enemies can find us," said Omar. "But Hassam will join us at nightfall."

"It shouldn't take him that long to dig the graves," said Lara. "Why don't we help him, or at least wait for him?"

"He will join us at nightfall," repeated Omar.

"Why not now?"

"Because he is a proud man, and he does not want you to see him cry."

"He had no choice," said Lara. "Otherwise the man would have escaped and brought back reinforcements."

"I know that," said Omar. "And so does Hassam."

"Then if it wasn't his fault, why . . . ?"

"Because the horse is just as dead."

She was silent for a long moment.

"What are you thinking, Lara Croft?" asked Omar at last.

"That I could have fallen in with worse companions," she replied.

17

They reached Dongola in two more days, gave it a wide berth, then did the same when they came to Ed Debba three days after that. There was never a lack of food for the camels; everything within a mile or two of each side of the Nile was green and growing, and the river supplied all the water they needed.

"I am surprised that you haven't become sick yet," remarked Omar as they put Ed Debba well behind them.

"I was sick when you met me," answered Lara. "I'm my old self now."

"I mean because of the water."

She laughed. "I have been in so many filthy places and drunk such foul water during my life that my stomach probably thinks the Nile is the finest, purest distilled water I've ever given it."

"I keep forgetting," said Omar. "You are not just some ordinary Englishwoman. You are Lara Croft."

"Don't underestimate my fellow Englishwomen," she said. "The first Elizabeth was a pretty tough old bird, Victoria ruled the world, and Maggie Thatcher could have reconquered it if she'd felt like it."

"I meant no offense," said Omar quickly.

"None taken."

"Have you given any thought to the Amulet?"

"Of course I have. Frankly, between you and me, I wish I'd never heard of it."

"That was not precisely the kind of thought I was referring to," said Omar.

"I know," said Lara. "I don't know enough yet to have any

serious thoughts on where to look. I've been to Khartoum a couple of times, but it's a very large, very old city. Chinese Gordon could have hidden it anywhere."

"Chinese?" repeated Omar. "You are mistaken. General Gordon was British."

"It was a nickname," she explained. "The press gave it to him after he'd conducted a successful series of campaigns in China. Anyway, he's the key to it. Obviously Colonel Stewart was in Edfu for some other reason, so the Amulet stayed with Gordon. I have to learn more about him, see where he lived and where he worked, read his writings, walk the city where he walked it. In short, I have to *become* Gordon. I have to learn to think as he did—and once I do that, I'll know where I would hide the Amulet, which means I'll know where *he* hid it."

"And you will bring all your training and experience to bear," said Omar.

"I'm not sure how useful my experience is going to be."

"I do not understand. You have found many lost treasures. Everyone knows this."

"It's not the same," she said. "You find ancient artifacts by studying ancient peoples—but much of the time, the reason the artifacts are lost is not because anyone hid them, but because the society no longer exists. You study their history, their culture, so that you can figure out where to dig, where they kept their most valuable treasures." She sighed deeply. "But we're not talking about that. We're talking about a man who lived little more than a century ago, who was a serving officer in the British army, who knew that hundreds, perhaps thousands of men would be searching for the Amulet the instant Khartoum fell—and he didn't want them to find it." She looked at Omar. "Do you see the difference? No one set out to hide an artifact like the Rosetta Stone. It became lost in the mists of time. That's not the case with the Amulet. Gordon actively hid it, and I have to figure out where, which is why I have to learn exactly how his mind worked. It's not much, but it's all I've got. If I were laying bets, I'd put my money on Kevin finding it, not me. He's the Gordon student."

"If I had put my money on Kevin Mason instead of you, all

four of us would have died five days ago," said Omar, referring to the incident with the five riflemen. "We have more faith in you than you have in yourself."

"I've never been plagued by self-doubt," said Lara. "But you have to understand that you're asking me to find a century-old needle that's hidden in a haystack a third the size of Europe. That's quite a daunting challenge."

"If it was easy, we wouldn't need your expertise," responded Omar. "So I ask again: What are your thoughts concerning the Amulet?"

"Just that it's very well hidden."

"Come now," said Omar. "You knew General Gordon's nickname. You are not totally ignorant of him. Doubtless you have read of his campaigns, perhaps even read biographies of him. Surely you can hazard a guess."

"People have been hazarding guesses since 1885," answered Lara, "and the Amulet is still missing." She paused. "You know," she suggested, "there is always the possibility that he destroyed it."

"He could not destroy it."

"What makes you so sure?"

"It is a magical amulet. It can only be destroyed by magic," said Omar with absolute certainty.

"That spell you mentioned, the one Abdul said was a fairy tale?"

Omar nodded. "General Gordon did not possess the spell."

"Then maybe he threw it in the Nile."

"No," said Omar firmly. "The course of the Nile has changed many times. Drought, earthquake, build-up of silt—any of these things could alter its course and expose the Amulet on the river bed."

"But would Gordon have known that?" asked Lara.

"If not, and if he planned to throw the Amulet into the Nile, he would certainly have asked," said Omar. "Not in so many words, of course. He would not walk up to an aide and ask if it was safe to hide the Amulet in the river. But he would have asked if the Nile always stayed within its boundaries. Remember, he was diverting some of the flow to turn Khartoum into a defensible island, so it would have been a natural question from a commander who had to know all the conditions he might be called upon to deal with."

"All right," conceded Lara. "That makes sense. So he didn't throw it in the Nile. But that doesn't give us any better idea of where he *did* hide it."

They rode until twilight, then dismounted and prepared to sleep in the shade of a large boulder that seemed to rise up out of the sand for no logical reason. Lara took a long drink from her canteen, then pulled out her pistols and began cleaning and oiling them. The three men did the same with their rifles.

"I have been thinking," said Omar after a few minutes. "By now they know we're going to Khartoum and approaching it on camels, and they know we've traveled by *felluca*, so they'll be watching the river as well. What if we release the camels when we are about thirty miles out of the city, and take public transportation the rest of the way? They would never think to look for us on a crowded bus."

"Won't your rifles give you away?" asked Lara.

All three men laughed. "It is more likely that your *lack* of a rifle will give us away," said Hassam.

"I assume I'll be wearing robes and being a boy again?" she said glumly.

"Only until we get to the Bortai Hotel, and get word to our people," answered Omar. "Then you can become Lara Croft once more."

"The robes worked when observers were a few hundred feet away," said Lara. "Can I pass for a boy in a crowded bus?"

Omar studied her. "Your face is too smooth," he said at last. "Even Circassian women do not have skin texture like that, not after years in the desert. I suppose the easiest remedy is to slap some mud and dirt on it."

"And don't speak," added Gaafar.

"I know. My voice is too high."

"Some boys have high voices," he said. "But you have a thick accent, and it is easily identified as English."

"All right, I won't speak."

"And bury your chin in your robes," said Gaafar.

"It won't be for long," Omar assured her. "The bus will

cover the distance in no more than an hour, and we will get off it within a short walk of the Bortai."

"We're still ahead of the *Amenhotep* unless it passed one night while we were sleeping," said Lara. "And its engine is so noisy I doubt that that could happen. How will we get word to Kevin?"

"We have allies in Khartoum," replied Omar. "Someone will come on board—a new deckhand, a cargo inspector, someone—and give Dr. Mason the information he needs. We will rent a room for him at the Bortai, under a false name of course, so that he will be able to move right in." He paused. "Then the two of you will find the Amulet."

Always assuming it wants me to find it, thought Lara.

The next two days were uneventful, and finally they came to the rarely used railroad tracks and the highway, in serious need of repair, that paralleled them. When they came to a landmark that Omar knew—it was just a trio of rocks at the roadside, meaningless to Lara but as clear as a street sign to him—they dismounted, took the bridles and saddles off their camels and hid them behind some thick bushes, then chased the camels off.

After waiting two hours for a bus, Lara turned to Omar.

"You're sure the bus drives on this road?" she said. "So far all we've seen are two cars and a mule-cart."

"This is its regular route," he assured her.

"Then where is it?"

Omar shrugged. "It breaks down a lot."

They waited another twenty minutes, and finally a rusted, dilapidated minivan pulled up.

"That's the bus?" asked Lara.

"That's the bus."

"The four of us will fill it up."

"I have seen it carry as many as fifteen grown men," said Gaafar.

"On the inside?"

Gaafar laughed. "Remember to hide your face," he said, and the four of them climbed into the minivan. Sure enough, it stopped twice more to pick up three more men, and Lara decided she was in more danger of being crushed to death than identified.

When the minivan was about ten miles out of Khartoum it hit a pothole and blew its left front tire. The driver had everyone climb out while he went around to the back and removed the spare, only to find that it was flat as well.

Lara was about to ask Omar what they should do next, then remembered not to speak aloud, and simply looked at him questioningly. He gestured her to follow him, Gaafar and Hassam fell into step, and the four of them began walking toward Khartoum.

"There will be another bus along soon, perhaps a real one," said Omar when they were out of earshot.

"That was some bus," said Lara. "I felt safer when people were shooting at us back in the desert."

"We are still in the desert," said Hassam. "*Khartoum* is in the desert."

"Quiet!" whispered Omar sharply before Lara could reply. She turned and saw that the other three passengers were approaching them. Omar began walking again, and soon all seven of them—the six men and the false boy—were trudging along the pothole-filled tarmac toward Khartoum.

Finally a large bus, every bit as filthy and rusty as the minivan, honked once and pulled up to a stop, and all seven got on. Omar paid for his party, and they walked past a few seated passengers to the back.

The leather had been ripped off the seats, and Lara elected to stand, holding onto a strap that hung down from the ceiling. One of the passengers from the van walked back and was soon standing next to her.

They lurched over the terrible road for a mile, then another, and suddenly the passenger had a knife in his hand and was plunging it into Lara's robe. The only thing that saved her was the bulkiness of the robe, which concealed the precise location of her body. The knife missed her ribs by inches, and she wasn't about to give her attacker a second chance. She grabbed his wrist and twisted sharply. There was an audible *crack* and the man's mouth opened in a moan, giving Lara a glimpse of the stub of a mutilated tongue. He dropped to one knee, just in time for his face to come into contact with Lara's swiftly rising knee. As his head shot back, she caught him on the throat with the edge of her hand, and he collapsed.

"Turn away!" whispered Omar so softly that only Lara could hear him. "You're humiliated and can't meet anyone's eyes!"

All the passengers turned to stare at her. She was fully prepared to pull her guns and hold them at bay until the bus reached Khartoum, but then Omar stepped forward.

"This scum actually had the nerve to try to kiss my baby brother!" he announced in outraged tones.

Then, as one, the passengers applauded.

"Serves you right, you son of a pig!" said Omar, landing a heavy kick to the unconscious assassin's rib cage.

Fifteen minutes later the bus came to a stop, the driver announced that they had reached the end of his route, and Lara, after many days and narrow escapes, climbed down the shaky stairs and finally set foot in Khartoum.

She looked around, trying to get her bearings based on her one previous trip to the city.

At least we should be all through with riflemen on horseback and slashers in buses, she thought.

"Welcome to Khartoum," said Omar. "I hope you enjoyed the journey, because now is when things start getting dangerous."

18

They walked three blocks to the Bortai Hotel. They paused before the entrance, and then Omar shook his head.

"Too many people know you're in the country now," he said, "and they know we have used the Bortai in the past." He whispered to Hassam. "Hassam will go ahead and get us lodgings at the one other hotel where we can provide security. Most of the Mahdists don't know we have any contacts there, so it should be safe—from them, at least—for the few days we'll be here before you find the Amulet."

"It could be months or even years looking for it," said Lara.

"You are Lara Croft," said Gaafar. "You will find it sooner than anyone thinks."

"I appreciate your confidence," she said. "I hope it's not misplaced." She turned to Omar. "Where will we be staying?"

"The Arak Hotel. It is half a mile from here."

They walked slowly, pretending to window-shop, giving Hassam time to make the arrangements. When they arrived, the Arak turned out to actually be nicer than Lara had anticipated. During the colonial era it had been nicer still, and the management had made every effort to keep it up during the intervening half century of war, drought, and poverty.

Omar walked up to the desk, nodded to the clerk, and came away a moment later with a number of keys. He handed one to Lara and one to Gaafar.

"You will be staying in a suite on the third floor," he announced. "Winston Churchill once stayed there." He paused. "Gaafar and Hassam will be on one side of you, and I will be on the other."

The elevator wasn't working—she suspected it hadn't

worked in some time—and they climbed the winding stair-case, then walked down the broad corridor until they came to her suite. She unlocked the door and walked in.

There was a large parlor with a number of chairs and couches, and best of all, given the heat, a bowl filled with fruit and figs on a small table. The bedroom and bathroom were off to the left.

"I hope the accommodation is acceptable," said Omar.

"It will be just fine," she said. "Come on in and have some grapes or a fig."

The three men entered the parlor. Gaafar and Omar seemed unimpressed; Hassam's jaw dropped, and she had the feeling that these, threadbare as they were, comprised the most luxurious surroundings in which he had ever found himself.

"Where will Kevin stay when he arrives?" she asked.

"Before I answer that, I am afraid I must ask an indelicate question," said Omar uncomfortably.

"We're just friends," she said. "I never met him before I went to Edfu."

"Then he will room with me," said Omar. "Assuming he is still on the *Amenhotep*."

"Why wouldn't he be?"

"The Mahdists or the Silent Ones may have killed him," answered Omar. "Or he may be as brilliant as you believe. He may have figured out where the Amulet is hidden, and left the boat to go retrieve it."

"He doesn't know where it is," said Lara.

"You are sure?"

"The Sudan is his area of expertise," she explained. "Yet he was looking for the Amulet at Edfu. That means he hasn't been able to find it here."

"*You* will find it," said Gaafar with conviction.

"He's the expert," replied Lara.

"But you are—"

"I know," she interrupted wearily. "I'm Lara Croft."

"Precisely."

"It gets to be a burden after a while," said Lara.

"Where will you begin looking for the Amulet?" asked Omar.

"I have no idea," she answered. "After all those days riding El Khobar and Nasrullah, and then what passed for a bus ride, I think I deserve the evening off. Tomorrow I'd like to see where Gordon lived, where his headquarters were, and if any of his writings are in the local library or museum I'll need to read them."

"I will arrange it," promised Omar. He turned to Hassam. "Ask Ismail when the *Amenhotep* is expected. If he doesn't know, go to the docks and make inquiry."

Hassam nodded and left.

"Who is Ismail?" asked Lara.

"The desk clerk—and my cousin," said Omar.

"Well, it's comforting to know you have a man on duty here."

Omar and Gaafar both laughed.

"What's so funny?" she asked.

"*A* man," repeated Omar. "Hassam has seen to it that we now have *eleven* men on duty at the Arak. There is at least one on each floor, and two in the kitchen to make sure your food is not poisoned."

"Are they all your cousins?"

"No," he replied. "Some are Gaafar's."

"Now I know why you felt we'd be safe in the Arak," said Lara.

"You are not safe anywhere," Omar corrected her. "Remember Abdul—he is my cousin, too. You are merely in less danger here."

She noticed Gaafar eyeing the fruit bowl and urged him to take one.

"They are for you," he said.

"I'm not hungry."

"But later you will be."

"Then I'll have room service bring more," she replied. "I assume somebody's cousin will deliver them, after someone else's cousin makes sure they're safe."

"You are sure?"

"I'm sure. Now eat." Then, suddenly, she hissed: *"Stop!"*

She pulled Gaafar's knife from its sheath and plunged it

into the fruit bowl. There was a crunching noise and she came away with a scorpion impaled on the blade.

She held the scorpion up and studied it. "This fellow is a *Lemurus quinquestriatus*—a Deathstalker scorpion. One sting and you're dead inside of five minutes. He's smaller than *Pandinas imperator*, the African emperor scorpion, but he's much deadlier."

"How do you know so much about scorpions?" asked Gaafar, clearly impressed.

"I spend a lot of time in the desert. If I didn't know what was dangerous and what wasn't, I couldn't survive a week." She returned Gaafar's knife and turned to Omar. "I think you need to hire more cousins."

"No," answered Omar. "We need to eliminate at least one of the cousins we already have." He turned to Gaafar. "You know what to do."

Gaafar nodded and walked to the door.

"Whoever it is," added Omar, "do not kill him so swiftly that he has no chance to name any confederates."

Gaafar stepped out into the corridor and closed the door behind him.

"Why didn't whoever placed the scorpion here simply walk up and shoot me?" mused Lara. "Why go to all this trouble? Not only did he take the chance that we'd spot it, but there was only a one-in-four chance that it would sting *me* instead of one of you."

"He couldn't walk up and kill all four of us before one of us killed him," answered Omar. "This way he hides his identity. If the scorpion failed, as it did, he is still alive and able to make another attempt on your life." He paused. "And never forget—killing you is important to the Mahdists, but it is not the ultimate goal. Their mission is to find the Amulet, so even if you are dead, the race for the Amulet continues, and it is to their advantage to have a spy in our midst."

"Then we can expect more indirect attacks?"

"It depends exactly who is doing the attacking," replied Omar. "If it is a known Mahdist, he has no reason to conceal his identity or work indirectly. If it is a traitor, he'll do everything he can to conceal his identity. The Silent Ones, of course, may strike at any time."

"That's very reassuring," said Lara.

"By the way, you can get out of the robes whenever you wish," said Omar. "I had hoped we could keep your presence a secret for another day or two, but obviously our enemies already know you are here."

"How do you suppose they found out so soon?" asked Lara, removing her robes. "We were just given this suite ten minutes ago."

Omar shrugged. "Perhaps all the other rooms are full. Perhaps the traitor knew we would give an Englishwoman the Churchill Suite. Perhaps our enemies didn't have to see through your disguise at all; perhaps they merely saw Gaafar and Hassam and myself with a slight stranger and drew the logical conclusion."

"Should we change hotels?"

"I don't think it would help," said Omar. "They know you're here; they'll be watching us from now on. If we move to another hotel, they'll know it instantly—and despite the scorpion, we can still provide better protection here. There is one traitor in our midst, but we have ten men working in the Arak who are willing to sacrifice themselves to keep you safe." He paused. "We not only have to worry about spies and Mahdists, but there are the Silent Ones, who never want the Amulet found and would be happy to kill you now, before you figure out where it is."

"That's stupid," she said. "It's becoming active. It seems to have a will of its own, and it *wants* to be found. If Kevin or I don't find it, then someone else will—but it's pretty clear that it's no longer content to be inactive."

"I know," agreed Omar. "But we cannot convince all of those who *should* be our allies, who oppose the Mahdists as we do."

"We'll worry about each in turn as we come to them," said Lara, tiring of the conversation, which seemed to be about how many different factions wanted to kill her. She laid her robes onto a sofa. "They're useful in the desert, but they're awkward when I'm inside."

"I do not think you will have to return to the desert. Never forget that Gordon was surrounded. The Amulet *must* be in Khartoum."

"He sent Colonel Stewart all the way to Edfu," noted Lara. "What makes you think he couldn't have sent someone else out of the country with the Amulet?"

"Let us hope he didn't," said Omar. "The Sudan is big enough. I would hate to think we had to search the entire world."

"It would make life much easier if you were right—but it's always possible that he was using Stewart as a decoy, that while his enemies watched him and Stewart, he gave it to some Sudanese man or woman to take into the desert, or to Somalia, or to Libya, or somewhere else."

"Do you really think so?"

"I don't know," answered Lara. "But you have to consider all possibilities. For example, Colonel Stewart traversed the Nile all the way from Khartoum to Edfu. What makes you so sure he didn't simply throw it overboard, or bury it in a riverbank hundreds of miles from Edfu?"

"Because history tells us that he did not travel alone until he reached Edfu, and he would not take the chance that someone might be observing him."

"Someone observed him going into the Temple of Horus," she pointed out.

"But we know now that he was acting as a decoy," answered Omar. "If he actually had the Amulet with him, he would have waited until the middle of the night, and approached it by a circuitous route, making sure that he wasn't being observed."

"Well, it sounds good, anyway," said Lara.

"You know it was not at the Temple of Horus or you would have found it."

"I keep telling you: I wasn't looking for it," she replied. "Besides, do you know how *big* that temple is? You could hide a hundred Amulets in it."

"But no one did," said Omar with certainty. "Since the journalist's memoir was found, the Mahdists have searched the temple top to bottom. If neither you nor they nor Dr. Mason found it, it was not there."

"I hope you're right," said Lara. "At least, I'm going to proceed on that assumption."

There was a knock at the door.

"Come in," said Lara. "It's not locked."

Hassam entered the parlor. "The *Amenhotep* is four days overdue," he announced.

Lara looked at Omar with concern, but Omar merely smiled. "That's faster than usual. Are they in radio contact with the port authority?"

Hassam nodded. "They expect to be here tomorrow morning."

"Mason is still in good health?" continued Omar.

"They have not reported any unusual incidents, and I thought it best not to ask about him."

"You were right," said Omar approvingly.

"I saw Gaafar walking through the lobby on my way back to the suite," said Hassam. "Is something wrong?"

"There has already been an attempt to kill Lara Croft," confirmed Omar.

"I will get my rifle," said Hassam instantly.

Omar shook his head. "That will not be necessary. Gaafar will take care of it."

"But—"

"I want you to stay here to protect her."

"I can protect myself," said Lara firmly.

"Right now you are the most important person in the whole of the Sudan," said Omar. "Through no fault of your own, you also have the most enemies. There is no question that you are able to protect yourself under normal circumstances, but you must acknowledge that these circumstances are anything but normal."

Suddenly a hideous scream echoed through the corridors of the hotel. A moment later Gaafar, the front of his robe spattered with blood, entered the room and closed the door behind him.

"My family just became smaller," he announced.

"Who was it?" asked Omar.

"Abdullahi."

"He prepared the fruit bowl?"

"No, that was Khalifa," answered Gaafar. "Abdullahi is the one who placed it in the room."

"You are sure Khalifa was not a confederate?" asked Omar.

"I am sure."

"How sure?" persisted Omar.

"He will be out of hospital the day after tomorrow."

"I think we had better have Ismail and Suliman make sure there are no other traitors on the staff."

"I can do that," said Gaafar.

"I know you can—but we cannot continue finding trusted replacements for each one you question." He turned to Lara and said, only half-jokingly, "I hope you can find the Amulet before we run out of family members."

19

Lara awoke shortly after sunrise, washed her hands and face in the trickle of water that came out of the bathroom faucet, dressed in her shorts and top, donned Omar's robes over them, and went down to the lobby, where she found her three companions waiting for her.

"I know we agreed there was no more need for a disguise," she said, indicating the robes, "but somehow I don't think my usual outfit would go over too well. Besides, this way I can still wear my pistols."

"You are always thinking ahead," said Hassam admiringly.

"Right now the only thing I'm thinking about is breakfast. Where's the restaurant?"

"It is closed," said Omar.

"When does it open? I'm famished!"

Hassam smiled wanly. "In three weeks."

"All right," she said. "Where can I find some food?"

"We're just a few blocks from the Sudan Club," said Omar.

"The Sudan Club?" she repeated. "What's that?"

"A private club for your countrymen," he said. "It numbered more than twelve hundred members at Independence back in 1956. Today it has less than one hundred and fifty members, and the building is in serious need of repair, but it does serve English breakfasts."

"I could kill for a good English breakfast!" said Lara enthusiastically. "Let's go."

"We will take you there, and we will wait for you," said Omar. "But we are not allowed inside."

"But this is *your* country," she protested.

"True. But it is *your* country's private club." He paused. "It has the only squash court and the best swimming pool in the city."

"Do any of your relatives work there?" she asked.

"A few," answered Omar. "And doubtless some Mahdists as well. No one of them is quite sure who is on which side, so I think you'll be safe there as long as you remain in the public rooms."

"All right," said Lara. "We'll go there, I'll have some breakfast, I'll join the three of you while you eat, and then we'll go meet the *Amenhotep*."

"We have already eaten," said Gaafar.

"Right," said Lara. "I forgot: This place is teeming with your relatives." She lowered her voice. "What did the police say when they found the man you killed last night?"

"They will not find him," answered Gaafar.

"We're not air-conditioned. Even if you hid him, he's not going to smell very good by tomorrow."

Gaafar smiled. "He is not in the hotel."

"Where is he?"

"After you were asleep, I left Hassam guarding your door and I took him swimming."

"Dead men can't swim," said Lara.

"I know."

"The hotel's pool or the Nile?"

"We're in the middle of another drought," answered Gaafar. "There hasn't been water in the Arak's pool all year."

"And no one saw you drop him in the Nile?"

"Probably someone did," interjected Omar.

"And they didn't report it?"

"You wouldn't believe all the things that get dropped into the Nile at night," said Omar. "Most of them are never reported. Shall we go?"

He led her out the door, and the four of them walked the half-mile to a white building that had seen better days and better decades. A large bronze plaque next to the door proclaimed that it was the Sudan Club. Then, beneath its name, in smaller letters, was the inscription: *For Members Only*.

A tall, lean Sudanese man opened the door.

"Welcome to the Sudan Club, Lara Croft," he said. "I hope you will enjoy your meal here."

Lara was surprised to hear her name spoken, and turned questioningly to Omar.

"Another cousin?" she asked.

"Almost," replied Omar. "He is my half-brother Mustafa. He will take you to your table and watch over you until you are ready to leave."

Lara followed Mustafa through a large entryway, then turned left, and found herself in a walled courtyard. Some fifteen diners, all but two of them male, presumably all of them British, were seated at various umbrella-shaded tables. Most stared disapprovingly at her when she entered; at first she thought it was because she was an unescorted woman, but she quickly realized that it was because she was dressed in Sudanese robes.

A single sheet of paper, with the day's menu mimeographed on it, was handed to her. She studied it and then turned to the waiter.

"I'll have porridge, scrambled eggs with sausage, and tea."

"No sausage," said the waiter.

"You're out of it?" she said. "What else have you got? Bacon, perhaps?"

"No bacon," he said severely.

"Let me think about it," said Lara. "Come back in a few moments."

The waiter walked away, and a white-haired gentleman at the next table leaned over.

"Excuse me for interfering, my dear," he said. "I couldn't help overhearing. You are an Englishwoman, are you not?"

"Yes."

"I won't even ask why you are dressed in such apparel," he said. "Let me give you a piece of advice: If you ask for sausage or any other pork products, you will be refused and told they don't have any."

"What's the secret?" asked Lara. "I notice *you* have sausage on your plate."

"You just have to speak a little British," he said with a smile. "Ask for bangers. They don't know it's our informal word for sausages. They just open the banger package and fry them. They probably think it's beef or lamb."

"Thanks," said Lara. "I'll try it."

She ordered bangers with her eggs, and got them. When her food arrived she closed her eyes and just enjoyed inhaling the odors for a minute before she began eating. It was possible she'd had another meal this good since she was trapped in the tomb back in Edfu, but she couldn't remember one.

With the exception of the man who had given her the hint, none of the other club members made any effort to introduce themselves or start up a conversation, and for that she was grateful. She didn't feel like lying, and she had no intention of telling anyone the real reason she was here. She was aware that Mustafa was hovering near the entrance to the kitchen, making himself as inconspicuous as possible, but never letting her out of his sight. When she finished she left some Egyptian pounds on the table and got to her feet. Mustafa came over, picked up the money and returned it to her, explained that she was a guest of the club—a statement no one challenged or seemed to care about—and led her back to the club's front door, where Omar and Gaafar were waiting for her.

"Where's Hassam?" she asked.

"He's gone ahead, just in case the *Amenhotep* has already arrived," said Omar. "We wouldn't want Kevin Mason wandering off in the wrong direction."

The three of them walked to the riverfront, where Hassam was waiting for them.

"Soon," he said. Then he shrugged. "That is probably exactly what they said the last four mornings."

"Almost everything in this country needs fixing," complained Omar bitterly. "The one thing we absolutely do not need is a charismatic leader who is intent on destroying what's left. You and Mason *must* find the Amulet before the Mahdists do."

"We'll do our best," said Lara. "You know," she added, looking at the buildings all crowded together by the river, "it's not London or Paris or New York, but it's a lot bigger and more built up than when General Gordon was here. So much has changed in more than a century. It's always possible that the Amulet is encased in cement, buried beneath the corner-stone of some five-story building."

Omar shook his head. "Gordon was a careful man, and he knew what he had in his possession. He would never have simply buried it in the empty streets of Khartoum and hoped that someday someone would erect a building over it."

"Probably not," agreed Lara. "But I hope you're wrong."

"Why?"

"Because if it's part of a building, or beneath a slab foun-dation, it will never be found, which I gather will please you as much as my finding it."

"Yes and no," he answered. "If I *knew* it was in such a place, inaccessible for all time to come, I *think* I would be sat-isfied. . . . But there is always a chance that if you do not find it on your own, it will lead or call or direct you—or someone—to where it lays hidden."

Suddenly Gaafar nudged him with an elbow. "I see the boat."

Lara and Omar looked down the river, and sure enough, the rusted, decrepit *Amenhotep* was finally in sight.

"It will be here in ten minutes," announced Omar.

His prediction was optimistic. It took the *Amenhotep* more than half an hour to reach them, and another five to attach the gangplank.

The first one off the ship was the captain himself. He was followed by half a dozen men who looked like they had just escaped from jail or were destined to wind up there before long. Then Mason appeared and walked down the gangplank and onto the shore.

Lara was about to approach him, but Omar grabbed her arm and held her back.

"What's the matter?" she said.

"Wait."

"Why?"

"I have spotted three Mahdists. Let's see if they are here for Mason, or if they have some other reason for meeting the boat."

Lara spent the next couple of minutes scanning the faces in

the crowd, trying to pick out the Mahdists. As she did so, Mason walked slowly through the mass of people, obviously looking for her. Finally he gave up and began walking toward the Bortai Hotel, as she'd instructed in the note she'd left him.

"All right, they are not here for him," said Omar.

Lara walked ahead and caught up with Mason before he had gone another hundred feet. She reached out and touched his shoulder.

He turned and looked at her, eyes widening in surprise and pleasure. "Lara!"

"Did you have a pleasant voyage?" she asked, returning his smile, surprised at how glad she was to see him.

"I searched all over that damned boat for a few hours, looking for you, before I found your note and realized you were all right," he answered. "The trip was pretty dull. There was nothing to read, so I spent most of my time on deck and got to brush up on a couple of local dialects." He looked around. "Are you alone?"

"No, I have friends with me. I just thought I'd better speak to you first, so you'll know you can trust them. They have been with me since I left the boat." She turned and nodded to Omar and the others, who approached them. "This is Omar, this is Gaafar, and this is Hassam. I don't know their last names, and frankly, it's probably safer for all of us if neither you or I ever learn them."

"I recognize two of you from the boat," said Mason.

"Only two?" asked Omar with an amused grin.

"Oh, hell!" said Mason after studying his face once again. "You were the waiter!"

Omar bowed. "At your service, Dr. Mason."

"I'm pleased to meet you all," said Mason. "And if Lara vouches for you, that's good enough for me. I hope your trip was as uneventful as mine."

"We've had our share of events," said Lara. "I'll tell you about them later."

"Later?" he repeated. "What are we doing now?"

"Have you eaten breakfast?" she asked.

"Well, I ate *something*," replied Mason, making a face. "I'd hesitate to call it breakfast."

"You don't have any luggage, right?"

"As you'll recall, we left Cairo in rather a hurry."

"Then there's no need to feed you or to take you to our hotel right now," said Lara. "So we might as well get to work."

"An hour from now will be soon enough," said Omar.

"Oh?" said Lara. "What do you suggest we do first?"

"Lose the men who are following us."

20

Omar led them on a torturous route as the morning temperature topped the one hundred degree Fahrenheit mark, a sign of worse to come by midday. They circled city blocks, cut through alleyways, walked into the Aeropole Hotel and walked out through a side entrance. After half an hour the little group came to a stop.

"Well?" asked Mason.

"We have eluded all but one of them," announced Omar.

"What happens now?"

"Now you and Lara go to work." He turned to Gaafar. "You know what to do."

Gaafar nodded and walked into the open doorway of a small fabric store.

"We just walk?" asked Mason.

"That is correct," answered Omar. "Hassam and I will accompany you."

"And what about the man who's following us?"

"He won't be following us once he passes the fabric store," said Omar with a grim smile.

"Well," said Lara to Mason, "where do you want to go first—the library, the National Museum, or the Ethnographical Museum?"

"I don't suppose it matters," answered Mason. "Sooner or later we have to see them all."

"Let's start at the National Museum, then," she said. "It's the largest of the three."

"Sounds good to me," said Mason. He looked around. "Which way is it?"

"You're kidding!" said Lara. "Your father contributed two

rooms' worth to it. They named the Kevin Mason Gallery after him."

"I'm all turned around," he explained. "It was eluding those men. I couldn't even tell you where the Nile is."

"Follow me," said Lara, leading the party to El Gamaa Avenue. They reached the Botanical Gardens in a couple of blocks, and a large brick building loomed up behind all the foliage.

"Do you know where you are now?" asked Lara.

"Of course," said Mason.

She turned to Omar. "Are you two coming in with us?"

"I will join you," he answered. "Hassam will guard the entrance."

"Why bother?" asked Mason. "He can't stop anyone from entering."

"You'd be surprised at what he can do," replied Omar.

"I mean, it would draw too much attention."

"To whom?" asked Omar with a smile.

"Ah!" said Mason approvingly. "I see! It will cause enough of a commotion that we'll be forewarned and can leave by a different exit."

"All right," said Lara. "If we hear a fight, we'll find another way out."

"And if they're already waiting inside," added Mason, "I've got a gun in my shoulder holster and I'm sure you've got your pistols under those robes. But I doubt they'll attack us here. They've got to have figured out that if we're here researching Gordon and the Mahdi, we don't have the Amulet yet, so why rush things when we still might lead them to it?"

"That logic might work for the Mahdists," said Lara. "But not the Silent Ones."

"The who?" asked Mason.

Lara explained as they climbed the stairs leading to the main entrance of the museum. Omar, Mason, and Lara walked through it; Hassam remained behind.

"All right," said Lara. "Shall we split up or do it together?"

"Together," said Omar before Mason could answer. "If you split up, I can't watch you both."

"Watch Lara," said Mason. "I can take care of myself."

"If you insist," said Omar. "We'll meet you back here in two hours."

Mason headed off to the far end of the museum, and Lara turned to Omar.

"You agreed awfully fast," she said. "I thought you wanted to keep an eye on both of us."

"That was just good manners," replied Omar. "*You* are the one we are counting on, so you are the one I will guard."

"All right," she said. "It's too hot to argue. Let me get to a museum directory. I need to find what they have on Gordon and the Mahdi, and if possible I'd like to see a map of Khartoum as it was in 1885."

She soon found herself in the Gordon Room, which was filled with photos of the man, medals he'd won in China and the Sudan, a proclamation he had signed years before the siege in which he abolished all slavery in the Sudan, a portrait that had been painted in his home in England a year before he'd been summoned to defend Khartoum, and a trio of original manuscripts for religious monographs he had written. His sword and pistol were in display cases, as were three of his uniforms. There was even a glass case containing the saddle he had used when directing the Battle of Omdurman, and another displaying the telescope with which he studied the Mahdi's forces across the river during the siege.

There were no photos of the Mahdi, but there was a jeweled dagger that was said to have belonged to him, and a pair of letters he had written to his generals.

She looked around at the photographs and exhibits. "He was quite a man, that Gordon. It's just amazing that he could have held out for so long with no army, no artillery, hardly any food. . . ."

"He had his God," answered Omar. "And they say his faith was as strong as the Mahdi's."

"He also took comfort from the knowledge that a relief column would arrive at any moment," said Lara. "The column arrived two days after Khartoum fell, and Lord Kitchener didn't retake the city for a dozen years." She paused. "Of course, Gordon didn't know that. All his information said that he had only to hold out a few more days or weeks until the column arrived. He may have lost, but it was a truly remarkable bit of soldiering."

"He was a remarkable man. They both were. And they were both sure that they had Allah's blessing."

Lara sighed. "Well, I'd better see what I can glean from all this."

She began examining each item, each photograph, with a single-minded intensity. After she'd been through the entire room twice in an hour and was starting to go through it a third time, Omar stepped forward.

"What exactly is it that you are looking for?" he asked. "Perhaps I can help."

She shook her head. "I'm just trying to learn how his mind worked—why he did this instead of that. Did he ever feel self-doubt or fear? Did he have any respect or compassion for his enemies? When did he know for certain that he couldn't save Khartoum, and when he finally did know it, why didn't he at least save himself?"

"And have you discovered anything about his mental processes?"

"He was more than simply a religious man. He had such absolute certainty that whatever he did was right, that God would direct and protect him. . . ." She grimaced. "He was a great man, but he must have been hell to get along with—especially if you disagreed with him."

Omar watched in silence for another forty-five minutes, then approached and told her it was almost time to meet Mason.

"All right," she said. "I'm not going to learn any more here."

"Have you any ideas?"

"All I can think of after seeing this exhibit is to examine every church that was standing in 1885. Where else would a man of such faith hide something he believed belonged to a servant of the devil?"

"They *have* been searched."

"Perhaps not thoroughly enough," said Lara. "We'll try

again. But first I have to get to the library and the Ethno-graphical Museum."

They reached the main lobby and found Mason waiting for them.

"Learn anything?" he asked.

"Not really. Just that we should probably go through the churches with a fine-toothed comb."

"I did that before I went to Edfu," he said. "Still, it can't hurt to do it again. Might as well be thorough."

"Well, that's helpful, anyway," said Lara.

"What is?" asked Mason, puzzled. "I didn't find it."

"No, but you knew where to look—so you must have a list of the churches that were built before 1885 and are still standing, and where they are."

He seemed surprised. "I'll be damned! I hadn't realized how valuable such a list would be. I got rid of it when I couldn't find anything in the churches."

"No problem. It shouldn't be difficult to put it together again. How many churches were there?"

"Four," said Mason.

"We can search them tomorrow or the next day," said Lara. "For the moment, I think we ought to get over to the Ethno-graphical Museum and see if they have anything useful—though I have my doubts. There won't be anything on Gordon, but they might have something on the Mahdi, and I'm still looking for a map of 1885 Khartoum."

The three of them walked out of the museum, and were immediately joined by Hassam.

"No Mahdists?" asked Omar.

Hassam shrugged. "Here and there. None of them chose to walk past me." He turned to Lara. "Was the museum productive?"

"Probably not," she said. "You have to understand: We're on an awfully old, awfully cold trail."

"You will find it," he said with certainty.

"I appreciate your confidence, but it may be misplaced," said Lara. "It's getting very hot out, and we have a bit of a walk to get to the next museum. Let's get something cold to drink first."

"The Al Bustan restaurant is close by," suggested Hassam.

They made their way to the restaurant and were ushered to a small table, where the waiter took their orders.

"Where is Gaafar?" asked Lara. "Shouldn't he have joined us by now?"

"Don't worry about Gaafar," replied Omar. "He is probably just questioning the Mahdist."

"For two and a half hours?" said Mason.

"He asks very thorough questions," said Omar with an amused smile.

The drinks came, and Lara gratefully accepted an iced tea from the waiter.

"I never did ask," she said. "Did you come up with anything at the museum?"

"Not really," he said. "You were in the Gordon exhibit. I just wandered the rest of the place, looking for . . . hell, for I don't know what. For anything that might jog my mind into gear, give me a hint."

"Gordon and the Mahdi were well matched," said Lara. "They were born leaders, they were brilliant generals, and they each had the absolute knowledge that God was on their side. Under other circumstances, they might have been great friends, even brothers."

"I doubt it," said Mason. "I don't think either of them could ever tolerate the fact that the other spoke directly to God."

She chuckled in amusement. "You're probably right."

"Finish your drink," said Omar. "If we hurry, you can get to the Ethnographical Museum and the library today, and tomorrow the search can begin."

"You're being a little too optimistic," said Lara. "Right now the only thought I have is to search through the churches, and Kevin's already done that. We probably won't learn anything from the next museum, and whatever books and papers I find in the library may take days to go through before I know if they're any use."

"And if they are not?" asked Hassam.

"Then we'll study more," said Lara. "Omdurman isn't very

far across the Nile. If I can't learn anything from where Gordon died, maybe I can learn something from where he defeated the Mahdi. After all, if he came into possession of the Amulet before the Battle of Omdurman, perhaps he never brought it back to Khartoum at all. Maybe it's across the Nile somewhere."

"Do you really think so?" asked Omar.

"I don't know."

"I know how much it means to you and how badly you want it," said Mason to the two Sudanese men, "but never forget: If it was easy to find, someone would have found it already."

Gaafar caught up to them on the street outside the restaurant.

"How did your morning go?" he asked as he joined them.

"About as expected," replied Lara. "How did *yours* go?"

"We were aware that the Mahdists know you are in Khartoum," said Gaafar. "But they also know *why*. I think it likely that they will leave you alone until you find the Amulet or lead them to it."

"As we thought," said Lara. "Maybe we can relax a little now."

"Except for those tongueless killers you mentioned," said Mason.

"I said, 'a little,' " Lara said.

Just then, a bread truck careened crazily around the corner, jumped the curb, and bore down upon them.

21

Lara leaped to her left and reached for her pistols, but they were tangled in her robe. She saw Mason push Omar and Hassam out of the way, then almost elude the truck himself, but the passenger's mirror, sticking out from the door, caught his shoulder and sent him hurtling into the middle of the street.

"Kevin!" she yelled. "Are you all right?"

"Don't worry about me!" he grated. "Just watch yourself!"

Two women screamed as the truck remained on the sidewalk, plowing through carts and kiosks. Then it turned and headed back toward her.

Lara positioned herself in front of the concrete block wall of the building on the corner. There was an awning overhead, and as the truck raced toward her, she reached up to the awning's crossbar and in an almost perfect gymnastic maneuver swung herself up to the top of it, avoiding the truck by less than a second.

This time the truck crunched into concrete and cement. The hood sprang open, and steam burst from the engine. The driver was momentarily blinded as the awning fell across his windshield.

Lara didn't know if the truck could still move, and she wasn't about to wait and find out. She rushed to the door, flung it open, and pulled the driver out of the truck, throwing him to the ground. As the motor stalled and steam continued to fill the air, two more men emerged from the back of the truck, both of them brandishing guns.

The driver, still on the ground, lunged at her. Lara could have dispatched him with a quick kick to the thorax, but she knew she'd be a sitting duck for the two gunmen, so instead she allowed him to trip her up. As she fell and rolled she finally managed to get her hands on her pistols, and she came to a kneeling position, both Black Demons spitting .32-caliber death. One man dropped instantly. The other ducked under the truck, firing awkwardly without a clear view of his target.

Lara had no intention of laying on her belly to get a good shot at him and give him an equally good shot at her. Instead she jumped into the cab of the truck. The engine was still sputtering, and she put it into reverse. There was a scream, and then, after backing up no more than a dozen feet, the motor died.

Lara leaped out of the cab, pistols at the ready, looking for any sign of life. The driver, who had leaped out of the way, was getting groggily to his feet. She swung her hand with a Black Demon still in it and caught him in the temple. He dropped to the ground, senseless. She stepped back and saw that the truck had indeed backed over the final gunman, pinning him to the ground. His face wore a hideous death mask.

Mason had staggered to his feet and was walking over to her.

"Are you all right?" she asked.

"I'm fine," he said ruefully. "Serves me right for trying to be a hero."

They walked over to Omar and Hassam, who were just getting to their feet.

"I appreciate your saving our lives," said Omar. "But next time," he added with a grin, "don't push so hard. For a moment there I wasn't sure who was the enemy."

Lara led them to the three bodies, two dead, one unconscious. "Are they Mahdists or Silent Ones?" she asked.

Mason squatted and propped open the unconscious man's mouth. "He's got a tongue, so I guess that means Mahdists."

"Unfortunately not," said Omar. "That a man has a tongue in his mouth proves nothing. By that definition, we would all be Mahdists. We'll have Gaafar question this man when he wakes up, and then we will know for sure."

Lara looked around. "Where *is* Gaafar?"

"I think I know," said Mason grimly. He pointed to the huge Sudanese, who was lying about ten yards behind the truck. "He caught a stray bullet from the man you pinned under the wheel."

Omar and Hassam raced over and knelt down. Hassam began cursing in Arabic. Omar remained motionless for a full minute, then stood up and turned to Lara and Mason.

"He is dead," he said softly.

"You're sure?" asked Mason.

"I am sure."

"I'm sorry," said Lara. "If I hadn't backed over that last man, maybe he wouldn't have gotten off a wild shot."

"You saved two of us," said Omar. "His death is hardly your fault."

"He was a good man," said Lara, replacing her pistols in her holsters beneath her robes.

"The best," replied Omar. "I will tell his brothers and his cousins. They will claim the body after the police examine it. And now we must go. If they were willing to make one attempt on your life in the daylight, in front of witnesses, they will surely make more."

"I'm not going to let them succeed," said Mason firmly.

"Then we'd better get you healthy first," said Lara.

"What are you talking about?" he demanded.

She pointed to his neck and shoulder. "You're bleeding."

"I am?" he said, surprised. "I must have cut myself when I was rolling across the street."

"Or when the truck hit you," she said.

"It wasn't the truck," he said, obviously annoyed with himself for being hurt at all. "It was that goddamned side mirror."

"Whatever it was, we should get you to a doctor."

"It's just a scratch," he protested.

"I'm not walking into a museum or a library with a man whose shirt is drenched in blood," said Lara.

"All right, all right," he said. "But I'll be damned if I'm going to a doctor or a hospital with a little scratch like this. I'll go to the hotel and clean up."

"And buy a shirt along the way," said Lara. "You don't have any luggage, remember?"

"What about you?"

"I'll go to the museum and meet you at the library."

"All right. It beats arguing with you." He paused. "We're at the Bortai, right?"

"Not anymore," said Omar. "Now we are at the Arak. Do you know where it is?"

"I'll find it."

"I'll see you in a couple of hours," said Lara as he started off. "And be sure to use a disinfectant on that cut. There's a pharmacy just down the block from the hotel."

Mason resisted the urge to salute her, and simply turned and began walking toward the city center.

"Should we tell him it's closer to the Nile?" asked Hassam.

"No," said Lara. "The more haberdashers he passes, the more likely he is to actually buy some clothes." She turned back to Omar, who was once again kneeling next to Gaafar's body. "Come on," she said gently. "The police will be here any minute. I can hear the sirens already, and I don't think it would be a good idea for them to ask me any questions."

Omar stood up, a dagger in his hand. "We will go now." He reached out and presented Gaafar's knife to her, handle first. "He would have wanted you to have this."

"The Scalpel of Isis," she said. "You're sure?"

"I am sure."

She tucked the blade inside her robe. "Then I'm honored."

"We must go," said Hassam as the sirens became louder.

It took them ten minutes to reach the Ethnographical Museum, keeping off the main thoroughfares, and as Lara had predicted, there was nothing of use there.

Hassam walked her to the library while Omar went off to pass the word of Gaafar's death, not only to inform his family of it, but also to try to find out who was responsible for the truck attack. Lara had a feeling that Omar's people were involved. It made perfect sense to her that the Mahdists would let her live as long as they thought she might find the Amulet; it was men like Abdul who wanted it to remain lost or hidden forever.

Mason, dressed in all-new khaki shirt and slacks, with white bandages climbing up his neck from his shoulder, and a felt hat shading his eyes from the sun, was waiting for them on the steps of the library.

"Well, you're looking fit," she said. "If they ever remake

King Solomon's Mines, you should be a natural for the part of Allan Quatermain. Are you feeling better?"

"I was never feeling badly," he said. "Where's Omar?"

"Spreading word of what happened, and trying to find out who ordered it," she said.

"I'm not without my own sources in the city, and I'll bet they're different from his," said Mason. "I'll tell you what. You do what you have to do in the library, and while you're at it I'll see if I can get some answers."

"Omar will find out," said Hassam.

"I'm sure he will," said Mason. "But it won't hurt to have it confirmed from independent sources."

"You do what you want," said Lara. "As for me, I'm going to hunt up Siwar."

"Siwar? One of Omar's lieutenants?"

"One of Khartoum's historians," she replied.

"Oh, of course," said Mason. "I'm still not thinking clearly. I'd better get going before I say anything else stupid. Besides, the sooner we find out who sent the truck after you—"

"It doesn't really matter," she interrupted. "As far as I'm concerned, I don't care which side tried to kill me. The sooner we find the Amulet, the sooner they'll leave me alone." She gestured toward the library. "I'm going in there."

Mason went off on his own, and Lara and Hassam entered the library. After a moment she noticed that tears were streaming down his face.

"I know he was a good friend and ally," she whispered, "but try not to think of him, at least until we're out of here. People are starting to stare at you and wonder what's wrong."

"You are right," he said, making an almost physical effort to cast the image of his dead comrade from his mind. "I will not embarrass you again."

"I'm not embarrassed," replied Lara. "I just don't want to attract any extra attention."

He nodded his acquiescence, and the two of them walked to the back of the building, where she found a few dozen volumes on Gordon and the siege of Khartoum.

"I'm going to be here for a few minutes," she whispered to

him. "Why don't you rinse your face off? The tears have left streaks across the dust. You almost look like you're wearing a mask."

"You'll remain here?" said Hassam.

"I won't leave this section until you come back," she promised.

He turned and headed off to the rest room, and Lara pulled down a volume that was written in Arabic, thumbed through it looking for a map, couldn't find one, and pulled another book out. This one did have a map, and she studied it for a few minutes. A frown spread over her face, and she began thumbing through the pages—and suddenly she felt the sharp point of a knife against her rib cage.

"Not a sound," whispered a voice in Arabic. "I want you to walk slowly to the exit on your left."

"If you're going to kill me, why should I make it easy for you?" she whispered back. "Do it right here, surrounded by witnesses, and be assured that I don't plan to die silently."

"How you die is of no concern to me," said the man. "I am offering you a chance to live. I know you found the Amulet of Mareish in the Temple of Horus. Just tell me where it is."

Okay, she thought, *so you're a Mahdist. I guess not all of you are willing to sit on the sidelines while I hunt for it.*

"I don't even know yet what it looks like," she replied.

"You lie."

"If I had it, why would I be here, trying to learn about it from books?"

"To learn how to use its power, of course," said the man. "Now, do you walk or do you die right here?"

I don't know how many more Mahdists are in the library. Let's get outside where it's just you and me, and then we'll see how tough you are.

She walked meekly to a side door, and a moment later the pair of them were alone in a deserted alley.

"Now tell me where it is, or by Allah I will cut the answer out of you."

He pushed the point of his weapon against her. She gasped and bent over, ostensibly in pain—but as she bent over, her right hand snaked inside her robes and made contact with the hilt of the Scalpel of Isis. She grabbed it and maneuvered it loose from her belt, where she had tucked it.

"Now you see what happens when you do not cooperate," hissed the man.

"What happens," she said, "is that I lose my temper!"

With that she spun around, dagger in hand, and slashed upward. The man screamed as her blade cut deep into his free arm, then took a step back, and she got her first good look at her attacker. He was a huge man, six and a half feet tall, close to three hundred pounds, without any fat on him.

"You could have told me what I wanted to know and saved yourself!" he rasped. "Now you will die whether you tell me or not!"

She knew better than to close with him when he outweighed her by more than two-to-one. As he approached her, she looked around the alley for anything she could use to her advantage.

There was an insulated power line stretched across it, but it was about twelve feet up, and she knew she couldn't jump high enough to reach it. Then she saw the garbage piled up beside the building—wooden packing crates, heavy boxes, all discarded by the library. As he took another step toward her she raced up the pile of boxes and leaped toward the power line. Her fingers closed on the rubber insulation, and she swung herself up.

"You think you can hide on a wire?" said the man with a contemptuous laugh.

She got her feet under her and stood up, walking along the wire, scanning the rooftops until she found what she was looking for.

"Catch me if you can!" she said, laughing back at him.

"You think I cannot reach the wire?" he said. "Then watch!"

He leaped straight up, and his fingers closed on the wire.

"You should have stayed on the Sudanese basketball team!" she said, jumping off the vibrating wire onto the roof of a small building.

He couldn't walk the wire the way she could, but he swung himself along it, hand over hand, with remarkable speed, and a moment later he was standing on the edge of the roof.

She waited until he began running after her, and then she turned and ran to the edge of the roof and jumped the five-foot gap to the next roof.

She landed on the brick border, and raced along it, following its right angle at the corner. When she was halfway down the length of it, she turned to see her pursuer. He was just leaping from the first roof to the second and he had built up such momentum that he didn't stop at the border but began running across the wooden roof at an angle, trying to cut off her line of retreat.

And suddenly there was a *crash* as the roof gave way and, with a scream, the man fell heavily to the ground floor.

Lara walked gingerly across the roof to the hole he had made and looked down. He lay on his back, staring up at nothing, his arms and legs at impossible angles.

"Lots of dry rot in this climate," said Lara. "Three-hundred-pounders really shouldn't be running across rooftops."

A moment later she leaped lightly to the alley and reentered the library. She sought out Hassam and told him what had happened.

"I think it's time to return to the Arak," he said.

"So much for the theory that the Mahdists will leave me alone now."

"There are obviously rogue elements among the Mahdists," said Hassam as they walked out the main entrance. "What happened was my fault. I should never have left your side. I must report myself to Omar."

"I won't tell him if you don't," said Lara.

"I would be no better than our enemies if I lied to my leader."

"Nonsense," said Lara. "Our enemies want to rule the world. We just want to save it."

"Sometimes I think we will never find the Amulet," said Hassam morbidly.

"We'll find it," said Lara.

"Then you did learn something today?"

"Almost certainly," she replied. "Now I just have to figure out what it was."

22

They returned to the hotel, and Lara went up to her suite, where she gratefully threw off her robes and reveled in her newfound freedom of motion. After walking around for a moment she turned to Hassam.

"Go down to the lobby and have one of Omar's cousins visit either the main library or a local branch and take out half a dozen books on Gordon."

"Are there any particular titles?"

"No, not really. I've got to start somewhere. Eventually I'll read them all."

"All?" asked Hassam.

"Don't look so surprised. You don't search for treasure in a vacuum. If you're going to be successful, you do your research first."

"I will go downstairs as soon as Omar returns."

"He might not get back until dinnertime," said Lara. "Do it now, before the libraries close. The sooner we find it, the sooner everyone will stop trying to kill me. There's no sense wasting a night."

"I can't leave you alone."

She drew her pistols as fast as Doc Holliday or Johnny Ringo could have done more than a century earlier. "I'm not alone," she said. "I have these."

He looked hesitant. "I don't know. . . ."

"What's more important to you?" she asked. "Finding the Amulet, or taking a chance that someone will get past all your friends and relations in broad daylight, make his way up to the suite, and sneak up on me before I can shoot him?"

Hassam sighed in defeat. "When you put it that way . . ."

"I do."

He walked to the door. "At least promise to lock it behind me."

"All right."

"I will knock three times when I return."

"Everybody knocks three times," said Lara. "Why don't you just take the key with you? You ought to be back in less than ten minutes."

"What if Omar or Dr. Mason shows up first?"

"Then they'll have to wait in the corridor until you return," said Lara, tossing him the key. "The sooner you go, the sooner you can get back."

Hassam walked into the hallway, closed and locked the door behind him, and went off to find someone he trusted to get what Lara needed from the library. As soon as she was sure he was gone, she pulled one of the Black Demons and pointed it toward the heavy draperies that were gathered to the side of a set of French doors that led out to a small balcony.

"I really do need the books, but that's not why I sent him away," she said. "You can come out now—and keep your hands where I can see them."

There was no response.

"I know you're there," she continued. "You've got exactly three seconds to come out or I'll put fifteen bullets into the curtain."

A tall, lean, bearded man stepped out from behind the drapes, his hands in the air.

"There's no fire escape," she said. "You either bribed the maid or picked the lock. Why?"

"I must speak to you."

"I've been in Khartoum for a day and a half."

"This is the first time you've been alone."

"Okay, we're alone. Now speak—and keep those hands where I can see them. Who are you and what do you want?"

"My name is Abdel el-Dahib. Omar is my cousin."

"Didn't his family ever have a hobby?" she said sardonically. "He seems to be everybody's cousin. Why couldn't you approach me when Omar was around?"

"Because we are on opposite sides," said the man. "He wants the Amulet found. I do not."

"Are you behind the attempts to kill me since I arrived here?"

"No," he said. "The Silent Ones wish to kill you because you are looking for the Amulet. Some of the Mahdists wish to kill you because they fear you have already found it."

"Tell me something I don't know," she said. "For instance, why you wish to kill me."

"I have told you, I do not. I wish only that you stop looking for the Amulet."

"So you thought you'd pay me a polite visit and ask me nicely to stop my search. How very civilized of you."

"I am a scholar," said Abdel. "I seek to persuade you with words, not threats or weapons."

"I'm afraid it's too late for that," she said. "Though I must say, I wish more people around here shared your philosophy."

"Why is it too late?" asked Abdel. "You don't mean . . ."

"No, I haven't found the Amulet," said Lara, seeing his alarm. "But someone will, and soon."

"How can you be sure of this when it has gone undiscovered for more than one hundred years?"

"Because the Amulet itself wants to be found."

Abdel nodded grimly. "Some of the Mahdi's writings hint that the Amulet is a conscious entity in its own right: a demon-possessed artifact, perhaps."

"Whatever it is," said Lara, "if it insists on being found, I think it's better for our side to find it than the Mahdists." She finally lowered her pistol. "You should be in favor of that. If those who oppose the Mahdists possess it, you'll be invincible in battle. The Mahdists won't be able to defeat you or take it away from you."

"Do not tempt me!" he said passionately.

"Tempt you?" she asked curiously.

"The Amulet is pure, unbridled power, and with absolute power comes absolute corruption. Only those who are totally selfless and noble in thought dare to so much as *touch* it. If we were to use the Amulet, we would become no better than those we oppose, just as the Silent Ones have become twisted reflections of the Mahdists they were originally formed to combat."

Lara stared at him for a long moment. "You are an honorable man, Abdel el-Dahib," she said sincerely, "but you cannot convince me to stop my search."

"Have you thought about what you will do with it if you do find it?"

"Not yet," she replied. "First I have to find it."

"At least you have been honest with me," he said. "And there is always the chance that you will not find it."

"*Someone* is going to find it," said Lara. "It might as well be someone from our side." She paused. "Will you try to stop me?"

"No," he replied. "I am no murderer. But I cannot speak for all of my allies."

"What will Hassam or Omar do if they find you here?"

"I truly do not know."

"Well, there's no sense finding out the hard way." She looked around the suite. "Go wait in the bedroom. They have Moslem sensibilities; that is one room they will not enter unbidden. When we go out for dinner, I'll leave the suite unlocked. Let yourself out and go in peace, Abdel el-Dahib."

"Thank you, Lara Croft," he said. "I do not wish to kill my cousin, and I know he does not wish to kill me. Continue your search if you must, and may a compassionate Allah misguide you."

He walked into the bedroom and closed the door.

It was less than a minute later that Hassam unlocked the door to the suite and entered the parlor.

"Ismail himself has gone for the books," he announced. "He should be back within an hour."

"Good." She walked to a sofa and sat down. "I'm going to be hungry in another hour or two . . . and I've lost my faith in this hotel's room service. Why don't we go back to that restaurant we had a drink at earlier? It looked good."

Hassam's face lit up. "You mean the Al Bustan?"

"That's the one."

"Then that is where we shall go—if Omar approves."

"Contrary to what he believes, Omar doesn't run my life,"

said Lara bluntly. "He can eat where he wants. I'm going to the Al Bustan."

"Good choice," said Mason, entering and walking into the parlor. "I've eaten there before. Try the grilled chicken."

"Kevin!" she exclaimed, walking over and hugging him. "I didn't even hear the door open."

"I'm getting better at all this cloak-and-dagger stuff," he said, not without a trace of pride. "Did you have any luck at the library?"

"I'm still alive," she said. "Some might say that was a stroke of luck."

"There was another attack?"

"Nothing I couldn't handle," replied Lara. "How about you—did you get the information you were after?"

"They were Mahdists, all right," he confirmed. "And working on their own. My source says that if they'd succeeded, their own people would have killed them. They want you watched, not murdered or even hindered." He checked his wristwatch. "When do you expect Omar back?"

"I don't know."

"Well, if there's any other place you want to go today . . ."

"I've got to stay here," she said. "I'm waiting for Ismail."

"Who's Ismail?"

"A friend," replied Lara. "I sent him to the library to pick up some books."

He frowned. "I thought you just came from the library?"

"I left in rather a hurry."

"What did you ask him to bring you?"

"Books on Gordon," she answered.

"Any titles in particular?"

"No. I just need to know more about him, to learn how his mind worked. I know he was a brilliant general, and I know he was almost fanatically religious, but that's hardly enough to go on. I've got to put myself in his shoes. He's got the Amulet, and the Mahdi has declared a sixty-day cease-fire. He doesn't know for a fact that the city can hold out for the ten months that it did; it might fall in two months, or six weeks, or the day the cease-fire ends. He's got to hide the Amulet soon. He knows he's being watched, so he sends

Colonel Stewart all the way to Edfu as a decoy. Now what does he do next?"

"He hides it, of course," said Mason. "And he's got to hide it within the city limits."

"Not necessarily."

"But he turned the city into an island," noted Mason. "He couldn't leave it."

"He didn't flood the ditch and isolate the city until a month before the siege began," said Lara. "I learned that much at the National Museum this morning. So he had thirty days in which to get it out of Khartoum."

"I don't think so," said Mason. "He was the most recognizable man in the Sudan, probably even including the Mahdi. There's no way he could have left without being spotted."

"He didn't leave," answered Lara. "He kept a diary, so we know he was here the whole time, but that doesn't mean that the Amulet didn't leave."

"You're reaching," said Mason firmly. "It's somewhere in Khartoum."

"Maybe," she admitted. "I'm just pointing out that he *could* have sent it away with a trusted aide—probably a Sudanese, since any of the British he was here to save would be too easy to spot."

"He *could* have done a lot of things," said Mason. "You're making it too complex. The answer is right here in Khartoum."

"Perhaps," she said. "I'm just trying to be thorough, and to see the city—and the enemy, and the world—as Gordon himself would have seen them."

"What I can't figure out is why he didn't use the damned thing," said Mason. "Once he had it, why didn't he turn its power on the Mahdi? How could he make himself part with it?"

"You're forgetting his nature," answered Lara. "He was a devout Christian, and he would have believed that the Amulet was a tool of Satan. He'd sooner have surrendered the city to the Mahdi without a fight than blacken his soul by using it."

"Based on the intimations you've received, wouldn't the Amulet itself have something to say about that? Nothing wants to die, or be hidden away, not even a mystic artifact."

"It might be able to contact you or me," said Lara, "but if it tried to influence Gordon, he'd never have touched it again. He'd have locked it in some box and gotten rid of it as soon as he could."

They fell to discussing Gordon for the next hour, and then there was a gentle knocking at the door. Hassam walked over to it, dagger in hand, cracked it open, saw that it was Ismail with a pile of books, sheathed his blade, took the books, and closed the door again.

"Good!" said Lara. "Tonight's homework."

Hassam set the books down on a coffee table.

"Six volumes," she said to Mason. "That's three for each of us."

"Fair enough," said Mason. "They look pretty old, and it wouldn't hurt to run a cloth over them. I'll wager they haven't been read in years." He studied the spines. "At least they're all in English. Have you any preference?"

She shook her head. "Take the top three when you leave; I'll go through the others."

They waited another twenty minutes, and when Omar still hadn't shown up they decided to go out for dinner.

Hassam looked at her strangely as she made for the door.

"What is it?" she asked.

"Your robes," he said. "Are you not going to wear them?"

"Why? Is there something wrong with how I'm dressed?"

Hassam's eyes flicked over her bare legs and the open top buttons of her shirt, but he said nothing.

"You won't be able to wear your guns," Mason observed. "At least with the robes, you could still wear them underneath."

"I'll have the Scalpel of Isis tucked in my boot. That will have to do for now." Then, looking at their doubtful faces, she added: "Guns are useful, but it's a weakness to grow too dependent on them."

As they passed through the lobby Hassam told Ismail, who was working the reception desk, where they would be and to send Omar along if he appeared within the next half hour.

The Al Bustan was on Sharia al Baladiya, just a few blocks in from the Nile, and offered what most foreigners considered to be a typical North African bill of fare. Lara ordered the grilled chicken, as Mason had suggested, while he himself had lamb. They both had sweet figs for dessert, then splurged with a pair of lemonades.

She was aware that she was attracting a lot of stares. Being a beautiful woman, she was used to it, but on this occasion she knew that most of them were coming from people who were offended by her bare arms and legs, and a few were probably coming from men who wanted her dead.

They finally returned to the hotel and went back up to her suite, where she gave Mason the books and sent him and Hassam off to their room, while she prepared to sit down and plunge into the remaining volumes after making sure that Abdel el-Dahib had left while they were at dinner.

She had just opened the first book when Omar entered the room.

"You should lock your door," he said severely.

"I knew you'd be coming by," she said. "I'll lock it when I go to bed. What did you find out?"

"They were not *my* men, but they were men who did not want you to find the Amulet."

"That's strange," she said. "Kevin's source said they were Mahdists."

"Then his source is mistaken."

"He seemed pretty sure."

"I'll check further tomorrow," said Omar. "Or perhaps even tonight."

"Go ahead," she said. "You don't have to chaperone me. I'm spending the night reading."

Omar walked to the door, then turned to her. "He was certain, you say?"

"Yes."

"Maybe I had better check my own sources." He opened the door and stepped into the corridor. "Remember to lock the door behind me."

"I will."

Then he was gone, and Lara locked and bolted the door. She knew there was no fire escape, but she walked over and closed the French doors to the balcony just to be on the safe side, then bolted them shut.

Finally she settled back on an easy chair to read about the fabulous life of General Charles Gordon. Four hours later she had worked her way up to his correspondence with the great Victorian explorer, Sir Richard Burton, and was reading in rapt fascination when she came to a page that was missing. She didn't think much of it; it was a very old volume, and perhaps six or seven other pages were missing as well. But in a later letter to Burton, Gordon referred to his letter of June 3, 1883, and mentioned that he had used it as the basis for a magazine article. When she turned back to see what he had said on June 3, she found that was the letter that was missing.

She tried to continue reading.

The letter. Find the letter.

"Who was that?" she said, leaping to her feet, pistol in hand.

The letter. June 3, 1883.

It wasn't a voice. It was more as if the wind itself had formed the words.

The letter.

"All right, all right!" she said to the empty room. "I heard you."

The letter.

She walked to the door, then thought better of it. There was no way she could go down to the lobby and walk out the front entrance without picking up an escort, and she definitely didn't want an escort for what she was about to do.

She decided to leave the Black Demons behind again. The last thing she needed was to be stopped by the police for walking around with weapons in the middle of the night, and robes were too bulky for what she had in mind.

She opened the French doors and stepped out on the balcony. There was no fire escape, but every room on this side of the hotel had balconies. She climbed over the edge, holding on to the railing, and lowered herself as much as she could. Then she began swinging her legs back and forth, and when they were over the balcony below she released her grip and landed lightly, then repeated the process, landing on the sidewalk.

She looked around to make sure she hadn't been seen, then

began walking quickly to the library. It was locked, of course, but she had known it would be. She walked around to the alley where she had fought the huge man earlier in the day, again used the pile of discarded crates and boxes to reach the insulated power line, and walked along it to the nearest roof. Then she walked over to the library. Its roof was twenty feet higher than the roof she was on, but there was an ornamental chimney—she was sure it was never used, not in this climate—with enough handholds that she felt confident she would be able to catch it without falling to the alley below.

Her decision made, she hurled herself through the air. Her outstretched fingers latched onto a pair of weeping bricks that extended out from the chimney, and she slowly pulled herself up. Her feet found purchase, and she began climbing the chimney. She reached the roof a moment later.

She had hoped to find a door, or some means of entering the library, but there wasn't any. She walked to the edge, leaned over, and checked the nearest window. Closed. She methodically made her way around the building, checking each window—and finally came to one that was cracked open.

She slung her legs over the side of the roof and lowered herself until she was hanging by one arm, opposite the window. With her free hand she raised the window until it was fully open.

Her problems didn't end there. This wasn't like a balcony she could drop onto. Any kind of straight drop would send her to the pavement thirty feet below. She could have swung her body, as she did on the hotel's balcony, and crashed her feet through the window, but she didn't want to alert any guards or passing police.

She extended her body to its utmost, and found to her relief that her toes just reached the windowsill. She slowly released her grip on the edge of the roof, balancing precariously. She felt herself slipping, unable to hug the building as she lowered herself. Then, just before she fell to the ground, she managed to slide feet inside the window, and she now slid down until she was sitting on the ledge with her legs inside the building. From there it was just another few seconds before she was totally inside. She closed the window behind her, descending to the ground floor, and, using a pocket flashlight, began her search for the missing letter.

There were two dozen books on Gordon still on the shelf, and she picked them up, one by one, thumbing through the index to each—and on the seventeenth book she hit paydirt.

"All right," she muttered, sure that whatever had directed her here could hear her. "I've found it. But if you don't mind, I'm going to take it back to the hotel and read it there."

There was no response, nor had she really expected one.

Tucking the book under her arm, she walked to the same side exit she had used earlier in the day and twisted the handle. It was as she had thought: locked from the outside, but not the inside. A moment later she was back in the alley, and heading back to the Arak Hotel, but before she had taken a dozen steps, her way was barred by a glowing skeleton of something that stood erect but would never be mistaken for human, or even primate.

It reached a bony hand out to take the book from her. She backed away.

All right, she thought. *The Amulet wants me to read this, so it didn't send you. That means you're from the Mahdists or anti-Mahdists, and their magic isn't as strong as the Amulet's. I hope.*

The hand reached out again, and this time she grabbed it—and was mildly surprised to find that it was substantial, rather than just an illusion. She bent one of the fingers back. It broke off, but the skeleton seemed not to notice.

Its jaws moved, and though it had no tongue, no larynx, no means of making a sound, the words *"I want!"* seemed to emanate from its missing lips.

"You can't always have what you want!" said Lara, backing up another step, her eyes searching the alley. Finally she found what she was looking for—a metal garbage can, one of the few. She picked up the lid and, using it as a warrior might use a shield, charged into the skeleton, holding it in front of her.

The bones shattered and the skeleton collapsed, but where each bone fell there was now a small, growling, vicious dog. The closest one launched himself at her ankles, and she kicked it through the air like a football. Before it could fall to the ground it sprouted wings, metamorphosed into a black crow, and flew off, squawking its anger.

Then she was among them, kicking some, picking others up by the scruff of the neck and hurling them away, pounding on some with her shield. Every time contact was made the dog turned into a crow and flapped noisily away.

Finally just one small dog remained.

"You tell your creator that I don't scare easily," said Lara, approaching it.

Suddenly the dog's entire demeanor changed. It turned away, tucked its tail between its legs, and ran off, yipping like a terrified puppy, leaving her to ponder whether the sorcerer had given up or a real dog had accidentally wandered into a pack of its supernatural brethren.

She held up the book to show whatever had directed her to the library that she still possessed it.

"I hope you're satisfied," she said into the dark, empty night.

The sigh of a breeze was her only answer.

There was a knock on Lara's door.

"Are you awake?" said Mason's voice.

"Just a minute," she said, getting up off the couch, where she'd fallen asleep reading the book. She walked to the door and opened it.

"It's three in the afternoon," said Mason. "Were you planning on sleeping the day away?"

"I was up all night reading," she said. "Have you been out?"

"Yes," replied Mason. "I picked up a little .22 caliber Beretta; I've got it tucked away in my belt."

"If you shoot anyone with it, you'll just make them mad," said Lara. "Why didn't you pick up an AK-47? They're for sale in almost every alley in the city."

"Because I couldn't hide it under my coat," he admitted awkwardly.

"We don't want to get in a shooting war with a million Mahdists," she said. "The whole purpose of having a gun is to frighten people off, or make them think about the consequences of shooting at us. If they can't see it, it can hardly serve as a deterrent."

"I disagree," said Mason. "I'm not interested in handheld deterrents. The only purpose of a gun is to kill your enemies."

"If I start killing my enemies, I could very quickly turn this megalopolis into the smallest village you ever saw," said Lara.

"No harm is going to come to you," said Mason. "I didn't let it happen in Egypt, and I'm not going to let it happen here in the Sudan."

"I wasn't able to defend myself in Cairo," replied Lara. "Anyone who attacks me now will know he's been in a fight."

"I'm sure he will," said Mason. "It seems a shame, though. . . ."

"What does?"

"Attacking you."

"I'll take that as a compliment."

"It was," said Mason.

"Thank you."

He stared at her for a moment. "If I may say so," he began, "I find you—"

"Stop," she interrupted him, holding up a hand. "One compliment a day is all I can handle when people are plotting to kill me."

He laughed. "All right. But when this is over, I think I just might show you how romantic an archaeologist can be."

"When this is over, I might be interested in finding out," replied Lara.

There was an awkward silence, and then Mason spoke up. "So what were you reading that kept you up all night?"

"There was a series of letters from Gordon to Sir Richard Burton."

"The explorer?"

"And the man who translated the *Arabian Nights*," she said. "Anyway, Gordon later referred to one of the letters and mentioned that whatever he'd said had got him to thinking, and he'd even written an article about it. I was hoping it might be something about his favorite location in Khartoum, something that could lead us to the Amulet."

"But it wasn't?"

She shook her head. "As far as I can tell it was just a religious tract, nothing about Khartoum at all. I'm still hunting for it—but these are *thick* books. This one"—she held up the volume she'd stolen—"is thirteen hundred pages, and two of the others don't even have indices."

"If it's just a religious tract, why bother?"

Because the Amulet told me to. But if I say that aloud, the believers will kill me and the nonbelievers will lock me away at the funny farm.

They spoke for a few more minutes, discussing what research they planned to do next, what parts of the city to search. Mason mentioned once again that he planned to visit the Bureau of Information and try to get a list of all Khartoum's pre-1885 structures.

"It would be all but impossible to come up with such a list in most Third World cities," he said. "But 1885 was the most important year in Khartoum's history, so there just might be a record somewhere."

"I would guess from what Omar has told me that he thinks 1956 is the most important year," suggested Lara.

"Why 1956?" asked Mason.

"Independence."

"Oh, of course." Mason got to his feet. "Well, if I'm going to get that list, I might as well get started."

He walked to the door, and then turned. "Dinner?"

"I'll be too busy reading."

He looked his disappointment. "I'll see you tomorrow, then," he said, leaving the suite.

Lara picked up the book again, and spent a few more hours reading and rereading the Gordon-Burton correspondence, never noticing that she had not only slept through breakfast and lunch but that dinnertime had come and gone as well. For perhaps the fiftieth time since she returned from her nocturnal visit to the library she read the letter of June 3, 1883.

I don't understand, she thought in frustration. *There's nothing to it! He's just talking about religion. There's not a word about Khartoum, and not a word about you.*

And the answer came on the wind, through the open French doors: *Think, Lara Croft. Use your brain and think.*

She picked up the book again, and read the letter once more. But this time as she read, she blinked her eyes several times, frowned, looked away, then read it again—and suddenly she picked up the other books and began thumbing through them until she found what she was looking for.

"Well, how about that?" she muttered when she had finished reading it. "You sly devil, Gordon! There it is in black-and-white where anyone who read it could figure out where you hid it, and no one ever did."

She smiled triumphantly.

"Until tonight!"

24

The sun was just rising when Lara, who had been awake all night, picked up the phone and called down to the desk.

"May I help you?" asked the clerk on duty.

"I need to speak to Ismail," she said.

"Hold on a moment, and I'll get him."

She looked out at Khartoum through the French doors. With any luck, this would be the last morning she'd see the city—at least for a while.

"This is Ismail," said a familiar voice. "What can I do for you, Miss Croft?"

"I need a favor," said Lara. "A very important one."

"If it's within my power . . ."

"It is," she said. "I need to speak to Omar, and I need to speak to him alone, in my suite. He may be asleep, he may be awake, I have no idea. But he's sharing a room with Dr. Mason, and it's essential that Dr. Mason doesn't know he is meeting with me. I don't care what excuse he makes—he can say he's buying information from an informant, or visiting his girlfriend, or anything else—but he has to understand: It is absolutely vital that I speak to him, and that no one else knows about it."

"I will take care of it," promised Ismail.

"Good. Tell him my door is unlocked."

"Trust me, Miss Croft."

"I do," she replied. "That is why I am asking you to do this."

She hung up the phone and paced the room restlessly for the next ten minutes. Finally the handle on her door turned, and Omar silently let himself in. He closed and locked the door behind him, then turned to face her.

"You know where it is," he said. It was a statement, not a question.

"What makes you think so?"

"You are practically jumping in place, and I have never seen such a smile on your face."

"I know where it is," she confirmed.

"And you did not when last I saw you, of that I am certain," said Omar. "What has happened since then?"

"I finished doing my homework."

"Explain, please."

"The answer has been in your library for one hundred years, right there for anybody to find."

"I still don't know what you are talking about," replied Omar.

"General Gordon and Sir Richard Burton discussed their religious beliefs, as well as their various adventures, in a series of letters to each other. One page was missing, but Gordon mentioned in a later letter that he had written and sold an article based on whatever it was he mentioned in that letter." She picked up a century-old biography and opened it. "I found the article."

"What is in it?" he asked eagerly.

"The answer," said Lara triumphantly. "The title is *Eden and Its Two Sacramental Trees*."

Omar frowned. "Eden?" he repeated. "The Biblical Eden? How can that possibly tell you where Gordon hid the Amulet of Mareish?"

"Listen," she said, and began reading aloud. " 'The following are the reasons for the theory that the Garden of Eden is at or near Seychelles. I could even put it at Praslin, a small island twenty miles south of Mahé. . . .' "

Omar frowned. "The Seychelles Islands?"

"Yes!" she said excitedly. "He believed there was once a land mass between the East Coast of Africa and India, and that the Seychelles were all that remained of it. I won't go into his reasoning, because some of it is pretty strange, but he believed that Praslin Island was the site of the Garden of Eden."

"And you think—?"

"I *know* it!" said Lara. "Remember I said that given his religious beliefs and his conviction that the Mahdi represented the devil, he would likely hide the Amulet in a Christian church? That was before I read this article. Given a chance, he'd hide it in the Christian Garden of Eden, a land where he was sure God would not allow the Mahdi to even set foot, let alone search for it."

Omar considered this revelation. "It makes sense," he admitted at last.

"Gordon couldn't take it there himself," she continued. "But"—she thumbed through the pages and held the book up—"he even drew maps of Praslin! All he had to do was show one of his loyal Sudanese lieutenants where to hide it, and he could rest secure that the Mahdi would never find it."

"You sound like a believer."

"I'm just trying to see things through Gordon's eyes," answered Lara. "It doesn't matter what *I* think about Eden. The only thing that matters is that Gordon was sure he'd found it." She paused. "I should have thought of this earlier. I've never seen an ad for Seychelles tourism that didn't mention the fact that General Gordon swore it was Eden! I just never put two and two together."

"And what made you put two and two together yesterday?" asked Omar.

"I had a coach."

"A coach?"

"Don't ask."

She picked up a pack of matches from the coffee table, ripped out the reprint of the article on Eden, and set fire to the corner of the pages. She held them over a large ashtray until they were thoroughly aflame, then dropped them.

"What are you doing?" demanded Omar.

"Making sure no one else knows what I've read," she said. "I've memorized the maps, and I've already burned the page with the June 3 letter from the book Ismail gave me last night. I hate the idea of destroying books, but this information is too dangerous to leave lying around. I want you to destroy the rest of the books after I've gone."

"You are going somewhere?"

"Yes," she said. "There's no direct flight to the Seychelles from Khartoum, so I want you to book me on the first flight to Kenya, and get me a connecting flight to the Seychelles. If there's any delay in Kenya—I seem to remember the Seychelles flight operates only two or three times a week—reserve a cottage for me at the Norfolk Hotel."

"There are Mahdists in Kenya," said Omar. "Hassam and I will accompany you."

"No," said Lara firmly. "That will just attract more attention."

"I cannot let you spend any time there alone," he said firmly.

"I won't be alone," she replied. "Once you make my reservations, get in touch with Malcolm Oliver and let him know I'm coming."

"Who is Malcolm Oliver?"

"An old friend. He used to be a white hunter and then a safari guide, but he retired a couple of years ago. He doesn't believe in computers, so you'll have to send a telex or try to raise him by phone. He knows Nairobi far better than you do, and he's as handy with a gun as I am."

"Is there anything else?"

"Yes. I need to change some money. I can't use Sudanese dinars once I'm out of the country, and Kenya and the Seychelles are much stricter about passing British currency than Khartoum is. I'll need Kenya shillings and Seychelles rupees."

"We will go to the Mashraq Bank."

"Let me guess," she said. "You have a brother or a cousin working there."

He smiled. "A half-sister."

"You've got a remarkable family," she said. Then, "Finally, I'll need a small shoulder bag."

"Why? You have no clothes to take."

"I can't wear my pistols on the plane, and I'll never get them past security in a carry-on."

"I will get one for you. Is there anything else?"

"No, that's all. I don't know the plane schedules, but I definitely want to leave today if it's possible," said Lara.

"I will book two seats on today's flight," said Omar.

"One," she corrected him.

"What about Dr. Mason?"

"If Kevin knew about this, nothing could keep him from coming with me," explained Lara. "And if we both leave, the Mahdists will *know* that the Amulet isn't in the Sudan. If Kevin stays here, my guess is that most of them will think I've given up and he's still searching."

"He will be angry."

"I know," she said unhappily. "That's why I'm letting *you* tell him. We'll have breakfast together, and when it's over I'll suggest we go off in opposite directions and meet at some appointed spot in midafternoon. With any luck I'll be out of the country by then."

"And if I cannot obtain passage for you on today's flight?"

"Then I'll meet him where I said I would, and we'll try again tomorrow."

"I will begin to make arrangements right after breakfast," said Omar.

He opened the door and walked out into the corridor. Lara went into the bathroom, splashed cold water on her face, then took the ashes of the burned pages and flushed them down the toilet.

Breakfast was uneventful. Lara announced that she wanted to visit a small library in Omdurman, Mason decided to check the various churches again, and they agreed to meet at the centrally-located French Cultural Centre.

After they had split up, Lara returned to the hotel, and Omar showed up about ninety minutes later.

"Well?" she asked as he entered the suite.

"Your flight leaves at twelve-thirty P.M.," he announced.

"Good. What about the connecting flight to the Seychelles?"

"That is a problem," he reported. "The next flight from Kenya to the Seychelles is on Tuesday."

"From Nairobi?"

"Yes."

"Is there an earlier flight from Mombasa?"

He shook his head. "The Nairobi flight will stop on the coast to pick up more passengers from Mombasa."

She shrugged. "Well, if I have to spend three days in

Kenya, I have to." She looked around. "What about a shoulder bag?"

"Mustafa has purchased it, and will meet us at the airport. I'm sure you're being watched. Why walk out of the Arak with luggage and alert them to the fact that you're leaving?"

"I can't walk into the airport wearing my guns," she pointed out.

"You won't have to. He'll be waiting for us in the parking lot." He paused. "Malcolm Oliver was not answering his phone, so I sent a telex. I hope he receives it, but just in case he does not, I stopped by a cyber café and e-mailed one of my uncles who lives in Nairobi to make sure the message reaches him."

"Good," she said. "Then all I have to do is change some money."

"You have to do something else," said Omar. He produced a piece of paper and proceeded to write eight words on it.

She stared, frowning. "This isn't Arabic or Sudanese," she said. "Or any other language I know."

"It is a phonetic transcription of the language of the Sudan from the time of Mareish," said Omar. "It has been passed from father to son, from leader to leader, since the death of the great sorcerer."

"What is this all about?"

"Mareish knew the evil that the Amulet could do in the wrong hands. He had every intention of destroying it, but he died prematurely, and the Amulet was buried with him."

"I know that," said Lara.

"But what you don't know is that after he created the Amulet, he told his apprentice how it could be destroyed—indeed, the only way to destroy it."

"This is the spell you mentioned to Abdul. The one he called a fairy tale."

"This is no fairy tale," said Omar.

"Then why didn't Mareish's apprentice use the spell to destroy the Amulet?"

"Because the apprentice knew the seductive power of the Amulet, its ability to corrupt even a man of noble character, and he feared to touch it, so he passed the secret on to his son, who passed it to his son . . . and it has been passed down to me, and now to you." Omar pointed to the paper. "Commit those eight words to memory, and then destroy the paper."

"If they'll destroy the Amulet, why not just say them now and be done with it?" she asked.

"They will only work when the person who utters them is in physical contact with the Amulet. Gordon hid the Amulet because he did not know how to destroy it. It is our most deeply guarded secret, and I have entrusted it to you. Do not let us down, Lara Croft."

"I'll try not to." She read the words, repeated them four times, and when she was sure she had memorized them, she handed the paper back to Omar, who immediately set fire to it, then got to his feet.

"Shall we go?" he said.

She nodded and followed him out.

The staff at the Mashraq Bank seemed surprised to see a European enter the premises, but Omar's half-sister handled the transaction swiftly and efficiently, and soon Lara and Omar were riding a beat-up, rust-covered thirty-year-old cab to the airport.

Mustafa was waiting for them with a secondhand leather bag, a small lock, and the key.

After stowing her guns and locking them away, she shook his hand, then did the same with Omar, and walked into the airport. She handed in her ticket, showed her passport, waited tensely while the computer read its bar code and approved it, and walked through to the terminal.

She had sat down on a bench to await her flight, when a uniformed man approached her.

"Lara Croft?" he said.

"Yes."

"You are flying to Kenya, are you not?"

"Yes," she answered. "Is anything wrong?"

"There is a two-hundred-dinar exit fee required of all passengers leaving the country, and our computer says you have not yet paid it."

"I'm sorry," she said. "I thought the man who bought my ticket would have paid it." She reached into her pocket, and pulled out some bills. "I'm afraid I've traded in all my dinars. Will you accept British pounds?"

"I'm sure that can be arranged," said the man. "Please come with me. I will take you to our currency exchange."

He headed off to the left.

"Just a minute," she said, pointing to a small Citibank kiosk. "It's that way."

"They will charge you an exorbitant fee for changing your money," said the man. "As a courtesy to our passengers, we will do it for free." •

Something's wrong here, she thought. *If Citibank thought you were changing money for free, they'd pull out of here so fast it'd make your head spin.*

She followed him to a small unmarked door.

"This is our office," he said.

Sure it is. That's why your name's not on the door.

He opened the door and stepped aside to allow her to enter first. A large uniformed man sat behind an ancient wooden desk; a smaller man, wearing an ill-fitting suit, stood next to it. Both smiled at her—and suddenly, without warning, the man who had accompanied her shoved her into the small office and closed the door behind her.

She saw the smaller man swinging at her head and ducked. His hand crashed into the wall, and he howled in pain. The larger man got up from behind the desk, but before he could walk around it she had leaped onto it with the grace of a leopard and delivered a powerful kick to his chin. He staggered back a step, came into contact with his chair, and fell awkwardly into it. She was beside him before he could get up again, and delivered a lightning-fast one-two punch to his face. She could feel his cheekbone shatter beneath the second blow, and she turned to face the smaller man.

He had picked up the phone from the desk and was holding it like a weapon, ready to crush her skull with it. She saw that the cord was still attached to the wall, and dove across the desk, grabbing the cord and yanking it with all her strength, and simultaneously pulling the phone out of his hand and into his face.

He groaned and staggered, and before he could recover she was all over him, pummeling him with her fists, and finally dispatching him with a karate chop across the back of his neck. He dropped like a brick.

She knelt down next to him, going through his pockets to see if there was anything to show which side he was on, when the door opened again, and the man who had led her there took a step inside, gun in hand.

"You're as hard to kill as they said," he informed her. "What a pity they aren't offering a reward to the man who accomplishes it."

"It's a reward you'll never collect," she said, as she pulled the Scalpel of Isis out of her boot and hurled it at him in a single motion. It buried itself in his throat. For just an instant a look of total surprise crossed his face, as if he couldn't believe what had happened. Then he dropped his gun and fell to the floor, dead.

She withdrew the knife, wiped the blade off on his uniform, and stuck it back in her boot. She wanted to search the men and the office, but the public address system announced that her flight was boarding, and it was one flight she didn't plan to miss.

She stuck her head out of the room, made sure no one was nearby, walked out, closed the door behind her, and walked to the boarding area. Then she was ushered aboard the refurbished DC-3, and less than an hour later she was flying toward Kenya. As she leaned back and relaxed for the first time in days, she decided to take a nap until the plane touched down in Nairobi, but the more she tried, the more uneasy she became.

What's the matter with me? she thought. *I know where the Amulet is. I solved the puzzle that mystified everyone for more than a century. In a little while, the world will be safe from the Mahdists. Why do I feel that I'm overlooking something very important?*

She tried to concentrate, but it was useless: She had absolutely no idea what she was trying to concentrate *on*.

Yet every time she started to drift off, she came back to wakefulness with the certainty that there was one more piece of the puzzle to solve, perhaps the most important piece. She was still wondering what it was when the plane touched down at the Jomo Kenyatta Airport in Nairobi.

PART III

———— · ————

KENYA

25

No one was waiting for Lara in the terminal when she got off the plane. She showed her passport to the immigration officer, then went to the baggage claim. She half-expected that her leather shoulder bag wouldn't make it through, but it was there, waiting for her.

She looked around for Malcolm Oliver, couldn't find him, and finally decided to take a cab to the Norfolk Hotel. As she stepped through the doors leading from baggage claim to the airport's entrance, a tanned, white-haired man wearing a khaki shirt and shorts walked up to her and threw his arms around her.

"Welcome back!" said Malcolm Oliver. "It's been a while."

"I'm glad to see you," responded Lara. "I expected to find you at the gate."

"International flight," he said. "We're not allowed to meet you until you've passed through immigration and customs."

"Of course," she said. "I forgot. I've had a lot on my mind lately."

"Well, come along, and you can tell me about it over dinner." He stared at her and frowned. "You've lost some weight."

"A bit," she acknowledged.

"The message I got was rather mysterious," said Oliver, as he led her to his car. "Some Arab phoned me, explained that he was Omar's uncle—as if I was expected to know who Omar is—and told me your life was in danger and I had to meet you here. Then I checked and found your telex, which was a lot less melodramatic, but on the other hand, you've never come here on just a few hours' notice before. What's going on?"

"We'll talk in the car or during dinner," said Lara. "I don't want to be overheard."

"Whatever you say."

They reached his green Land Rover and he opened the door for her.

"A new one, I see," she noted.

"Same as the old one, but with a lot less safaris under her belt," answered Malcolm. "Removable top, four-wheel drive"—he reached under his seat and carefully pulled out a .44 Magnum—"and this."

She smiled. "Why should I be the only one with illegal weapons?"

"Oh, I'm legal," he answered. "I spent a year on the police force back in seventy-eight, right after they put an end to hunting. I never quite resigned, so I'm still permitted to carry it."

"What do you mean, you never quite resigned?" she asked as he pulled out of the airport and turned onto Langata Road.

"I wasn't corrupt enough for that particular administration," he replied. "So after I arrested a number of politicians, I was asked to take a leave of absence. It's been about a quarter of a century, and no one has ever actually fired me, so I'm still officially on the force. I've even made an occasional arrest up in the Northern Frontier District, when Somali bandits would stop my car and try to rob my clients."

"Keep it loaded," she said, nodding toward the gun. "We might run into worse things than bandits."

"Happy to," said Oliver. "You can tell me what kind of things in a moment."

"Why are you slowing down?" she asked. "The Norfolk is fifteen or twenty minutes away yet."

"You need some meat on those bones," said Oliver. "We're pulling in here."

"Where is here?"

"The Carnivore," he said. "I took you here on your last safari, remember?"

"Yes," she said. "I loved it. But we went after dark. I had no idea it was so close to the airport."

Oliver parked and escorted her to an outdoor table. There was a huge, Brazilian-style spit, and at least a dozen game meats of varying types were cooking on it. It smelled so good, and she'd been hungry for so many days, that Lara was afraid she might begin salivating.

"What would you like to drink?" asked Oliver as a waiter approached.

"Just a cola or an orange pop."

He ordered two gin and tonics plus a Coke, and the waiter went off to the bar to get them.

"Two?" she said, raising an eyebrow.

"The other's for you, just in case you change your mind."

"It's not going to happen. I don't drink—and even if I did, I need to keep all my wits about me."

"Perhaps it's time to tell me what this is all about," said Oliver. "I was rather hoping you'd come to enlist me in the hunt for King Solomon's Mines, the way we once discussed."

"Perhaps next time," she said, and began telling him everything that had happened since Kevin Mason had found her buried in the rubble beneath the Temple of Horus and brought her to the Cairo Hospital.

She was interrupted a number of times, as waiters kept approaching the table, each with a different side of meat on a skewer. She chose the impala, the Thomson's gazelle, and the hartebeest, which they sliced off in turn, and passed on the zebra and the crocodile.

She finished her story at about the same time she finished her meal. Oliver signed for the check, got up, and walked her to the safari car. A few moments later they were driving through the center of the huge city, past the Kenyatta International Conference Centre, the New Stanley Hotel, the High Court, all the familiar landmarks.

"It's hard to believe that Nairobi consisted of nothing but two tin-roofed shacks in 1895," she remarked. "I wonder if any city ever grew this big this fast."

"It was tiny back then," agreed Oliver. "The problem is that it's too damned big now. Everyone comes here looking for work. We've got about three million people living here, and the water supply and sewage system weren't built to handle even half that."

"So what happens?"

"What happens is a lot of these poor bastards live in squalor that no one deserves," he said with a sigh. "I wish I could help, but what can an aging safari guide do?"

"Well," replied Lara, "if we ever go hunting for Solomon's treasure and actually find it, you can put your share to use here."

"I suppose there are worse things to do with it," he agreed.

Oliver turned onto Harry Thuku Road and pulled up to the front of the venerable Norfolk a moment later. He opened the door for Lara, then tipped an attendant to park the car.

"I believe you have a room for me," said Lara as they walked up to the registration desk. "My name is—"

"I remember you from your last visit, *Memsaab* Croft," said the desk clerk. "And we have a cottage for you, not a room." He paused. "With two bedrooms, as Mr. Oliver requested."

She stared at Oliver in surprise.

"I didn't know what the problem was," he said. "But I knew you weren't coming on safari. I live in the Ngong Hills, about ten miles from here. If you're going to need help in a hurry, I can't stay there."

"That was very thoughtful," she said. "I'll cover all your expenses."

"Too late," he replied with a grin. "I've already paid for three nights."

"What's a girl to do?" said Lara. "You win."

A porter came up and tried to take her bag from her.

"I'll carry it myself," she said.

"But—" began the man.

"You'll get your tip anyway," said Oliver in Swahili. "But the lady always carries her own bag."

The porter looked at them as if they were crazy, but he finally shrugged and led them through a courtyard, past an aviary, and to their cottage.

"Cottage Number Five," he announced. "This is known as

the Writers' Cottage. Many famous authors have stayed here—
Ernest Hemingway, Robert Ruark, Daniel Mannix . . ."

"I'm sure it will be fine," said Lara before he could continue his litany of writers.

He opened the door, ushered them in, puttered around
showing them the light switches and fans until Oliver gave
him his tip, and then departed.

"What a pleasure it is to be back here!" she said, plopping
down on an oversized chair. "An uneventful flight, a great
meal, and now I'm in the Norfolk. I haven't felt this safe in
quite a while."

"You're not *that* safe," said Oliver.

"What are you talking about, Malcolm?" said Lara. "This
is the *Norfolk*! I don't know about writers, but it's been host-
ing American Presidents and British royalty since Teddy Roo-
sevelt's day. Where could we find better security?"

"I guess you didn't know that the front of the place was
blown apart by a fanatic's bomb on New Year's Eve back in
1981," said Oliver. "They rebuilt it to look just like it's always
looked, but it's hardly attack-proof. Actually, I feel a little uneasy being here, since you registered under your own name.
The bad guys will know where you are by now."

"I told you: The bad guys won't bother me until I find the
Amulet," she said. "It's the good guys who are out to kill me."

"That's my Lara," he said. "All I ever did was hunt angry
elephants and man-eating lions and the like. You're the one
who leads an exciting life."

"Right at this moment I could do with a little less excitement."

"Well, with a little luck, you'll have three days to rest and
relax before you go to the Seychelles."

"I certainly hope so," she said.

They visited and discussed old times for another hour, then
both walked over to the gift shop to purchase some much-
needed bathroom equipment.

When they returned to the cottage, Lara found a robe that
the hotel supplied, laid it out on the bed, then carried the
toothpaste and toothbrushes they had just bought into the
bathroom.

"I've got the blue one," she said. "You can have the red one."

"Whatever you say," replied Oliver from the next room.

She put the toothbrushes in the medicine cabinet, rinsed her hands and face off, turned to the door—and froze.

"Malcolm," she said softly.

"Speak up," he replied. "I can't hear you."

"Malcolm, get over here—fast!"

He got up and walked to the bathroom, where the door was still open.

"Is it dangerous?" asked Lara.

Oliver looked at the snake that lay coiled on the floor between them.

"Don't move!" he said tersely.

"What is it?"

"A black mamba," he replied. "It's the deadliest snake in Africa."

The snake, annoyed by their voices, began raising its head. She stared into its cold reptilian eyes, almost mesmerized for a second.

"I'd better get my Magnum!" he said. "Don't excite him!" He raced out the door before she could tell him to get her pistols out of her bag.

The mamba hissed and raised its head even higher.

Lara slowly, ever so slowly, began crouching down. The snake's head lowered as it kept its eyes level with hers. When she felt she could reach her boot without any awkward motions, she moved her right hand down and slowly, gently pulled out the Scalpel of Isis.

She straightened up, and again the mamba raised its head. The snake was no more than two feet from her, within easy striking distance.

But I'm within easy striking distance of you, too, she thought.

She reached her left hand out very slowly. The snake watched it, unblinking. There was a box of tissues on the sink. Ever so carefully she pulled one out of the box and slowly moved it toward the mamba until it hissed again.

Then, tensing, she dropped the tissue. It fluttered toward

the floor, and the mamba struck—and as its deadly fangs went through the tissue, she grabbed it just behind its head with her left hand and stuck the dagger up through its underjaw with all her strength. The blade went up through the mamba's tongue and out the top of its mouth, pinning its jaws shut.

It began struggling in her grip, but it was unable to sink its fangs into her. She brought the snake's head down again and again against the hard enamel edge of the sink. At some point she realized that it was dead, had been dead for a few moments and was simply jerking spasmodically. She walked to the door of the cottage, pulled the Scalpel of Isis out, and tossed the dead mamba onto the stone patio.

Oliver arrived less than a minute later, Magnum in hand, and saw the dead snake.

"I'm sorry," he said. "Those bastards parked my car a block away."

"He couldn't just have crawled in here on his own, could he?" asked Lara, gesturing to the mamba.

Oliver shook his head. "There hasn't been a mamba in town in years. They're actually getting rather difficult to find." He lifted up the snake's body. "I'd better dump him in the garbage before all the guests start leaving in a panic."

He picked up the mamba and carried it off, returning a few minutes later.

"Well, nothing good is going to happen here," he said. "They know where you are. You'd better get your bag. If they want a second chance at you, they're going to have to find you first, and I know this country about as well as anyone."

26

"So where are we going?" asked Lara as the safari car made its way up the winding road.

"We're going to stop by my house first," answered Oliver. "It's where I've got my old hunting rifle, and Max is there, too."

"Who's Max?"

"He's my dog—a Jack Russell terrier. He's got a hell of a mouth on him. Believe me, nobody's going to sneak up on you when Max is around."

She looked out the window. "I can't really see it clearly, but it looks like the land's very beautiful."

"It is," he said. "Karen Blixen's old estate is just a couple of miles from here."

"And where do you live?" she asked. "I've never visited your house."

"We were always going out into the bush," he said. "You weren't paying to see a house. But it's very close by, on Windy Ridge Road."

"Windy Ridge?"

"It's well-named," replied Oliver. "The way the wind whips through here, especially in the rainy season, it could put Chicago to shame."

"I'll take your word for it," said Lara. "How much property do you have?"

"Four acres," he said. "There are a couple of local leopards living in the neighborhood, but Max lets me know whenever they're around."

"Leopards?" she repeated, surprised.

He smiled. "This isn't Nairobi. This used to be farming

country. Now it's filled with British ex-pats and it's the ex-urbs, which is as built-up as it's ever gotten to be. And as long as there are places to hide, and dogs and horses to eat, there are going to be leopards. They're like coyotes in America; just when you're sure they're gone, when you haven't seen any in a year and you've searched every inch of the countryside and declared the place free of them, suddenly you've got a leop-ard in your lap."

"Now I know why you keep your rifle."

"The rifle's for bandits," he replied. "Oh, I've shot over the leopards' heads a couple of times to scare them off, but my hunting days are over. I've come around to the view that leopardskins look better on the leopards and ivory looks bet-ter in an elephant's mouth."

He turned to the right, and she saw a small sign telling them that they were on Windy Ridge. A quarter mile later he pulled up to a large old wooden house, surrounded by veran-das and patios, and with immaculate grounds.

"It's lovely," commented Lara.

"I wish I had something to do with it, but I only bought it a few years ago, and the gardeners came with it."

The car came to a stop and they got out.

"That's curious," said Oliver.

"What is?"

"Max. He's always here to greet me."

"Maybe he's sleeping."

He shook his head. "Something's wrong."

"Why don't you look for him in the house and I'll check the yard?" suggested Lara.

"All right."

"A Jack Russell terrier, right?"

"Yes."

While Oliver entered the house, Lara began walking around the grounds. There was no outdoor lighting, but wher-ever one of the rooms was lit, it cast some light out onto the yard. It was when she went around the back of the house that she found herself in near-total darkness.

She could see the outline of a small wooden shed about fifty yards behind the house and decided to walk over and check it out in case the dog was there. She was just reaching for the door when she heard a rustling sound behind her and spun around to see what had made it.

She found herself facing the largest leopard she had ever seen. She reached for her pistols and realized that they were still packed away. She pulled out the Scalpel of Isis, prepared to sell her life as dearly as possible.

And then, rather than leaping upon her, the leopard spoke. His mouth didn't move, but she could hear the same hollow tones, the same insubstantial voice, that had told her to find Gordon's letter.

Why are you here? it demanded. *Your path must take you elsewhere, across the sea. Find me, free me, release me, and I will give you dominion over the lives of men.*

"I'm on my way," she said, "but—"

Do not speak aloud, said the leopard silently. *I can hear your thoughts.*

I will be on Praslin Island soon, thought Lara.

Many will still try to stop you.

I know, she thought. Then: *You seem to want me to find you. Will you protect me?*

The leopard snarled.

I yearn to be found, to be used as Mareish wanted me to be used. But I protect no one. If you are worthy of me, you will come to me. If you can be stopped, then you were not the One.

"Fair enough," she said aloud. "Just don't hinder me."

This meeting is done. Move away, for when I release the animal, it will do as it pleases. It has already killed the dog you are looking for.

Lara backed away a few feet and bumped into the shed.

"Fine," she muttered to herself. "I'll wait inside here until you go away or Malcolm sees you and blows you away with his rifle."

She entered the shed and felt around for the back wall, and her hand came into contact with one of Oliver's old hunting rifles. She checked the bolt to see if it was loaded. It wasn't, but she felt numerous boxes of cartridges on a small shelf.

She opened one up and slid it into the rifle, only to find that it was the wrong size.

She looked out the door at the leopard, and could tell by his eyes, by his entire demeanor, that he had regained possession of his body. He began slinking through the grass toward her.

She slipped another bullet into the rifle, and this time it fit. She lined the leopard up in its sights as best she could in the darkness, then stood motionless at he stalked closer and closer, his tail twitching nervously.

Finally, when she was sure that the leopard was about to spring, she fired the rifle over its head. The leopard leapt back, snarling, and dashed away into the night when she raised the rifle again.

Oliver came racing out of the house, rifle in hand.

"What happened?" he shouted. "Are you all right?"

"I'm fine, Malcolm," she said. "Just a close encounter with a leopard."

"Did you wound him?" Malcolm asked urgently.

Lara shook her head. "I also believe leopardskins look better on their original owners. I fired a shot to scare him off."

"I'm surprised that old rifle didn't break your shoulder," he said. "It's a .550 Nitro Express." He looked around. "Did you see any sign of Max? I hope he didn't run into that leopard."

If I tell you the leopard killed him, you'll ask how I know, and I don't think it's an answer you're prepared to hear.

"No," she said truthfully. "I haven't seen him."

"I guess he went off on a hunting expedition of his own," said Oliver. "He does that every now and then. Ah, well, no sense waiting around all night, maybe all weekend, for him. I've got my rifle; that's what I came for."

They returned to the car, where the first thing Lara did was unpack her pistols and wrap her holsters around her hips. She tossed the shoulder bag on the rear seat, and then they drove down out of the Ngong Hills and were soon back on a level road again.

After a few miles she turned to him, and said, "You're heading for the Rift Valley. Why?"

"We're not going that far," he replied. "This is Old Limuru Road. We're only taking it to Banana Hill."

"Never heard of it."

"It's about twenty miles out of Nairobi," answered Oliver.

"What's there?"

"A very pleasant, very peaceful, almost-unknown little hostelry called the Kentmere Club."

"The Kentmere Club?" she repeated. "Didn't we eat there once on the way back from a safari?"

"Did I take you there?" he said. "I don't remember."

"Well, *I* remember," said Lara. "Duck was the specialty of the house, and I also had a wonderful chocolate roulade for dessert."

"That's the place, all right."

"But it's just a restaurant."

"Most people think so," answered Oliver, "but it's actually a hotel. It's got about a dozen rooms."

"Okay," she said. "Why there?"

"It's not in Nairobi, it's not in Naivasha, it's not in Nanyuki, it's not in Nyeri, it's not in any city. And as I say, very few people know it's a hotel."

"Can we stay hidden there until Tuesday?" she asked doubtfully.

"I don't know," replied Oliver. "I hope so. I suppose it depends on how well-organized the other side is. You'd know that better than I do."

If he expected a reply he was disappointed, because Lara remained silent. A few minutes later they pulled up to a lovely old Tudor mansion that looked like it would be more at home in Surrey or Tumbridge Wells.

Oliver walked up to the desk, spoke softly in Swahili, then turned to Lara.

"Do you have any Kenya shillings with you?" he asked.

She pulled out a wad, and he took half of it, handing it to the desk clerk.

"I thought they knew you here," she said as he walked her up the stairs to their adjacent rooms.

"They do," said Oliver.

"Then why did they ask you to pay up front? And why don't they take credit cards?"

"Credit cards can be traced," he said. "And I didn't pay up front."

"Then what was that all about?"

"A third of it was to keep their mouths shut if anyone should come around asking about us."

"And the other two-thirds?"

He smiled. "To make them pretend they didn't see you walk in wearing a pair of pistols. They may seem like part of your clothing to you, but they do tend to make other people very nervous."

"Damn! I forgot all about them!"

"No problem. It's all taken care of." They stopped in front of a heavy oak door and he handed her a key. "Now I suggest you get a good night's sleep. I'll see you for breakfast."

She entered the room. It needed some decorating and updating, but it was clean, and that was all that mattered to her. She took a quick shower, then lay down and was asleep as soon as her head hit the pillow.

She awoke to the singing of birds. She put on her clothes, then walked to the window and looked out. The sun was up, a handful of diners were sitting at tables on the lawn, and the sight and smell of the food seemed to have attracted all the local birdlife.

She walked down the stairs and went outside, where she found Oliver already seated at a table, sipping a cup of coffee.

"Coffee?" she said, arching an eyebrow.

"I know it's sinful for an Englishman," he explained, "but I've had so many American clients who insist on starting the day with it that I've fallen into the habit."

A white-jacketed Kikuyu waiter approached and asked for her order.

"I haven't seen the menu yet," she said. "I'll have some tea when you bring it."

"Yes, *Memsaab,*" he said, bowing slightly and heading off to the kitchen.

"Have a banana or a piece of melon while you're waiting," suggested Oliver, indicating the bowl of fruit in the middle of the table.

She reached for the bowl and a small starling started screeching.

"What's the matter with you?" she asked it. "Hasn't anyone ever told you it's impolite to beg at the table?"

Nobody ever had, and it walked boldly up to her.

"All right," she said, picking up a small grape and holding it out for him.

It stared at the grape for a moment, then reached forward and took it out of her hand.

"How did you sleep?" inquired Oliver.

"Better than I have in days," she replied. "I was exhausted, and that was a very comfortable bed. Now I'm ready to eat." She paused. "What's on the agenda for today?"

"We're leaving," said Oliver, suddenly tense.

"When?"

"Right this second."

"What about breakfast?"

"You don't want it," said Oliver, pointing to the starling, which lay on the ground, twitching feebly. As she turned to look at it, it died.

"No, I don't," she agreed, getting to her feet.

"Let's go!" said Oliver urgently.

"Just a minute," she said. "Someone tried to kill us. Let's find out who."

"They know who you are. You don't know who they are, or how they found you, or even how many of them there are. A betting man wouldn't take those odds."

She considered it for a moment, then nodded. "You're right. Let's get out of here."

She was actually surprised that they made it to the car without getting shot at.

27

Oliver drove north on unpaved bumpy roads for an hour, then headed east toward the mountains.

"Mount Kenya?" asked Lara, staring at the white-capped peak to the country's tallest mountain.

He shook his head. "Too many tourists up at Bill Holden's old place."

"You mean the Mount Kenya Safari Club?"

"Yes."

"Where are we going, then?"

"The Aberdares," answered Oliver. "Except for Meru it's probably the least-frequented national park in the country. There are a couple of game-viewing lodges, but almost no one ever drives through the park. We'll go up into the mountains, and God help anyone who thinks he can sneak up on us there."

"So we'll spend the night out in the park?"

"No, it's too dangerous—and not from your Mahdists and such," said Oliver. "It's no longer politically correct to shoot lions that eat cattle or attack men, so if they can capture them without killing them, they turn them loose up toward the top of the Aberdares mountain range. There's plenty of game for them up there—buffalo, bongo, bushbuck, some other stuff—but they've developed a taste for men. It's the one park where I don't feel comfortable spending the night without even a tent."

"So what are we doing there?"

"Buying a few hours. When it's twilight, I'll drive us to one of the lodges, either Treetops or the Ark. They lock up the approaches at dark, so if we time it right, even if someone figures out that we're going there, they won't be able to get in.

And if they do, well, these lodges are raised on stilts and over-look spotlighted salt licks and water holes, and people tend to stay up all night watching the game. That's a lot of witnesses." He paused. "The lodges use retired white hunters as their animal spotters. I know just about all of them, so wherever we go, I should be able to get a little help guarding you when I get tired."

"I'm pretty good at guarding myself," said Lara.

"I know you are, but there are an awful lot of them and only one of you."

After passing miles of cultivated fields punctuated by little groups of circular thatched huts they entered a small town that was a blend of old colonial structures, a few new stores on the major thoroughfare, and rows of shanties just off the main streets.

"Where are we?" asked Lara.

"This is Nyeri," answered Oliver. "You've passed through here before. We just never stopped when we were on safari." He pointed to a brick building. "That's the White Rhino Inn, the counter-insurgents' headquarters during the Mau Mau Emergency, which the politically correct types now refer to as the Battle for Independence."

"You look like you're pulling in there."

"I am," he said as the car came to a stop. "Wait here for a minute."

It stretched to five minutes, but then he emerged from the inn, carrying two cardboard boxes and a sack filled with cans.

"What have you got?" she asked.

"Some box lunches and a dozen cans of soda pop," he said. "Once we're in the park there's nothing to eat, and you were hungry two hours ago."

"I still am," she said. "It smells delicious."

"There's no law that says you can't munch on a drum-stick while we drive," suggested Oliver, and she took him at his word, pulling out a piece of fried chicken and eating it ravenously.

They came to the entrance to the park a few moments later. Oliver left the car to enter a small kiosk and pay an entry fee, then got back in when a ranger emerged to open the gates and let him through.

"I think this is my favorite park," he remarked as they began driving up the dirt road that wound its sinewy way up the mountain range.

"I thought all you ex-hunters liked the Northern Frontier District best."

"For hunting, yes," said Oliver. "They always had the biggest tuskers up there. But for beauty, I'll take the Aberdares every time. They're always green, and because of the altitude they're never too hot."

"Not that many animals, though," she noted.

"There's tons of animals up here, as many as anywhere except the Maasai Mara," he replied. "But most of them are in the forest, and it's almost impossible to get off the road until we're above eight thousand feet in altitude." He came to a gentle stop. "Take a look off to the side."

She looked out the window. The mountain towered above the driver's side of the car, but her side was parallel with the tops of some trees that grew on the downslope, and she could almost reach out and touch a family of black-and-white Colobus monkeys that were sitting on a limb, grooming each other and staring in curiosity at the vehicle.

"That's another thing I like about the Aberdares," commented Oliver. "Anywhere else you'd have to stand fifty feet below the Colobus colonies and look at them through binoculars—if you could see them at all through all the foliage. But up here they're almost in your lap."

He started the car again, and they drove another two miles, stopping frequently to observe more Colobus monkeys, and once to let a huge bull elephant get off the road before trying to drive past him.

"Did you ever do any hunting here?" she asked.

"Not animals."

"What, then?"

"This was where the King's African Rifles fought the Mau Mau prior to independence, here and over on Mount Kenya." He grimaced. "We won the war, and then Parliament decided it was too expensive to keep an empire, so we gave them independence anyway. Think of the lives we could have saved on both sides if someone had thought of that before the war began."

"It's terrible terrain for a war," she remarked.

"I know," agreed Oliver. "Sometimes you'd look off in the distance, and see your opposite number on a slope, and you knew it would take you at least three or four hours to climb over there and he'd be long gone by then . . . so you just smiled and waved at each other."

"I'm amazed that there's so little residual bitterness," she said. "Everyone in Kenya seems to get along well these days."

"Well, most of the men who fought that war are either dead or else getting up there in years," he replied. "Hell, I was just a teenager when I saw my first action on this mountain. But strangely enough, there was never any lasting enmity, not on either side. It was a war, we all got it out of our system, they got their independence a couple of years later, we got out of the colonization business, they joined the Commonwealth, and everybody was happy."

The road began leveling off, and suddenly they were driving over a flat field. Finally he stopped the car near a waterfall, pulled out his Magnum and tucked it in his belt, got out, and took the box lunches and a couple of cans of pop with him, and Lara climbed out from her side of the car.

"The Gura Falls," announced Oliver.

"You couldn't have chosen a lovelier place for a picnic," said Lara.

"I didn't choose it for its beauty," replied Oliver. "I chose it because there's not a tree or a bush for three hundred yards. If anything from a lion to a Mahdist approaches, we'll have plenty of warning."

"What *do* we do if a lion approaches?" she asked. "I don't imagine my pistols would have much effect from more than a few feet away."

"The only thing to remember is not to run," said Oliver. "They're hard-wired to chase about anything that runs away from them. And don't talk. Human voices seem to irritate the bejabbers out of them."

"So what *do* we do?"

"Just stare at them," he replied. "They don't like to meet your gaze."

"And that's it?"

He chuckled. "Lara, the car's only ten yards away, and I promise you'll see any approaching lions at three hundred yards. But even if the car wasn't there, they probably wouldn't bother us."

"Even man-eaters?"

"I don't like to take chances with man-eaters, which is why we're not spending the night up here, but you have to remember that most of them became man-eaters because the spread of farms and villages had rid them of their natural prey. There's plenty to eat up here, and one of Man's greatest survival traits seems to be that we don't smell very appetizing or taste very good. Feed a hungry lion, or give him a chance to feed himself, and ninety percent of your man-eaters go back to eating what they're supposed to eat." He smiled. "It's the other ten percent I don't trust."

They opened the boxes and began eating the fried chicken and some roast beef sandwiches, washing them down with the soda. When they were done Oliver gathered the boxes and put them in the back of the safari car.

A small family of elephants, four females and two youngsters, broke into the clearing, seemed surprised to see the two humans and the safari car, and gave it a wide berth as they made a sweeping semicircle and disappeared into the bush a few minutes later.

Oliver looked at his wristwatch. "It's just past noon," he said. "We can loaf here for the next few hours, or drive around and pretend we're on safari."

"I'd love to look around the Aberdares," said Lara. "But the Mahdists seem so well-organized that I think it makes a lot more sense to stay here in the open where no one can sneak up on us."

"Whatever you say," replied Oliver, opening another can of soda and taking a long swallow.

"It's nice to just sit and relax and not be shot at," she remarked.

"It's hard to believe all this is because of some trinket that Chinese Gordon stole from the Mahdi more than a century ago." He paused. "What do you plan to do with it if you find it?"

"I'm not sure."

"You can't very well turn it over to a government or give it to a museum, not if a million men are willing to kill whoever you give it to."

"I haven't figured it out yet," she admitted.

"If it was me, I'd take it to Europe and sell it for top dollar. Get filthy rich, retire, and let the Mahdists chase the new owner."

A pair of vultures began circling lazily overhead, riding the warm thermals, and the discussion changed to raptors and other birds, then to the habits of the animals that lived on the mountain range, and before she quite realized it four hours had passed and Oliver got to his feet and announced that it was time to leave.

"We don't want to be in the park at sunset," he explained, "because they lock the gates then and we won't be able to get out until morning. Also, I lied about our identities when I registered at the gate, but by tomorrow, when we don't turn up anywhere else, the Mahdists will figure out who we are, so it's best to be out of here."

"Which lodge will we go to?"

"The Ark. It's closer. If we'd kept driving, we'd probably have wound up at Treetops."

She opened the car door, and suddenly stopped. "Do you smell something?" she said.

"Half-eaten chicken."

"No," she said. "I think it's . . . I don't know . . . maybe gasoline?"

He sniffed deeply. "Yeah, I smell it." He frowned. "Might be a little leak." He handed her the keys. "Start it up and I'll see if anything's wrong."

She climbed onto the driver's seat and turned on the ignition.

"Gun it," said Oliver, who had raised the hood and was peering underneath it.

She put her foot down hard.

"Damned if I can see anything wrong." He lowered the

hood, then pulled himself up onto the passenger's seat. "Long as you're sitting there, you might as well drive. It's not often I get to just lean back and appreciate the sights."

"So we're not losing any fuel?"

"Not that I can tell."

"I still smell that odor."

"Start driving. If we've got a fuel leak, the gauge will show it sooner or later. And I'll check it out thoroughly after we reach the Ark. They've got a pretty well-equipped garage there."

She drove across the flat open area, moved onto the road, and began heading back down the mountain.

"The turn-off's in about three and a half miles," he told her. "We'll still be pretty high up."

The car began going faster, and raced into a sharp turn on only two wheels.

"Go a little slower," said Oliver. "You almost went off the road."

Lara frowned. "I can't!"

"What's the matter?"

"The brakes aren't working!"

"They worked fine all the way up here!" said Oliver.

"Someone at the hotel must have tampered with them!" she said, struggling to hold the road. "We've probably been losing fluid all day!"

They came to another curve. Lara floored the brake pedal. There was no response.

"Try the hand brake!" Malcolm shouted.

Lara yanked the hand brake back; there was no response.

The car kept going faster and faster as it raced downhill. She downshifted to second, and they felt the gears strip. Oliver didn't say a word; he didn't want to distract Lara while she was trying to negotiate the road at high speed.

It was Lara who finally spoke. "We are in *big* trouble!" she muttered, staring ahead out the window.

The brakeless safari car was racing downhill toward a herd of elephants that was standing right in the middle of the one-lane road.

28

On the right was the mountain; on the left were the tree-tops, and a dropoff that would surely kill them.

The car continued careening down the hill, and suddenly Lara leaned on the horn.

The sound panicked the elephants, and they broke for cover on the downslope, pushing the youngest to safety first. One matriarch turned to face the car, trumpeting her rage, ears spread, trunk extended, and Lara was sure they were going to collide with the six-ton behemoth, but at the last second the elephant lost her nerve and raced after the others. The car missed her by less than six inches.

But they weren't out of danger yet, because they still had no brakes and they were still racing down the steep, winding, single-lane mountain road. Every time they came to a curve she leaned on the horn again to warn whatever unseen animals or vehicles might be ahead. Once they almost ran head-first into a bull buffalo, and another time they barely avoided a greater kudu. A pair of baboons were too slow reacting to the horn, and their shattered bodies went flying down the mountain as Lara tried desperately to stay on the road.

Finally she spun onto a turnoff, where the ground leveled out, and a minute later she was able to bring the car to a halt. She sat, tense and motionless, her sweating hands still gripping the steering wheel.

"Where are we?" she asked at last. "Where does this road lead to?"

"We're a couple of miles from the Ark," said Oliver. "Just give my heart a minute to stop pounding and we'll start walking. Once we're there I'll send someone back to tow the car."

"I don't see any other car tracks," she noted, staring at the dirt road.

"Cars don't come to the Ark very often," replied Oliver. "Usually a bus picks up all the tourists at the Aberdares Country Club and drives them here as a group. This is just a service road; it probably gets used twice a week, tops." He opened the door. "Come on. If we hurry we'll make it there before dark."

"Will the place be full, do you think?" she asked, getting out of the car. She unstrapped her holsters and put it and the pistols into Oliver's unused backpack, which she then slung over her shoulders.

"The animal spotter on duty tonight is Franz Theibolt," answered Oliver. "He's a friend from the old days. If there's nothing else available, you can have his room."

"I wasn't concerned about a room," she said. "I just wondered how many people we're going to have to check out before we can relax."

"We'll know when we get there," he replied. "There are maybe fifty-five or sixty rooms, and they usually run close to a full house."

They began walking along the dirt road. A few baboons stopped to watch them.

"Well, that's a comfort, anyway," remarked Oliver.

"The baboons?"

He nodded. "As long as they're out in the open, it means there aren't any leopards around."

A bushbuck loped across the road some twenty yards ahead of them, and then a pair of giant forest hogs appeared, rooting industriously through the high grasses that lined the road. Lara kept waiting for something bigger to come along and claim right-of-way, something like an elephant or a buffalo, but none appeared, and after ten minutes she finally saw the Ark in the distance.

"You know, from here it really does look like Noah's Ark," she remarked. "Or at least like I've always imagined it."

"Except that it's well over a mile above sea level."

"So's the real one."

He stopped and stared at her. "You mean you've actually *found* it?"

Lara laughed. "Sorry, Malcolm. I couldn't resist teasing you. No, I haven't found Noah's Ark. But then again, I haven't looked for it either. Not yet, anyway."

They reached the huge structure in another five minutes. A number of people on one of the viewing platforms spotted them and stared curiously as they walked to a door at ground level.

"Hey, fella!" said one of the tourists. "Can't you read? No one's allowed to go wandering around the area. You have to stay in the Ark."

Oliver ignored him and entered the Ark, then led Lara up a service stairway to the main level, the one that held the bedrooms, the dining room, and the viewing platforms and balconies.

An ancient, khaki-clad man, his thin white hair barely visible against the pink shine of his near-bald pate, walked up to them.

"Malcolm!" he said. "What the hell were you doing walking around here?"

Oliver gave him a cock-and-bull story about poachers and blown tires. Then he and Lara stepped out onto one of the platforms overlooking the salt lick and the water hole. They spent a few minutes watching some giant forest hogs, perhaps the same they had encountered on the service road, come by to drink. A bongo arrived next, went directly to the salt lick, had his fill, took a drink, and soon vanished back into the forest.

When the excitement over Oliver and Lara's sudden appearance had died down, Theibolt caught their eye and wandered down the hall to the very last room. They waited a moment to make sure no one was watching them, then followed him.

"All right, Malcolm," said Theibolt when they had entered his room and shut the door behind them, "what the hell is going on? I haven't heard a gunshot all week, and I'm not so old and blind that I can't tell the lady is carrying guns in her shoulder bag, or that you've got your Magnum tucked under your shirt."

"I can't tell you everything," said Oliver. "But this woman is a friend, and she's in serious danger. We need to stay here for the night."

"We've always got a couple of extra rooms the public doesn't know about," responded Theibolt. He turned to Lara. "What's your name, Miss—and who's after you?"

"You'll live longer if you don't know the answer to either question," said Lara.

"You make it sound very mysterious."

"It's very *dangerous*," said Oliver. "Trust me."

"I believe you," said Theibolt. "Is there anything I can do to help?"

"Yes," said Oliver. "I need to get to a phone tonight."

"We don't have any phones, but we've got a radio, if that'll do."

"Yeah, that'll be fine."

"Anything else?"

"Someone's messed my car up pretty badly. It's about two miles down the service road. Have it towed in and see if anyone can repair it in the next few days, and if not, tow it to the shop in Nyeri. It's going to need a brake job and a new transmission at the very least." Oliver paused. "And I'll need to borrow a vehicle tomorrow morning."

"No problem," said Theibolt. "We've got a few safari cars tucked away. We use them to patrol for poachers. It's about the only excitement I get these days."

"Let's hope we don't bring you any more," said Oliver. "Now, where's the radio?"

"In the manager's office," answered Theibolt. "I have to warn you that it's like the rest of the Ark. Except for the viewing decks, space is at a premium."

"I'll tell you what," said Oliver. "The lady and I will have dinner, and then, after we're sure it's safe, I'll go to the office with you and use the radio. I don't think it'll take more than fifteen or twenty minutes."

"Sounds good," said Theibolt. "It's starting to get dark now, so the money animals should be coming down to drink.

I'd better go back to the deck and tell the people what they're looking at."

"The money animals?" repeated Lara.

"Elephants, rhino, maybe a leopard or two," answered Theibolt. "The stuff the tourists pay their money to see."

He ushered them out into the corridor, locked the door to his room, and escorted them back to the deck. When he began pointing out the obvious to the tourists, Oliver and Lara decided it was time to go grab some dinner.

A burly waiter barred the way to the dining room. "Everyone eats at the same time," he announced.

Oliver pulled out his never-rescinded police badge. "Not quite everyone," he said, flashing it before the man's eyes and brushing by him before he could protest.

Lara joined him, and they sat at a table in the corner of the room, the walls at their backs.

"What do you need with the radio?" she asked as they waited for their food to arrive.

"Your Air Kenya flight is Tuesday, right?"

"Yes."

"At the rate people keep trying to kill you, I'm not sure either of us can last that long," said Oliver seriously. "There are a number of small charter companies operating out of Wilson Airport, the little airport near the Nairobi Game Park. I thought I'd see if I can get us a flight to the Seychelles tomorrow. That way we just might survive."

"We?"

He nodded. "They tried to kill me, too. I have a right to see this thing through to the end."

"I suppose maybe you do."

"Well, that's settled," said Oliver. "I'll try to arrange something for late morning. The kind of small plane we charter will never make it to the Seychelles without stopping to refuel in Mombasa. We're probably looking at anywhere from five to seven hours for the trip."

"Then let's leave earlier," said Lara.

"Can't be done. We're in a national park. They won't let us out until the gates open. If we try to crash through, they'll assume we're poachers and start shooting—and you really don't need any more people trying to shoot you. Anyway, it's a two-hour drive back to Nairobi, so late morning makes the most sense."

Dinner arrived, and they broke off their conversation while they ate. When they were finished Oliver took his leave of her, hunted up Theibolt, and went to the office to use the radio, while Lara began wandering around the Ark.

All the game-viewing activities were in the back, by the water hole, and since she wanted to avoid any crowds she strolled in the other direction. When she reached the front of the Ark she saw a long wooden walkway leading over a gorge to the area where the bus that had brought the tourists was parked for the night. She heard a deep cough, the type a lion might make, coming from the gorge. She went about halfway down the walkway and looked over the railing, but she couldn't see anything.

Then she became aware that she was no longer alone. The burly waiter was slowly approaching her, a wicked-looking butcher knife in his hand. She took a step toward the parking area, then stopped as a smaller man, clutching a dagger, climbed out of the bus and began approaching her.

Undaunted, she reached down for her pistols—and suddenly realized that they were still in her shoulder bag. Instead, she reached into her boot and withdrew the Scalpel of Isis.

Neither man made a sound as they approached her, and she, too, remained silent. Oliver and Theibolt were locked away in an office, working the radio, and the last thing she needed was for some unarmed tourist with delusions of grandeur to hear a commotion and come to her rescue.

She saw no advantage in waiting for them both to charge her from opposite directions, so she quickly appraised both men, decided that the one from the bus would be an easier adversary, and instantly raced toward him. Startled, he took a defensive posture, but instead of charging straight at him she ran toward the railing, leaped onto it, raced down its length until she was even with him, and delivered a swift kick to his head.

He spun around, staggered, and swung his knife blindly at her. She hurled herself through the air, turning a complete somersault eight feet above the ground, and landed directly behind him, where she slashed out with the dagger, sliced his wrist, and caused him to drop his own knife.

He took a swing at her, but it was obvious he wasn't used to fighting without a weapon. She blocked his blow, jabbed a thumb into his throat, then sidestepped his blind charge and listened to his scream as he plunged over the rail and into the gorge.

She turned to meet the waiter. He had the butcher knife held high above his head, and as it plunged down at her she grabbed his hand, fell backward, lifted her feet, and hurled him over her head. His own momentum carried him through the air and he landed heavily on his back, as the butcher knife went clattering along the walkway and finally fell through the wooden slats into the gorge.

The man was on his feet instantly. He reached out for her, and she grabbed his wrist, twisting it sharply. He dropped to one knee, and she landed a blow to the side of his head. He grunted in pain, but was on his feet again a moment later.

The big man began circling to his left, and Lara turned to face him. He took a step forward, she backed away, and suddenly felt the rail behind her.

"I have you now!" he rasped and dove for her.

She tried to sidestep, but his arms were spread too wide, and as he grabbed her the pair of them crashed against the railing. Lara felt it give way, and then they were rolling over the edge, into the gorge. Desperately she reached for the edge of the walkway, and her fingers barely grasped it. The waiter began falling and latched on to her leg.

The additional weight almost yanked her loose, but she kicked his head twice with her free foot, and just when she was sure she couldn't hold on any longer, he lost his own grip on her and fell into the gorge.

Lara looked down, saw both men getting to their feet, and after pulling herself back up onto the walkway, began rushing back to the Ark, planning to lock all the ground-level doors so they couldn't come after her again.

Then she heard an ear-splitting roar, followed by two shrieks of terror.

Well, she thought, recalling what Oliver had told her, *if you know enough not to run away, if you don't panic, you just might live through the night, which is more than you planned for me.*

She resisted the urge to see if they had enough self-control to survive, and went back inside the Ark to have a cup of tea before turning in for the night.

29

They were up at sunrise, and immediately sought out Franz Theibolt. Lara decided to wear her pistols and didn't much care what kind of commotion they caused, but almost everyone was asleep after watching animals all night long.

"Did you get us a car?" asked Oliver.

"Yes," answered the old hunter. "I also got a pretty interesting radio message about two hours ago. Seems a couple of our employees showed up at the park gate, pretty badly bruised, all cut up from running into thornbushes in the dark, and scared half to death. I don't suppose either of you know anything about them?"

"Why should we know anything?" asked Lara.

Theibolt chuckled at her exaggerated innocence, then turned to Oliver. "How long will you need the car?"

"Just a few hours," said Oliver. "I'll leave it at the airport."

"It could take hours to find it in that parking lot," complained Theibolt.

"Wilson Airport, not Kenyatta."

"Oh, that's okay then," said Theibolt. "Remember when that was the only airport in all of East Africa?"

"Yeah," said Oliver. "There are probably still a couple of us who remember."

"Damned jet planes damned near put it out of business," said Theibolt. "It had one of the best bars in town, too. You'd sit there, have a couple of gin and tonics waiting for the plane to land, pick up your clients, drive 'em through the Nairobi Park so they could get their first look at some of the game they'd be hunting, and then haul 'em off to the Norfolk or the New Stanley. Now everything is jet planes and computers and the like." He shook his head sadly. "Time just kind of snuck up when we weren't looking and passed us by, Malcolm."

"It happens to everyone sooner or later," answered Oliver. "At least we're still working."

"Pointing out elephants at sixty yards and explaining to the tourists why they can't walk up and pet one," snorted Theibolt. "Ah, well, I'm in a country I love and I'm getting paid for what I do. Not much sense feeling sorry for myself." He handed a set of keys to Oliver. "Here you are. It's the zebra-striped safari car."

"I hate those stripes," said Oliver disgustedly. "I'd love to have the tour operator who thought up those damned things lined up in my sights." He made a face. "They're just out-and-out ugly. When the game notices them at all, they run the other direction." He turned to Lara. "Are you ready?"

"Yes."

"Then let's go."

He led her to the car.

"What's all that stuff in the back?" asked Lara, looking in through the window.

"Looks like a tent," answered Oliver. He opened the back door. "Yeah, that's what it is. If the rangers can't make it back by dark, it's safer to set up the tent than risk running into an animal."

She put her pistols in the backpack, they got in, and twenty minutes later they passed through the gates and were out of the park. Oliver turned south and headed for Nairobi. When they were a few minutes out of the city Lara turned to him.

"It's only eight-thirty," she said, "and we left without eating. Have we got time for breakfast?"

"Yes, we've got a couple of hours. There's never a crowd at Wilson. Most of the flights are little five-seat charters, or the occasional DC-3 taking tourists to the Maasai Mara." He paused thoughtfully. "As long as we have time, I might as well take you to my favorite local restaurant."

"I thought that was the Carnivore."

"I said local—where I live."

Before long they were on Ngong Road, and they soon pulled up to a very British-looking Tudor-style building.

"The Horseman," announced Oliver, getting out of the car. He pointed to a rail in front of the building. "That's from the old days, when the only way to get here was on horseback. I think the Yanks call it a hitching post."

They entered the restaurant. The walls were covered in a burgundy fabric, and the curtains were held back with brass hooks. Prints of horses were everywhere. Most of the customers were ex-pat Brits who lived in the area.

"It's a nice place to come if you want to get away from the tourists," Oliver told her as they were ushered to a table. A waiter took their order, and a few moments later brought their breakfast to the table. Lara feasted on a mushroom omelet made from ostrich eggs.

"Interesting taste," she commented.

"You use what you've got," he explained. "Someday I'll get you a pizza made with eland cheese and warthog sausage."

When they finished they went back out to the car.

"We'll be an hour early," said Oliver, "but the airport's public rooms are comfortable. Besides, I don't know what our pilot looks like; he's going to have to hunt us up."

"I thought you knew him," said Lara.

"I know his boss," answered Oliver. "An American who flew close to a hundred missions in Vietnam, or so I'm told. When they told him he was too old to fly in the Gulf War, he came out here, bought himself a few Piper Cubs, and went into the charter business. I use his company whenever I have to take a client to Marsabit or Lamu."

"Why?"

"Marsabit's across two hundred and fifty miles of bandit-filled desert, and there are no roads to Lamu, so we fly to those two locations. Not many people go to Marsabit these days, but that's where the greatest elephant of them all used to live."

"Ahmed of Marsabit," said Lara. "I've read about him."

"He was the only elephant ever protected by presidential decree," said Oliver. "He had three or four armed guards who accompanied him everywhere he went until the day he died."

"Did you ever see him?"

"Not in the flesh, but his skeleton's at the Nairobi Museum. I'll take you there someday."

He turned onto Langata Road.

"Isn't that the Nairobi Game Park?" asked Lara as they began driving past a seemingly-endless fence.

"Right," answered Oliver.

"It's just amazing that you've got wild game within sight of the city's taller buildings."

"It's a lovely park," said Oliver. "Better than forty square miles, yet it's actually within the Nairobi city limits. I'll show it to you when we have some time."

"You'll show it to her *now*," said a deep voice from directly behind them. They both turned in surprise and the car almost swerved off the road.

A white-garbed Arab sat in the backseat, a pistol in each hand, pointing toward each of them.

"Remove your shoulder bag *very* carefully, Lara Croft. One false move and I will not hesitate to kill you both right now."

Alone, she might have ducked and gone for her knife, but she knew if she did he'd put a bullet into Oliver's head, so she slipped her bag off and passed it to the backseat.

"Thank you," he said. "Don't even think about looking for your Magnum. I have already appropriated it."

"You weren't in the car when we left the Ark," said Oliver. "You must have entered it at the Horseman when we were eating."

The man nodded his head. "It is well known that the Horseman is your favorite restaurant, Mr. Oliver. One of us has been posted there ever since Lara Croft arrived in Kenya. When you went inside I entered your vehicle and hid under the tents. Now we will enter the game park, and then I believe we can conclude our business."

"If you're going to kill us anyway, why should I drive into the park so you can do it with no witnesses?" said Oliver.

"Because like all other living things, you will do almost anything to extend your life another five minutes," said the man with total confidence. "I know the guard at the Langata Gate is a friend of yours. You will not stop the car or pay a fee, because I do not want you speaking to anyone. Just wave to him as you drive up and then continue through. He will not understand why you didn't stop, but he will not report you."

Oliver did as he was ordered, and a few minutes later they were driving through the park. As they came to the area known as Hyrax Valley, the Arab ordered him to stop the car.

"Get out."

Lara and Oliver got out of the car, followed by the Arab.

"Someone will hear the gunshots," said Lara.

"What makes you think I'm going to shoot you?" asked the man with a grin.

"Let me guess," she said. "You're going to talk us to death?"

"You know, I have always despised liberated women," he said. "You can't imagine how glad I will be to cause the death of one." He pointed to a small glade about two hundred yards away. "I have come here every day for a week. There is a pride of lions living in that glade, a huge black-maned male and four females. They are very hungry."

"What makes you think so?" asked Lara.

"Because every time they have gone hunting for the past three days, I've used my car and my horn to frighten away their prey. They will emerge from hiding any moment and you will be the first thing they see."

Lara glanced quickly at Oliver, who didn't seem unduly concerned.

"Yes, Mr. Oliver, I know that lions are nocturnal hunters, and under ordinary circumstances they might not appear for hours. I also know that men are not their prey of choice." He pulled a black plastic gun out of a pocket. "A child's water gun, available in almost any toy store," he announced. "But this one is filled not with water, but with the blood of a topi that I killed yesterday." Keeping his distance, he squirted Lara and Oliver thoroughly. "Now as soon as the wind changes, I think we can expect some company."

"You're staying until then?" asked Lara.

"Why not?" responded the man. "After all, *I* don't smell like a lion's favorite dinner. Besides, once they begin approaching, I'll watch from inside the car."

They stood motionless in the morning sun for another ten minutes.

"It won't be long now," said the Arab. "The breeze has just shifted."

"You're right about that," said Oliver, looking just past the man. "It won't be long now."

The Arab turned to see what Oliver was staring at and found himself facing a two-ton black rhino from a distance of about fifty yards. He aimed his pistol at the rhino and fired two quick shots. Both missed.

The rhino trotted forward, looking agitated. The Arab shot again at thirty yards. This time they could see the dust rise where the bullet had hit on the beast's massive chest, but it didn't seem to do him any harm. He began trotting toward the Arab, who got off one more shot. Then his nerve broke, and he turned and raced away.

The rhino snorted, increased his pace, and lowered his head as he charged. His horn caught the Arab in the middle of the back, and he hurled him high into the air. The man fell heavily to the ground and lay still. The rhino trotted back to him and gored him a few times with his horn, then seemed to see Lara and Oliver for the first time. He trotted off at an angle, then stopped, turned, snorted again, and pawed the earth. Two more mock charges followed; both times he stopped well short of them.

"He's getting ready to charge in earnest," said Oliver softly.

"What do we do?" asked Lara.

"Get out of his way."

"Have you got any more useful advice?" she said irritably.

"That's not a joke," said Oliver. "This is a lot better than having an elephant mad at you. Remember you told me how you dodged a truck back in Khartoum? Trust me—if you can dodge a truck, you can dodge a rhino."

"Our Arab friend didn't have much luck," she noted.

"He was a fool."

"I'm not a fool, I'm just ignorant," said Lara as the rhino trotted in a little semicircle to observe them from a new angle. "Tell me what the Arab didn't know."

"It just takes nerve, and you've always had an abundance

of that," said Oliver. "If you try to get away when he starts running toward you, the same thing that happened to the Arab will happen to you. But if you can stand your ground until he's ten yards away and lowers his head to impale you on his horn, you can evade him. A rhino is blind once he lowers his head to charge; all he can see is a few inches of grass. If you can sidestep a truck, you can sidestep a rhino."

"You'd better be right," she said tensely as the rhino began snorting again. "I think he's about to start."

The rhino raced toward her. She stood motionless, waiting for him to lower his head—but he didn't. Instead he veered off to the left at the last instant and ran another fifty yards before he stopped and turned back to her.

"What was that all about?" she asked.

"He knows he's blind when he charges," said Oliver, "so he was trying to scare you into running. Watch yourself. Here he comes again!"

Lara watched as the huge beast moved from a trot to a gallop to a dead run. Now he was forty yards away, now twenty, now ten, and finally he lowered his head and she saw the huge horn reach out for her. She took two quick steps to her left—and the rhino continued his charge, not slowing down until he was another forty yards past her.

"I'll be damned!" she exclaimed. "You were right!"

The rhino continued running in a straight direction. He stopped about one hundred yards away and began browsing on some bushes as if nothing had happened.

"He thinks he tossed you," said Oliver. "Otherwise he'd come back and try again." He paused. "They're not very bright animals; that's why they're so easy to poach. Before we get on the plane I'll tell the game department that he's walking around with a slug in his chest. I don't think it did him any damage, but he's going to be in a bad mood for the next few days."

"He's not the only one," said Lara. "I'm getting sick and tired of people trying to kill me."

"Uh . . . it's not just *people*," said Oliver suddenly.

"What do you mean?"

"The wind was changing when the rhino interrupted us," he said.

She turned toward the glade and saw three lionesses starting to approach them.

"I thought the Mahdist said there were four of them," said Lara.

"There are."

Oliver pointed to the roof of the car, where the fourth lioness perched, observing them like a housecat observing a mouse that she was about to have a little fun with.

30

"Don't run," said Oliver softly. "Lions are pretty conservative animals. These have never attacked men before. They may think twice about it."

"How do you know they've never attacked anyone?"

"As I told you, the Nairobi Park is within the city limits," he said. "If they'd killed anyone, the game department would have shot them."

Suddenly an idea occurred to Lara. "What will happen if I walk very slowly?"

"To the car?" he asked. "The old girl on the roof will probably pounce on you if you get too close and she feels threatened."

"No," said Lara. "To the Arab's body."

"Probably nothing," said Oliver. "But if I'm wrong, you'll have less than three seconds before the closest of them is on top of you."

"It's worth a try," she said. "Don't forget: They're hungry and we're covered with topi blood. They're not going to stand back and just watch us all day."

She took a step, then a second and a third. The lead lioness stopped and stared at her curiously.

Two more steps and she was next to the Arab's corpse. She knelt down very slowly, never taking her eyes off the lions, felt around under the man's body, and finally found what she was looking for.

She straightened up very slowly with Oliver's Magnum in her hand.

"It's got too strong a kick for you," said Oliver. "And even if you landed a lucky shot and killed the first one, the other three will be on you before you can take aim again."

"I'm not going to shoot them," said Lara as two of the lionesses began approaching cautiously. Suddenly the lioness atop the car jumped lightly to the ground, no more than twenty-five yards away.

"Then what did you get the guns for?"

"Quiet," she said. "I've got to concentrate."

She turned, lifted the Magnum in both hands, held it in front of her, and took aim at the rhino, who knew that the lions wouldn't bother him and was eating peacefully a hundred yards away.

"I can't kill him from this distance, can I?"

"No," answered Oliver. "But you can annoy the hell out of him."

"Good!" said Lara, squeezing the trigger.

The lions jumped and roared at the sound. She saw a puff of dust rise from the rhino's flanks, and it began galloping straight at her. She stood her ground as the huge creature came closer and closer. The lions, not knowing that the rhino was charging Lara rather than them, broke and ran for cover.

Lara yelled at the rhino to make sure he didn't turn away and give the lions a chance to regroup. He snorted, lowered his head, and increased his speed—and she sidestepped him like the bullfighters she had seen in the arena at Madrid and Barcelona. As he had done before, he kept running, and this time he disappeared over a nearby ridge.

Lara and Oliver raced to the car, and were safely inside it before the lions broke cover and began returning. Oliver put his key in the ignition and drove off. Lara's last sight of the lions was as they were cautiously approaching the dead Arab, determined to eat *some*thing this morning.

"That was quick thinking," said Oliver. "I don't suppose you'd like to join me in the safari business?"

"Some other lifetime," she replied. "I just want to get to the Seychelles."

"We'll get there, never fear."

They drove to the Langata Gate, where Oliver stopped the car and approached the guard's station. He spent a few moments talking, then returned to the car and drove out of the park.

"All right," said Oliver. "I smoothed things over with him and fed him a fable about how we were hot on the trail of a notorious poacher. We even took a couple of shots at him, but he escaped, which at least explains the gunshots if anyone asks about them."

"And the dead Arab?"

"The lions won't leave much, and the scavengers will take care of the rest. There won't be a trace of him by tomorrow."

Suddenly he pulled off the road and stopped at a small dry goods store.

"Why are we stopping here?" asked Lara as they pulled up to the door.

"We're covered with blood, remember?" said Oliver. "There aren't any carnivores at the airport or on the plane, but we're not going to be too fragrant."

"You know, I'd completely forgotten," said Lara, getting out of the car and joining him as he entered the store.

They each bought a khaki outfit, his rather nondescript, hers more elegant and form-fitting, and after another five minutes they pulled into the lot at the Wilson Airport.

"It looks bustling," Lara remarked as a plane touched down and another took off a few seconds later.

"Almost all the in-country flights take off and land here," replied Oliver as they walked to the entrance. "There are scheduled flights to the Mara, Samburu, Lamu, half a dozen other locations. And dozens of charters leave here every day."

"So where's our pilot?" she asked, looking around as they entered the small airport.

"Beats me," said Oliver. "We didn't have a set time—just late morning. These arrangements are always very informal."

"What do we do now?"

"We wait where he's most likely to look for us."

He took her to a small bar and restaurant at the far end of the building.

"This is called the Dambusters 77 Club," he informed her as they sat at a leather booth. "It's ostensibly for members only, but anyone can buy a one-day membership."

She noticed a number of men sitting at the bar, most of them wearing leather jackets despite the heat. "I assume those guys are all pilots?" she said.

He nodded. "Yeah, that's the uniform, all right. This is their hangout. If our guy doesn't show up soon I'll see if we can hire one of them."

He didn't have to worry. A tall, slender man approached them a few minutes later and introduced himself as Milo Jacobi. They could tell from his accent that he was American.

"Pleased to meet you," he said. "I just brought a couple back from the Ngorongoro Crater over in Tanzania. I've got more than enough fuel to reach Mombasa, so we can leave whenever you're ready. Once we refuel on the coast, it's a straight shot to the islands. The Seychelles are about a thousand miles east of the coast, and we'll make about two hundred miles an hour, so figure on a five-hour flight from Mombasa—and we'll get to Mombasa in about an hour and a half. I've stashed some sandwiches in the plane for you in case you get hungry, and a few soft drinks."

"Sounds good to me," said Lara. "Let's go."

He led them out to the airfield, and soon was standing beside his plane.

"It's a five-seater," he said, "so you can both sit in back, or one of you can sit up front with me."

"I'll take the back," said Lara.

"Me, too," said Oliver. "I don't mind flying, but I hate looking out the front window—when you see clouds zigzagging right and left you suddenly realize just how much the wind knocks you around."

Jacobi laughed in amusement. "All right, the backseat it is. Do you have any luggage?"

"Just my shoulder bag," answered Lara. "We'll buy whatever we need when we get there."

If Jacobi found that curious he didn't say so, and a couple of minutes later they raced down the runway and were soon aloft and heading east.

Lara leaned back, relaxed, and looked out the window at the clear blue African sky.

They touched down in Mombasa, refueled, and headed off to the Seychelles.

It was when they had traveled perhaps one hundred miles over the Indian Ocean and were cruising at about 7,500 feet that Jacobi lowered his head and began whispering to himself.

"What are you doing?" asked Lara curiously.

"Praying," he said. Suddenly he reached over to the control panel and killed the engines.

"What the hell have you done?" demanded Oliver, leaning forward.

"I have done what so many others have failed to do," he answered. "I have killed Lara Croft."

"You've killed us *all*!" shouted Oliver.

"Better death than a world ruled by the Mahdi," said Jacobi serenely.

Lara flung herself over the top of the copilot's seat and tried to restart the engines. Jacobi took a swing at her, catching her a glancing blow on the jaw.

She pulled the Scalpel of Isis from her boot and slashed him across the throat. His scream turned into a moist gurgle. She didn't even look at him as she worked the controls.

"Jettison him!" she ordered Oliver.

"The door's on the far side."

"Then lower his window and shove him out. We're losing altitude! We've got to make the plane lighter and buy some time, even a few seconds, while I try to restart the engines!"

Oliver spent about thirty seconds getting the window open, and the plane almost flipped over with the change of pressure, but Lara got the wings level again and Oliver managed to slide the dead pilot's body through the window, where it plunged some 3,800 feet into the ocean.

"Can I help?" asked Oliver.

"Do you know how to fly a plane?"

"No."

"Then you can't help," she said.

"How soon before we crash?"

"If this was a 747, we'd have about five seconds . . . but it's a small plane, relatively light. Even with the motor off and losing altitude, I can probably glide for about three more minutes before we hit the water."

Oliver sat perfectly still and kept quiet, not wanting to distract her. The altimeter showed them dropping to 2,800 feet, then 2,500, then 2,000. At 1,500 he thought he heard the engines trying to catch, but the plane continued to fall. At 800 feet he heard the sound again, longer this time, before it vanished.

He looked out the window. It seemed like the ocean was racing up to meet them—and then, at 300 feet, the engines caught again, and this time they purred to life.

The plane leveled out, then slowly began climbing.

"Crisis over," announced Lara.

"I've had a few more crises than I bargained for," said Oliver. "Do you mind if I move up to the front with you?"

"Not at all."

He carefully maneuvered himself to the empty seat. "I didn't know you could fly a plane," he said.

"You never asked me."

"Do you know how to get to the Seychelles?"

"He's got maps here, and we'll be in radio contact with the Mahé airport in another hour or so."

"Should we report what happened to Jacobi?"

"Who's Jacobi?" she asked innocently. "We rented this plane in Mombasa. We'll return it to your friend when we're done with it."

Oliver smiled and shook his head in wonderment. "You seem to make a habit of saving all the people who thought they were supposed to protect you," he said ironically.

"Not quite all," she replied. "I owe my life to Kevin Mason a few times over."

"Tell me more about this second-generation scholar who rescued you from that collapsed tomb," said Oliver. "We've been so busy just trying to stay alive that I haven't had a chance to ask you about him."

"He's spent most of his adult life searching for the Amulet," she replied. "He's bright, he seems well-read, and he's surprisingly good with his fists."

"You did mention something about that."

"Then what else do you want to know about him?" she asked. "He's the son of one of the world's foremost archaeologists, he's very personable, and he seems to be totally without fear. At least, he was more than willing to risk his life to save mine."

"He sounds like quite a man," said Oliver.

"I suppose he is."

"And handsome?" he asked.

"Why should you think so?"

"Just a hunch."

"Yes," she admitted. "Handsome, too."

"Anything else?"

"Just that he hates what he calls hugger-mugger—but it doesn't stop him from doing whatever has to be done."

Oliver smiled.

"What's so funny?" asked Lara.

"He sounds like a male version of you," he said. "At least he does if he's rich. Do you miss him much?"

"That's none of your business."

"*That* much?" he said, amused. "If you're right about the Amulet, we should conclude our business here in a day or two and then you can see him again."

"I'm right about it," she said with certainty.

"Well, if you're wrong, you can always become a ballet dancer, or maybe a broken-field runner in American football," said Oliver. "You dodged that rhino like you were born to it. Most people lose their nerve the first time—and of course if they do, there usually isn't a second time."

"It's an amazing piece of information," she said. "I'd never heard that about rhinos before."

"Nobody hunts them anymore," said Oliver. "But they're about as foul-tempered an animal as you'll ever find. These days poachers just spray them with AK-47s, but back in the old days, when it was still a sport, you'd just wait for a rhino to charge, then step aside and stick a bullet in his ear as he ran past." He shrugged. "I know it looks terrifying to the uninitiated, but actually it's quite routine."

"Shut up, Malcolm," said Lara. "I'm trying to compliment you."

"It's not necessary," he replied. "There are a lot of things I don't know. I'm totally ignorant about art and music and most of literature. I flunked math in school. I haven't seen a movie in thirty years, or a play in even longer. But if there's one thing I *do* know, it's my own business."

"I'm impressed anyway."

"No need to be," said Oliver. "What kind of guide would I be if I got lost in the bush or didn't know my animals?"

"Okay, you win," she said with a smile. "I was wrong. You're nothing special after all."

And suddenly, there was an almost audible *click* inside her head as the final piece of the puzzle, the one that had troubled her on the flight from Khartoum to Nairobi, suddenly fell into place.

PART IV

— • —

SEYCHELLES

31

They touched down and coasted to a stop, then taxied back to the terminal. It was an odd airport, with 747s from France side-by-side with small passenger aircraft that made the circuit of the out islands, and even smaller planes, such as Jacobi's, in among them.

"No one's questioned why you needed landing coordinates?" asked Oliver.

"No," she said. "It seems to be a very laid-back place. And given how many private planes there are here, it's only natural that some of the pilots would need directions." She climbed down to the ground. "I'm surprised that it's not more humid."

"Ocean breezes," suggested Oliver, joining her. "Besides," he added with a grin, "they wouldn't allow too much humidity in Eden. The Seychelles have been cashing in on General Gordon's description for a century or more." He looked around. "I wonder where Praslin is from here?"

"Twenty miles north and east," said a voice, and they turned to find themselves facing a tall man in his fifties, his grizzled face browned from the sun, a thick gray beard reaching down to his chest, piercing brown eyes trained upon Lara. He was dressed in a white outfit that wasn't exactly Western, wasn't exactly Indian, and wasn't exactly Arabic.

"Who are you and why have you approached us?" she demanded.

"Do not be afraid, Lara Croft," he said. "My name is Ibraham Mohammed el-Padir. My cousin told me you would be arriving and asked me to watch over you."

"You're another of Omar's cousins?"

"Yes. I am here to serve you."

"Prove it," said Lara.

The man nodded, as if he had expected her to test his claim. "Omar told me to tell you that he had 'burned the rest.' He said you would know what that meant."

Lara smiled. "Pleased to meet you, Ibraham," she said. "Now, I have something in my shoulder bag that I don't want to take through customs and immigration. Do you know a way to get it through unnoticed?"

"I can do that," said Ibraham. "But *you* must go through Customs."

"All right. Bring it to my hotel."

"Where are you staying?"

"I knew we'd be landing just before dark, and I thought it would be too late to take the ferry to Praslin Island, so I reserved at the Beau Vallon Beach Resort tonight. Then tomorrow we'll go over to Praslin." She took off the bag and held it out to Oliver. "I believe you have something you'd prefer not to take through Customs, too?"

"It's no problem for me," he answered. "As I told you, I'm still officially on the Kenya police force, and I have a license for the Magnum. They'll let me carry it through as a professional courtesy."

"You're sure?"

"I've done it in other countries."

"All right," she said. "Ibraham, we'll meet you at the hotel as soon as we get through all the red tape."

She left her bag with him, and she and Oliver went off to clear customs. They passed through quickly and without incident, had their passports examined and stamped, and soon caught a cab. It drove west for a few miles, then turned right and shortly thereafter pulled up to a sprawling, luxurious structure right on the beach.

They walked through the spacious tiled lobby to the desk that overlooked a huge T-shaped swimming pool. Lara stopped at the desk, waited while the clerk found her reservation, and picked up keys to adjacent rooms.

"Have you no luggage, Madame?" asked the clerk in a heavy French accent.

"It's coming from the airport," she answered. "Don't bother calling the bellboy. We'll find our own way."

She checked the numbers on the keys, then began walking down a long, cool corridor, the walls painted in muted colors, until she came to their rooms. She handed one key to Oliver, then opened her own door with the other.

The room was spacious and filled with all the amenities of a five-star hotel: mini-fridge, complimentary robes, a walk-in closet, coffeemaker, hair dryer, whirlpool tub, and sliding doors to a private patio facing the water. She was still exploring its features when there was a knock at the door.

"Come in, Malcolm," she said. "It's not locked."

"It should be," said Ibraham, entering the room and tossing her shoulder bag onto a leather chair. "You are not safe here."

"I won't be here that long," she said. "In the meantime, I have a question for you."

"Ask it, and I will do my best to answer."

"I know the Seychelles were a former British possession . . ."

"That is true."

"So why does almost everyone who works at the hotel and the airport speak with a French accent?"

Ibraham smiled. "Have you ever heard of the Chevalier Jean-Baptiste Queau de Quinssy?"

"No."

"At the dawn of the nineteenth century, the Seychelles were a French colony. Then came the Napoleonic Wars, and first the British claimed them and then the French did. De Quinssy was the administrator of the Seychelles, and though he was French by birth his only concern was for the islands, not for the politics of two nations that were thousands of miles away. So whenever a French fleet put in to port in Mahé he flew a French flag, and when a British fleet approached he flew the Union Jack. And since he never went to war with either side and was never conquered by either side, the English and French who lived here stayed here. Neither was ever forced to leave." He paused. "You mentioned that most of the people you'd met speak English with a pronounced French accent, and that is true; what you don't know is that most of the people you would meet at some of the other hotels or certain government offices speak French with a British accent. It is all because of the Chevalier de Quinssy, who refused to take sides in matters that were truly none of his concern."

"That's a fascinating story," said Lara.

"There are many interesting aspects of Seychelles history," replied Ibraham. "Perhaps over the next few days I can share some of them with you."

"Were you born here?"

He shook his head. "I come from the Sudan. I have been here for nine years."

"What are you doing here? You couldn't possibly have known I was coming."

"I grew tired of the desert. Only mad Englishmen like Gordon and Lawrence love the desert. Those of us who were born there prefer water and green things."

"Makes sense to me," she said.

She walked over to the shoulder bag, withdrew her holsters, strapped it on, and then began checking out the pistols.

"Those are remarkable weapons," said Ibraham admiringly.

"They're Wilkes and Hawkins Black Demon .32s. Fifteen shots to the clip, specially weighted, and with a palm print chip lock."

"They are very impressive," said Ibraham. "What do you call them?"

"What are you talking about?"

"Your weapons." He pulled out a small pistol from a hidden shoulder holster. "This, for instance, is the Spitting Cobra."

She sighed. "You guys and your toys."

Ibraham frowned. "You must have a name for your weapons," he said in a voice filled with concern. "It is customary."

"All right." She pulled out a pistol and twirled it around an index finger. "This one is called Lara's Gun, and this one"—she pulled out the remaining pistol—"is called Lara's Other Gun. Okay?"

He looked defeated. "Okay."

"Whoops—I forgot!" she said, suddenly removing the holsters.

"What is wrong?"

"I've got to go out, and I can't wear my guns out in the street." She stared at Ibraham. "Maybe you can help me."

"That's what I am here for." His voice took on a hopeful tone. "Would you like me to kill the man you arrived with—the man in the next room?"

"He's my friend," she said sharply. "Leave him alone."

"As you wish."

"I need to find a really fine artisan, someone who works in bronze. Do you know of such a person?"

"I know many."

"I want the best. Cost is no object."

"I can take you there."

"How far is it? I didn't see any shops when the cab drove up, except for the gift shop in the lobby."

"It is not far. I have an automobile here."

"Let's go," she said, returning her pistols and holsters to her bag. "This shouldn't take too long. There's no sense bothering Malcolm."

He led her out of the hotel to a small Japanese car that had seen better days and better decades, headed back to Victoria, and pulled up before a wooden shack a few minutes later.

"You wait here," she said, getting out of the car.

"I will come in and bargain for you."

"I don't need anyone to bargain for me," she said. "Stay here. I'll be fine."

"But—"

"Ibraham, are you going to do what I ask or not?"

"Yes, Lara Croft. I will do as you ask."

She turned and entered the shop, and emerged ten minutes later with her purchase in a small cardboard box.

"What did you buy?" asked Ibraham.

"A remembrance of the Seychelles," she said.

"Where can I drive you now?"

"Back to the hotel."

"Nowhere else?" he persisted. "You came out only to buy a gift?"

"That's right."

His expression said that he would never understand Western

women, but he did as she asked, and a few moments later they were back in the hotel.

"I'm going to go to my room for a minute and then see if my friend would like some dinner. Do you recommend the hotel's restaurant?"

"It is one of the best on the island, perhaps second only to the Scala, which is in the capital city of Victoria."

"Good," said Lara. "Then we'll eat here. Would you care to join us?"

He shook his head. "I am not staying here, and only residents may dine in the hotel restaurant. I will watch you from the lobby or the beach, depending on where you are seated."

"Then thank you for the ride, and I'll see you later. Or at least you'll see me, which is probably more important."

She went down the corridor, unlocked her room, tucked the box into her shoulder bag next to her guns, then stopped by Oliver's room.

"Ready for dinner?" she asked.

"Yes," he said. "I knocked on your door a few minutes ago, but you didn't answer."

"I was asleep; I just woke up."

They began walking to the lobby, then turned and entered the restaurant.

The maître d' escorted them to a table and a moment later a waiter came by to deliver menus and take their drink orders. He seemed offended, as only waiters in very fine French restaurants can seem, when they asked for tea instead of wine.

"By the way, Malcolm," she said, "there's a very nice casino just opposite the restaurant."

"I know. I saw it when I came in."

"I was thinking we might stop by for an hour or two when we're done with dinner."

"Sounds good to me."

They ordered the lobster thermidor, and followed it with Grand Marnier soufflés, then wandered over to the casino. Lara quickly lost more than ten thousand rupees at roulette, while Oliver bet far less and played far more conservatively at the baccarat table. She was looking around for a different game when an elegant young Frenchman approached her.

"I have a message for you, Lara Croft," he said.

"What is it?"

"Your table is waiting for you."

She frowned. "*My* table?"

"Yes. Please follow me."

"And if I don't want to?"

"Then you will continue to live in ignorance," he said. "I assure you that this is not a trap."

"What are your assurances worth?" she asked.

He smiled. "I will enter first. You can watch me every second, even use me for a shield if I have lied to you."

She considered his offer for a moment. "All right," she said. "Let's go."

He led her to a small door that she hadn't noticed at the side of the casino.

"This is it?" she asked.

"Yes."

"You go in first."

"Certainly."

The young Frenchman opened the door and entered the dimly lit room. She followed him in, and the door closed behind her.

"And now I must leave you," said the Frenchman.

He seemed to grow thinner and less substantial, and then he vanished completely.

"Welcome, Lara Croft," said a wispy voice to her right. She spun around to confront it, and found herself facing another manifestation of the sand creature she had seen in the desert. This one sat behind a table; it took human form, though its features were very vague, and it wore a hooded robe. "Sit down."

A chair popped into existence across the table from the sand creature, and she felt an almost irresistible compulsion to walk over and sit on it. She resisted for a moment, just to make sure she could, and then complied with its request.

"You are closer to finding me than anyone has ever been," said the creature. "Others may guess where I am hidden, but you *know*."

"Why do you talk to me through a sand demon?"

"I come from hot dry sands of the desert, and someday I shall return to them. I have power over many things, but foremost among them is the sand."

"Why have you brought me to this room?"

"I know your heart and I know your mind," said the creature. "You will be the one who finds me, but you cannot use me to my full power—yet."

"Yet?"

"I can make a true believer of you." Its clumsy hands pushed a deck of cards to the middle of the table. "Cut the deck, Lara Croft."

"You're going to convert me with card tricks?" she said sardonically.

"Cut the deck."

She cut to a three of spades.

The sand creature reached out and cut to the king of hearts.

"You win," said Lara. "For whatever it's worth."

"I lose. Observe your card."

She looked at the card, and somehow it had turned into an ace of diamonds.

"Good trick. So what?"

"These are not mere tricks, Lara Croft. This is the power you can have over your fellow man. You will never lose, not in battle, not in finance, not in anything."

"Why are you telling me all this?"

"I know what Omar gave you when you left Khartoum. I know you have the power to destroy me. I tell you, Lara Croft, that I will not allow myself to be destroyed. Of all those who have sought me, you are the brightest. Apply that wisdom to use me as I should be used and I shall willingly serve your ends as you will serve mine. But try to utter those eight words, and you will learn the true extent of my power."

And as the words left the sand creature's mouth, the ace of diamonds she was holding instantly metamorphosed into the living skeleton of a huge snake, growing bigger and bigger until it was larger than the black mamba she had killed.

Use me against your enemies, Lara Croft, said the snake silently, its words entering her brain, *or you yourself will become my enemy.*

She leaped out of the chair, pulled out the Scalpel of Isis, and swung it at an angle that would sever the snake's head—but when the blade reached it, the snake was gone.

"Are my skills and powers impressing you?" whispered the sand creature. "We could be effective partners, you and I."

Lara glared at it. "I'm impressed."

"You still have more foes to vanquish," it said. "And I see that you have intuited what is awaiting you on Praslin. I will not help you, but if you overcome the final obstacles, I am yours, and together we will rule the world. Strong men will tremble at the mention of your name, and we will carve a path of blood to the thrones of the world."

And then, suddenly, she was not looking at a humanoid sand demon, but at a tiny pile of sand on the floor, barely enough to fill a small hourglass.

She examined the empty room, and finally opened the door and walked back out into the casino. She went over to where Oliver was standing at a craps table and tapped him on the shoulder.

"Ready to call it a night?" she asked.

"I suppose so," he said. "I looked for you a couple of minutes ago. Where were you?"

"I had an interesting experience in that little side room," she said, pointing.

"What little side room?" he asked.

"*That* one," she said, and suddenly realized that she was pointing at an unbroken stretch of wall, with no sign that there had ever been a door there.

"Never mind," she muttered, and walked out of the casino.

She knew something was wrong as she approached her room. The door was wide open, and there were agonized moans coming from inside. She ran the last hundred feet, followed by Oliver, and found Ibraham lying on the floor in a pool of his own blood.

"What happened?" she asked, kneeling down next to him.

"A man," he gasped. "He was searching your room. I tried to stop him, but I was too clumsy. He knocked me down, and before I could get to my feet, he shot me. He had a silencer on his gun, so no one heard."

She opened his robe to stanch the bleeding.

"You haven't been shot," she said, surprised. "You've been stabbed."

"That came later. The Silent Ones also came looking for you. They were very . . . methodical," whispered Ibraham. "I refused to speak for as long as I could endure it, but finally I could not help myself."

"The man who shot you—was he a Mahdist?"

"Yes," said Ibraham weakly.

"Who was he?"

He tried twice to get the words out, and failed. "Praslin," he finally rasped. "They know you are going to Praslin."

Then his body jerked spasmodically, and he died.

"Maybe we'd better postpone our trip to Praslin until we can enlist some help," suggested Oliver.

"No," said Lara firmly. "I've had enough of Mahdists and Silent Ones and things that go bump in the night. Tomorrow we're going to Praslin after the Amulet of Mareish, and one way or another I'm going to settle matters."

"Meanwhile, what are we going to do about poor Ibraham?"

"Make sure he didn't die in vain, that's what."

"I mean, about his body. We can't just leave it lying here. We have to dispose of it somehow."

"I don't suppose you brought along a pride of hungry lions?" Lara asked.

"Sorry," said Malcolm. "I reckon we'll have to try and sneak him out without anyone seeing us. If the police start asking questions, you'll never get to the Amulet."

"Check and see if the coast is clear," said Lara. "Meanwhile, I'll get the sheets off my bed to wrap up the body."

When Lara returned to the room, the bedsheets bundled in her arms, she found Malcolm looking at the empty spot on the floor where the body had been. Now there was only a small pile of sand.

"You didn't take the body into the bedroom while I was gone, by any chance?" asked Malcolm.

"No," said Lara. "It was the Amulet. Like I said, it *wants* to be found. And it looks like it wants me to find it enough to smooth my path a little."

Malcolm looked pale. "But . . . what do you suppose happened to the body?"

Lara shook her head. "I don't know, and I don't want to know."

"Amen," said Malcolm.

32

Lara waited until the first rays of sunlight appeared on the horizon before knocking on Oliver's door. He emerged, totally dressed, a few seconds later, and they walked to the lobby and checked out of the hotel.

They hailed a cab and took it to the waterfront at Victoria, then transferred to the ferry, and two and a half hours later set foot on the smaller island of Praslin.

"It's everything Gordon said it was," remarked Lara, looking at the empty white sand beaches, the endless variety of flowering shrubbery and trees, and the palms looming over the beach. "It's not difficult to see why he thought he'd found Eden."

"I think it had something to do with the *coco de mer*," said Oliver. "I read somewhere that he was sure it was the forbidden fruit, and that the breadfruit tree was actually the biblical Tree of Life."

"I've seen photos of the *coco de mer*," replied Lara. "If he really thought it was the forbidden fruit, he must have thought Eve was thirty feet tall. Those things are the size of a basketball, and it would take an enormous set of jaws to bite into them."

"Well, we're here, for better or worse," said Oliver. "What now?"

"Now we stop by the Solare Car Hire and see if the car I reserved is waiting for us."

"You rented a car?" he asked. "Just to get to the hotel?"

"I may have other uses for it," said Lara, looking around at the various small buildings for the Solare agency. "Ah, there it is."

They walked over, and a moment later they were driving down the narrow tarmac road in a late-model Mercedes convertible.

"I don't even know where we're going," remarked Oliver.

"Our hotel."

"That's what I meant," he said. "Which hotel are we staying at?"

"Well, it's not exactly a hotel," she replied. "Don't look so distressed, Malcolm. The Chateau de Feuilles has a five-star rating."

"I'd have thought you'd be staying at L'Archipel," said Oliver. "It's supposed to be the most luxurious hotel in all the Seychelles, and I know you like your luxury."

"I wish you'd seen some of the places where I slept in the Sudan before you told me how much I liked luxury," she said with a smile. "Anyway, I chose the Chateau de Feuilles because it consists of one main house with half a dozen rooms and four cottages, all built into a hill. It's very difficult to get to, and it's so small that once you're there it should be even more difficult to hide. No Mahdists are going to sneak up on us, not at the Chateau de Feuilles."

"You make it sound inaccessible," he replied. "Can we actually drive there, or do we walk the last mile or two?"

"They assured me we could drive right up to the front door. They also told me that their driveway is quite long and drops off precipitously on both sides, which means they'll know if anyone follows us in a car."

"Where is this hidden paradise?"

"On the Baie Ste. Anne—Saint Anne's Bay to non-French-speakers."

"And where's that?"

"I'm not sure. But they told me how to get there. It's not difficult; there's only about twenty-five miles of road on the whole island, and only about half of it is paved. If we just keep going in this direction, we'll get to their turnoff sooner or later. They're about as far from the ferry dock as you can get, but on this small an island, that means they might be a fifteen- or twenty-minute drive, tops."

"I realize that you're the brains of this operation and I'm

just along to ride shotgun," said Oliver, "but wouldn't it make more sense to go to wherever you think the Amulet is right now, find it, and get the hell out of here?"

"We'll get around to it," she said. "Right now, though, I want to check in and have that breakfast we skipped on Mahé."

"It's your show," he said in resignation. "I don't even know what the damned thing looks like."

"No one does—not exactly, anyway."

"Then I don't know how you expect to find it."

"I've figured out where it is. All I have to do is go there and hunt for something that doesn't belong."

"I don't know why," said Oliver, "but I have a feeling you're making it sound easier than it's going to be."

"Perhaps," she said noncommittally.

"I also have the distinct impression that you're not telling me everything you know."

"I'm sorry you feel that way," said Lara.

"I'm sure you are," he replied. "But I notice you didn't deny it."

She made no reply, and they drove the next five miles in silence, just appreciating the scenery as they circled the island. They came to a sign proclaiming that they could turn left to the Vallée de Mai National Park—the center of Gordon's Eden, the lush green valley that boasted the *coco de mer* forest. She passed it and continued along the coastal road until she came to a small sign directing them to the Chateau de Feuilles. She turned onto the resort's narrow driveway, and finally the main building came into view.

She parked in front of it, went in, and registered in fluent French, then turned to Oliver as they walked back outside.

"Did you understand any of that?" she asked.

He shook his head. "I don't speak a word of French. It was hard enough to learn Swahili."

"Well, we each have a cottage of our own overlooking the bay. We'll find the keys in the locks. I've got to leave the car here. There's just a narrow path to the cottages. I got us the two that are farthest away from the Chateau." She began walking. "Let's put the guns away and see what the place looks like, and then we'll come back for breakfast—or lunch, if it's as late as I'm afraid it is."

Oliver followed her as she went down the path past a large swimming pool surrounded by lounge chairs. The path turned toward the bay, and suddenly they came upon a quartet of very elegant cottages. She walked past the first two, then stopped at the door to the third.

"I'll take this one," she said.

"Are you sure you wouldn't prefer the one that's closer to the water?"

"This'll do fine. I'm going to take a look inside. Why don't you check yours out, and I'll meet you right here in, say, five minutes?"

"Okay."

She entered her cottage as Oliver went off to inspect his own. The floors were a bronze-tinted tile, the walls were a cream-colored stucco, and there was a trio of ceiling fans. The bed was king-sized, and centered under mosquito netting that could be rolled down at night. There was a ceramic-tiled bathroom with everything she'd come to expect of a top-rated hostelry, and a stairway leading to a loft that had another bed.

She looked out the picture windows. There was a lot of foliage there, thick and heavy; it would be difficult, almost impossible, for any intruders to get past the main building unseen, but if they did, they could sneak up to her cabin with impunity. They could even approach by boat and come up from the bay. The Chateau de Feuilles may have been safer than L'Archipel, but no place was safe for her until she finally got her hands on the Amulet.

Still, there was no sense worrying about it. She'd come this far and survived; she had only a little farther to go.

She opened the door and stepped back out onto the path, where Oliver joined her a minute later.

"There're two bedrooms in mine," he said.

"I've got a bedroom and a sleeping loft."

"Why don't you move to my cottage?" he suggested. "I can protect you a lot better if we're in the same building."

"It's not necessary, Malcolm," she said.

"I'm an old man," he said. "I'm not making a play for you."

"I know you're not." Then, just to make him feel better, she added, "I'd be flattered if you were."

"I just think you'd be safer if—"

"I'm fine," she said so firmly that he let the subject drop.

They walked to the restaurant, which actually consisted of a series of linen-covered tables on a patio with a beautiful view of the bay.

"What next?" asked Oliver when their food had arrived and their waiter was out of earshot.

"It's such a pretty location, I think we'll just relax and spend the day here enjoying it," said Lara.

"Correct me if I'm wrong, but I thought we came here to find the Amulet before they kill you," he said, puzzled.

"They're not going to try to kill me until I find it," she replied. "I'm tired of being shot at. Let's take one day off."

He frowned. "You've got something up your sleeve, and you're not telling me what it is. How can I help you if you keep me in the dark?"

"I don't need any help today."

"Even superwomen need help," he continued. "You told me that your friend Mason saved you two or three times back in Egypt."

"I'll need help tomorrow," she said. "And I promise that I won't hesitate to ask you for it."

"Tomorrow?"

"Tomorrow. But today let's just enjoy Chinese Gordon's Eden. I might even take a drive to the Vallée de Mai."

"Not without me," said Oliver.

"Not without you," she agreed. "How about right after we eat?"

"Whatever you say."

Half an hour later they were in the Mercedes, driving into the valley of the famed *coco de mer*. The trees towered above them, a small stream ran alongside the road, the birdlife was profuse and noisy, and it seemed that every flower on the island was in bloom.

"It's gorgeous, isn't it?" said Lara, slowing the car down and studying her surroundings.

"Very," said Oliver.

"Then why do you look so uneasy?"

"I keep looking for assassins behind every one of those trees," he replied.

"Don't. They're not there."

"I can't help myself."

"Just enjoy it. It's a beautiful day."

"*You* enjoy it. I'll keep looking."

They drove from one end of the valley to the other, then took a newly created road that entirely circled the forest. They passed endless flowering shrubs and trees, a picturesque small stone chapel, even a few *coco de mer* trees that seemed almost to have fled the valley and taken up residence on its outskirts. Finally she turned the car back toward the Baie Ste. Anne, and in another quarter hour they were back at the Chateau.

"Wasn't that fabulous?" she enthused as they walked back toward their cabins. "I've spent too much time under the ground. Every now and then it's nice to remind myself of the beauty that's on top of it."

"It was pretty."

"Just pretty?"

"My tastes were formed in Africa," replied Oliver. "It's pretty, but I'll take the Ngorongoro Crater or the Northern Frontier District."

"That's all right," she said with a smile. "There's no shame in being a Philistine."

He laughed. "I'll say this for Praslin. Nothing bites. Except the people."

"Another argument for it being Eden."

"Well, it's early afternoon," said Oliver. "What now?"

"Now I think I'll take a nap."

"You're kidding, right?"

"Why should you think so?"

"People have been trying to kill you all across Africa. Now you're within miles of what you're after, and you're really going to sleep?"

"Got to get my beauty rest."

"You're not kidding?" he said. "You're really going to take a nap?"

"I'm really going to take a nap. Wake me about eight o'clock for dinner."

He stared at her as if she was crazy, but finally he walked back to his own cottage. And then Lara did the one thing Oliver was sure she wasn't going to do: She went into her cottage, lay down on the king-sized bed, and went to sleep.

She woke up as a cool breeze came through the window, and saw that it was already dark out. She washed her hands and face, then sat out on her patio until Oliver came by to take her to dinner.

"What did you do with your afternoon?" she asked as they ate.

"Not much. Walked around. Looked for ways an enemy could approach your cottage." He paused. "You're really not very safe there. They don't have to come down the driveway and past the desk. They can walk a mile or two through the underbrush, or even come up from the sea."

"I know. But the slope is very steep. If they slip, we'll hear them."

Besides, she thought, *I've done my sleeping for the day. I won't sleep again until this is ended one way or another.*

They spoke about Africa and the Seychelles, about old times and future plans, and finally dinner was over.

"I think I'll buy something to read," Lara announced, walking to the small gift shop. She looked over the selection, picked up a science fiction novel and a murder mystery, then joined Oliver as they walked back to their cottages.

"I'd offer to visit for awhile," he said. "But unlike you, I didn't take a six-hour nap, and we were up pretty early this morning."

"That's all right," said Lara. "I have my books."

"All right, then," he said. "I'll see you in the morning."

"Good night, Malcolm—and thanks for all your concern."

"I wish you meant it. I have a feeling it just annoys you."

"I do mean it." *Which is why,* she added mentally, *I'm not going to endanger you if I can help it.*

He went off to his cottage, and she entered her own. She closed the rest of the windows so the insects couldn't fly in, then turned on a light, sat down on an easy chair, and began reading.

When she finished the science fiction novel, it was three in the morning, late enough for everybody to be asleep. She picked up her holster and the item she had purchased on Mahé.

This is why I chose this cottage, Malcolm. You're an old hunter. Your senses are better than the average man's, and there's always a chance that you'd hear me if I had to walk past your cottage.

She opened the door, quietly stepped out onto the path, walked up to the parking lot, got into the Mercedes, and drove off.

She was back an hour later. She returned silently to her cabin and picked up the mystery novel.

After she'd read a couple of chapters she got up and paced the room nervously, then sat down and forced herself to continue reading. Sleep was out of the question, but she needed all the rest she could get.

This was going to be one hell of a day.

33

Lara looked out the window and estimated that the sun would be rising in about half an hour, and she knew that Malcolm Oliver usually awoke with the sun. She checked her pistols, made sure the clips were full, put half a dozen spares in her holster, then put everything into her shoulder bag. That done, she opened her door very quietly, and shut it gently behind her. Then she walked silently to the registration desk.

There was no clerk on duty, but the night watchman nodded a greeting to her. She looked around, found a piece of paper, and wrote a note to Oliver, stating that she'd driven to the Amitie airstrip to buy some more clothing, plus some other items she'd forgotten to bring along.

"Will you please see that Mr. Oliver sees this?" she said to the watchman. "He's the gentleman in the very last cottage."

The watchman stared at her and pointed to his ear. She repeated her request in French, and he picked up the note and began walking out the door with it.

"No," she said in French. "Don't wake him. Just make sure he sees it when he wanders over for breakfast. I'm sure he'll be looking for me; just tell him that I'll be back in a couple of hours."

"*Oui, Mademoiselle.*"

"*Merci.*"

She got into the Mercedes, started the engine, went up the long driveway, and turned onto the main road. The sun came up as she was driving to the little community of Grand Anse, about a third of the way around the island. She checked her side mirrors; the road behind her was empty.

As she neared Grand Anse she drove past three side roads and turned off on a fourth. A quarter mile away stood a small white brick church, its grounds immaculately kept. No one was anywhere to be seen.

She parked the car, opened her shoulder bag, and removed her pistols, sliding them into her holsters. Then she got out and began walking cautiously toward the church. Some birds set up a commotion, but she ignored them and concentrated on the sides of the building, looking for any lurking enemies.

Finally she reached the front door of the church and entered. A rather pudgy priest was standing beside the altar, and he turned to face her.

"How may I help you, my child?" he asked.

"You can't, Father," said Lara. "But I can help you."

"Oh?" he asked curiously.

"Get away from here."

"I beg your pardon?"

"There's probably going to be some trouble here in just a few minutes," she said seriously. "I want you to leave before it begins."

"If there's trouble, then this is the place for me," protested the priest.

Lara pulled out one of her Black Demons. "*This* kind of trouble, Father."

His eyes widened, and he gulped hard.

"Who is after you, my child?"

"I haven't got time to explain," said Lara. "Just leave. If any shooting starts while you're still here, I won't be able to protect you."

He looked at her guns again. "God be with you," he said, and walked rapidly out of the church.

Lara approached the altar and carefully began removing a loose stone at the back right-hand corner. Suddenly she heard a stick break as someone approached the church.

Tensing, she released the stone and pulled her guns, training them on the door.

A shot rang out, and she threw herself down behind the altar. She heard the sound of shattering glass hitting the stone floor and realized that the bullet had come through a window on the side of the building rather than the door.

She took a deep breath, then stood up and fired both guns at the window. Two, three, four, five shots rang out almost instantaneously, and a man screamed in agony.

She saw a flurry of motion out of the corner of her eye, and turned to face the door. Two men had rushed in. She fired again, and put a bullet between the eyes of the slower one. The other crouched behind a wooden pew.

She looked up, saw a ceiling fan spinning lazily above the man, and put three quick shots into the rod that held it in place. The rod broke, and the fan fell on the hiding man. He yelped in pain and surprise and jumped to his feet, and a Black Demon spat four .32 slugs into him.

A face appeared at another window. She fired half a dozen shots, and it vanished.

She knelt down behind the altar, pulled fresh clips out of her holster, inserted them, and then listened intently. When she heard the sound of feet shuffling, she stood up and began firing. Three more men dropped just inside the door. A fourth turned to flee, ran into the door frame, careened back into the church, and paid for his mistake as she riddled him with bullets.

She hid behind the altar again. When there was no more noise and no more gunfire, she slowly stood up, looked around carefully, then cautiously walked to the door. There was nobody else in sight, just bodies piled up by the door and beneath the two windows. Their silence throughout the fight made her sure that her attackers were Silent Ones, as she had expected. But if her guess was right this was just the beginning.

Could I have been wrong? she wondered, frowning. *Did I set this up for nothing? Where are you?*

She stepped over the bodies, and walked back to the altar. There had to be a back entrance, maybe two, but she didn't dare leave the main body of the church. It would be too easy for still more gunmen to enter and take up defensive positions behind the pews.

She stood there, almost motionless, guns trained on the

open door for the better part of ten minutes. Then, finally, she holstered her pistols and went back to work on the heavy stone at the end of the altar.

She never heard the bearded man sneak up behind her. By the time she sensed his presence and turned to face him, his knife was already plunging down toward her.

"Thank you for leading us to the Amulet," said the man. "Now prepare to—" A single shot rang out, the knife fell from the man's hand, and he flew backward as if kicked by a mule.

"I was almost too late," said Kevin Mason, standing in the doorway, a smoking pistol in his hand.

"Thank you, Kevin."

"I couldn't very well let him rob you of the Amulet," replied Mason.

"You can put the gun away now," said Lara.

"You didn't let me finish," said Mason, keeping his gun trained on her. "I couldn't let him rob you of the Amulet, because that's *my* job. Please remove your guns *very* carefully, and then lay them on the floor."

She withdrew her pistols and did as he ordered.

"Now kick them under one of the pews."

She shoved them under a pew with her foot.

"You don't seem very surprised, Lara," commented Mason.

"I'm not."

"Why don't you just stand by that wall over there, where you won't be tempted to dive for your guns? I'll finish extracting the Amulet myself."

Lara walked to the far wall of the church as Mason, never taking his gun off her, approached the altar.

"May I ask a question?" said Lara.

"Certainly. I owe you that much."

"Is there really a Kevin Mason Junior?"

"Not anymore. I killed him in Cairo after I brought you to hospital. That's what I was doing when I left you for a few hours to get a room at the Mena House."

"Why?"

"I knew that if you were going to lead me to the Amulet, I'd have to be someone you trusted. Mason's son was actually an engineer who specialized in building bridges. I figured you'd never heard of him. If you don't mind telling me, where did I slip up?"

"It was a bunch of little things," said Lara. "At the time I wrote it off to you being under pressure from all the 'hugger-mugger' you kept complaining about. Then Malcolm Oliver said something on the flight from Kenya to Mahé that brought it all home to me." He looked at her expectantly. "He said that he might be ignorant of art and science and history and culture, but if there was one thing he knew, it was his business."

"There's nothing profound about that."

"No, but it got me to thinking. You said that you examined four churches, but only two survived from Gordon's era. You didn't know that a dhow is a *felluca* in Egypt. You had theoretically made North Africa your life's work, and you didn't know that the Sudan became independent in 1956. You studied Sudanese history, and you never heard of Siwar, one of the great historians. You've been to Khartoum a number of times, and you didn't know where the museum that housed your father's collection was. Any one could be excused; add them up, and it's clear that you're an impostor." She paused. "And there was something else. You said your sources told you the men who attacked us in the truck were Mahdists. Omar found out they weren't. That means you didn't have any sources in Khartoum."

"Oh, but I do have sources in Khartoum," he said. "I just couldn't reveal their existence."

"Who are you?"

"I am Khaled Ahmed Mohammed el-Shakir. But you can keep calling me Kevin, if you like—or, in just another minute or two, Mahdi."

"You're no Arab."

"I'm a Circassian," he said. "Surely you know of us."

"The fair-skinned Arabs."

He nodded. "My parents immigrated to England when I was three. I grew up there, had all my schooling there, even took an English name, though of course it wasn't Kevin, but I always knew that my destiny, a great destiny, lay elsewhere. I first heard of the Amulet of Mareish almost sixteen years ago. That's when I joined the Mahdists. When I learned that the famous Lara Croft was in Edfu, indeed at the Temple of Horus, I figured you had to be looking for it. Then, after I searched through the rubble and couldn't find it, I realized that either you'd beaten me to it or it was hidden elsewhere. Either way, I had to rescue you. If you'd found it, I'd take it away and kill you; if not, I'd impersonate Mason's son and let you think we were partners while you hunted it down." He paused. "I must admit I never thought it would be in the Seychelles. How did you know it would be right here, in this church, inside this altar?"

"There were hints in Gordon's letters to Burton, and hidden clues in his diary and in the maps he drew. I just pieced them all together."

"Serves me right for never reading books," he said. He stared at the altar for a moment, then looked back at Lara. "It occurs to me that if I use both hands to move this cornerstone, I'll have to set my gun down, and I wouldn't want to encourage you to do anything rash, so why don't you come over and move the stone yourself?" He stepped back a few feet. "I'm fully aware of the damage you can do with that beautiful body of yours. Just remember that I'm beyond your reach, and that I've got a gun trained on you."

"Why didn't you just let your Mahdist henchmen get it for you?"

He laughed. "First of all, you killed the lot of them. And second, they weren't my henchmen. Every attempt on my life back there in Cairo and the Sudan was real. The Silent Ones were after me for the same reason they were after you. As for the Mahdists—I was assigned by them to get close to you, win your confidence. But not to claim the Amulet for myself." He paused and the smile left his face. "Eventually they realized that I was going to betray them and become the new Mahdi instead of turning over the Amulet to one of their choosing. Now move the stone, please."

Lara walked over, placed both hands on the stone, planted her feet, and pulled at it. It gave way, and finally came off the altar, revealing a bronze amulet the size of a drink coaster, perhaps three inches in diameter.

Khaled Ahmed Mohammed el-Shakir stared at it in rapt fascination, and took a step or two toward it—and as he got within reach, Lara hurled the stone at the hand that held the gun.

It clattered to the floor, and as el-Shakir reached for it, Lara kicked it across the floor of the church.

"Don't make me kill you," he said ominously. "I have other plans for you."

"Don't worry," she said. "You're not going to kill me."

He lunged for her, but she was too quick for him. She ducked under his outstretched arms and leaped lightly over a pew. He pivoted and ran for her again, and this time all he got for his trouble was a left to the stomach and a sneaky right that smashed the cartilage in his nose.

He bellowed in rage and landed a glancing blow on her shoulder. It spun her around, and he delivered a powerful left hook to her jaw.

He thought he'd slowed her down enough to retrieve his gun from the far side of the church, and he began running toward it, but Lara saw what he was trying to do. She jumped onto a pew, ran down the length of it, and flung herself into the air. Her outstretched hands reached what was left of the rod that had held the fan she'd shot down, and she swung as far as she could on it, then released her grip.

Her feet landed on el-Shakir's back, and plunged him face-first into the wall of the church. He staggered, then turned to face her just in time to see her kick his gun away again.

He approached her more cautiously this time, watching not only her hands but her feet, but again she was too quick, and landed a spinning kick to his ribs that knocked him backward to the wall.

Careful, she told herself. *You're showing too much skill. You'd better let him deliver a few blows or he'll never buy what you've got planned.*

She planted her feet and waited for him. Just as he got within reach she lowered her guard, not much, only a few inches, but enough to present him with her unprotected chin.

He delivered a roundhouse right that knocked her spinning against a pew. She made sure she fell over it and was slow getting to her feet.

She stood up just in time to catch a foot to the head, swung a couple of weak blows that landed but didn't do any damage, and braced herself for the haymaker she could see coming.

She almost lost consciousness when his fist crashed into her face. As it was, she fell to the floor, and it was no act when she found herself momentarily too weak and dizzy to get back to her feet.

"That was stupid!" he said angrily. He walked over to the altar, picked up the amulet, and placed it around his neck. "At last!"

"You win," muttered Lara, still on the floor.

"And I will never lose again." He frowned. "You know, there was something between us before, something real. I could feel it." He stared at her as she wiped the blood from her mouth. "I could have made you my queen." He put his hand on the amulet. "I still can. Come over here."

She got painfully to her feet and approached him.

"You hate me, don't you?" he said with an amused smile. "I can see it in your eyes."

She didn't answer.

"Now put your arms around me and kiss me," he ordered her. "And mean it."

She put her arms around his neck and gave him a long, passionate kiss.

"Yes," he said when they parted, "they certainly didn't lie about its charismatic powers."

"Am I to be your queen?"

"I'm afraid not," he said. "You still hate me. I could never turn my back on you."

"I love you," she insisted.

"That's the Amulet speaking. But some day I'll remove it, to shower or sleep or for some other reason, and then not only will you find that you hated me all along, but you'll also try to find ways to kill me before I can put it on again." He stared at her. "Still, you *did* lead me to it. I owe you something for that.

Say that you accept me as the Expected One, and I will reward you by letting you live."

"I acknowledge that you are the Expected One."

"All right," he said. "You have been Forerunner to my Messiah. I will not harm you further today, and nothing can harm me. I'll be leaving for the Sudan later this morning. It would be best if you never returned there, because if we should ever meet again I will consider you my blood enemy." He stared at her and a fanatical glow seemed to spread across his handsome face. "You have the Mahdi's solemn word on that."

And then Khaled Ahmed Mohammed el-Shakir walked out of the Grande Anse Church, his prize around his neck, ready to lay claim to the ownership of the world, and to cleanse the path to his throne with the blood of all who opposed him.

34

Lara picked up her pistols, then began walking to the Mercedes. On the way she encountered the pudgy priest, who was cautiously approaching the church.

"Are you all right, my child?" he asked her.

"I'm fine."

"I heard gunshots," he said. "Dozens of them. Perhaps hundreds. I waited until I was sure they were done, and then—"

"They're done," said Lara. He was about to continue toward the church when she blocked his way. "Father, you're about to see a sight that will probably sicken and terrify you and will surely make you want to summon the police."

"Is someone—?"

"A lot of someones," she said. "I want you to remember that I urged you to get away to a place of safety."

"I remember."

"That advice saved your life, Father. Now I want you to return the favor."

He looked puzzled. "How?"

"Don't report what you see here for three hours," said Lara. "Four would be even better. After that you can tell anyone you want."

"You are asking me to neglect my duty."

"Your duty is to the living," said Lara. "That's *me*—and I won't remain among the living if you don't help me." She stared at him. "Will you?"

He considered her request for an uncomfortably long moment, then finally nodded his agreement. "I'll do as you ask."

"You'd be a lot happier not even going to the church for a few hours."

"If someone's suffering or in pain, I must go to them."

"Nobody's suffering anymore," she said coldly.

"Go," said the priest. "Your three hours have already started."

She walked to the car without another word, got into it, and headed back to the Chateau de Feuilles. When she got there she found Oliver standing in front of the reception area, his Magnum tucked in his belt.

"Where the hell were you?" he demanded as he walked up to the Mercedes. "And don't give me any crap about the Amitie airstrip. You didn't need your pistols to buy new clothes."

"You didn't need a Magnum to eat your breakfast," she responded with a smile.

"Damn it, Lara, are you going to tell me what's going on or not?"

"It's all but over," she said. "Get in the car. I've got one last thing to do."

A moment later they were driving away from the Chateau again, this time toward the Valleé de Mai.

"So what happened?" persisted Oliver.

"I took care of business," she replied calmly. "In another few hours, all the Mahdists and Silent Ones will know that Khaled Ahmed Mohammed el-Shakir has the Amulet, and then they'll finally stop trying to kill me."

"Khaled Ahmed who?"

"A renegade Mahdist traveling under the name of Kevin Mason Junior."

"Mason! He followed you here?"

"That's right."

"And now he has the Amulet."

She smiled grimly. "Now he has *an* amulet."

"I don't understand."

"You said something on the flight here from Nairobi that got me to thinking, and I realized that Kevin was not who he said he was, that he'd rescued me and kept me alive for one reason and one reason only: the hope that I'd lead him to the Amulet. I knew by the time we touched down in Mahé that if I actually found the Amulet, he'd be waiting to take it away from me." She paused. "Do you remember when I had Ibraham take me to a gift shop in Victoria?"

"You bought an amulet?"

"That's right. No one knows what the real one looks like, just that it was bronze, and may have had a silver chain. They think it may have had a sword and a dagger emblazoned on it, but they're not sure. So I went to the best artisan on the island and picked out an amulet—complete with sword and dagger—that could pass for the Amulet of Mareish."

"I'll be damned," he said.

"The reason I took such a long nap yesterday was that I had to plant the amulet in the middle of the night, when no one was around to see what I was doing. I drove out to Grande Anse, got into the church, put it under a cornerstone of the altar, and came back to the Chateau about two hours before sunrise."

"So for all you know, the real Amulet was in the church, too," said Oliver.

"It's not."

"What makes you so sure? Did you search the church before you hid the false amulet?"

"I didn't have to," replied Lara. "I did my homework, and from all the mistakes he'd made, I knew that Kevin wouldn't do his."

"I don't understand."

"The church was built in 1903. Gordon died in 1885; he *couldn't* have hidden it there," she ended triumphantly. "Any questions?"

"Just one."

"Ask away."

"I know you, Lara, and I know how good you are with *those*," said Oliver, gesturing to her guns. "If you knew he was watching you, he couldn't have taken you by surprise. . . . So why didn't you shoot him?"

"You're not thinking clearly, Malcolm," she said. "What do you suppose would have happened if I'd killed him?"

"He'd be dead."

"And then what?"

"You're still a step ahead of me," said Oliver. "I don't know what you're getting at."

"Nothing would have changed," answered Lara. "Every Mahdist still would be out to kill me because they were sure I'd found it and killed him in a fight over it, and every Silent One would be out to kill me to make sure I never found it. This way Kevin—or rather, Khaled Ahmed Mohammed el-Shakir—becomes the lightning rod. Let them all think he's got it and leave me alone."

"But if it won't work . . ."

"When it doesn't work they'll blame the legend, or they'll blame Kevin—but they won't blame me or come looking for me."

"That leads to another question. He's clearly a dangerous man, so why didn't he kill you?"

"He thinks he's got the true Amulet. It gives him total power over me, which means I can't possibly be a threat to him. And," she added, "both of us were without our guns. If he'd tried to get his weapon to kill me after I threw the fistfight, I'd have dispatched him with *this*." She pulled the Scalpel of Isis far enough out of her boot for Oliver to see it, then pushed it back in.

"So it's finally over," said Oliver. "What do we do now—give him a day's head start and then leave for home?"

"No," she said. "Now we pick up the real Amulet—and we do it fast. I'm in a bit of a time bind. I have to get off Praslin before anyone reports what happened at the Grande Anse church."

"You sound like you know where the Amulet is."

"I've known since Khartoum."

"You never said a word about it, never confided in me," said Oliver in hurt tones.

"Let me amend that," replied Lara. "I've known what to look for since Khartoum. I found it when we were driving around the island yesterday."

"You did? I don't remember a damned thing."

"You didn't know what to look for," she said. "I did."

"What the hell did you see?"

"We're almost there."

"We're almost at the Vallée de Mai," he said. "There's nothing there but the *coco de mer* forest."

"Yes there is," she said, pulling off the road and coming to a stop. "Here we are." Oliver looked out and saw a very small stone building.

"This?" he asked unbelievingly. "We passed it yesterday."

"This," she said. "Take a look at the inscription above the door."

He read it aloud. "Church of the Chevalier, established 1856."

"No one uses it anymore, but it's the only church near the *coco de mer* valley still standing from Gordon's era," said Lara. "If he was going to hide the Amulet in his Eden, this is the place. I spotted it yesterday, and checked the inscription late last night when I was planting the false amulet. This is the place, all right."

She pushed against the door. It creaked open, and a beam of sunlight shone through the dust and cobwebs. There was a cross on the back wall, a small altar just in front of it, four benches—she wouldn't dignify them by calling them pews—and a pair of paintings of the crucifixion on facing walls to her right and left.

"Tiny room," remarked Oliver. He walked around it. "I don't see a thing. Could you have been wrong?"

"It's here, all right."

"Where?"

"Let's find out." Lara turned to the center of the room. "I made it this far. Are you going to help me the rest of the way?"

"Me?" asked Oliver, puzzled.

"No, not you."

Look before you, Lara Croft, whispered the non-voice.

And suddenly the Amulet, the *true* Amulet of Mareish, appeared on the small altar, attached to a thin silver chain.

"My God, there it is!" exclaimed Oliver, stepping forward.

Lara reached out and grabbed his arm. "Stop."

"What's the matter?"

"This is too easy," she said. "Let me think for a minute."

"But you said the Amulet wants to be found. Here's proof of it!"

"But the Amulet didn't hide itself. Gordon's man did—and Gordon would have booby-trapped it, just in case someone from the Mahdi's side ever found it."

"It was invisible," protested Oliver. "Isn't that protection enough?"

"From you and me and even el-Shakir, yes," said Lara. "But the Mahdists have enlisted sorcerers on their side, and for all I know so have the Silent Ones. I have a feeling invisibility doesn't work on them."

Come, Lara Croft. Step forward. Touch me. Feel the power course through your body.

"Just a minute!" said Lara. "Invisibility was the *Amulet's* protection! Gordon would have sent it with a normal man. It'll be booby-trapped the way a normal man would have done it back in 1885."

"But once he touched the Amulet he wouldn't have been a normal man," Oliver pointed out.

"The Amulet's still here," replied Lara. "That means he never touched it. Gordon would have wrapped it thoroughly, in such a way that no part of it could ever come into contact with his man. Once he was here he probably cut the wrappings, or pulled a string and had the wrappings come away, still without touching it." She stared at the Amulet. "All right, we know Gordon himself didn't bring it here, and neither did Colonel Stewart. So it would have been brought by a Sudanese, probably a relatively unsophisticated man who had never been out of the country before. So how would he have protected it?"

She walked slowly around the altar, studying it, trying to spot the trap.

"Knives?" she mused. "Poison dust?" She grimaced. "I'm approaching it wrong. He wouldn't know how to rig that. It's got to be simpler."

She stared at the ceiling above the altar. "It looks intact. Nothing's going to fall on me if I pick up the Amulet. And the walls are solid. Nothing's going to shoot out of them." She circled the altar again. "It wouldn't be something like a mamba, or even a Deathstalker scorpion. He'd know they wouldn't live that long." She leaned over the Amulet and studied the surface of the altar. "Nothing rough enough to break the skin, and even if there was, how long could a poison retain its potency? He may not have been sophisticated, but he wasn't stupid. Gordon would never have entrusted the mission to a stupid man."

She stepped back, still studying the Amulet.

"All right," she continued. "It's not the ceiling. It's not the walls. It's not the surface of the altar. It can't be the Amulet itself, because he never touched it. It's not an animal or an insect. What's left?"

And then: "Of course! Malcolm, go outside and find me a long branch. Trim the leaves off it and bring it back."

Oliver left the church.

I knew you would be the one. With your indomitable will and my limitless power, we will be the absolute rulers of the world. I will impart my secrets to you, and all shall tremble before us.

Oliver returned with a stripped branch and handed it to her. She walked over to the altar.

"Stand back, Malcolm," she said. "I don't know how far away we have to be. Not very, considering it's rigged to kill someone who actually grabs the Amulet, but it doesn't hurt to be on the safe side."

She held one end of the branch and reached out toward the altar, sliding the other end through the silver chain. She slowly lifted it up—and the instant it was no longer in contact with the altar, sharp spring-loaded spikes jumped out in all four directions.

"Not bad for 1885," said Lara. She pointed the branch toward the ceiling and let the Amulet slide down to her waiting hand. As her fingers closed around it, she felt a surge of power and energy such as she had never experienced in her life.

"So we've finally got it!" said Oliver.

"Yes," she said, still trying to adjust to the feeling. She held the Amulet up and stared at it. "It's everything they said it was, Malcolm."

"I know," said Oliver. "It seems to be calling out to me."

"You, too?" she said, surprised.

"It's like a magnet, drawing me to it," he said, a strange look in his eyes. "Whoever possesses the Amulet will never have to worry about money again. Or enemies. He can have every woman he desires. The Mahdi knew nothing but the desert . . . but think of what it could do for its owner in Europe or America!"

"That's why Gordon hid it," said Lara. "He wasn't just worried about the Mahdi. He knew its power to corrupt *any* man or woman."

"Let me see it for a minute, Lara," said Oliver, holding out his hand.

She shook her head. "I don't think that would be very wise."

"I'm not *asking* you," he said. "I'm *telling* you."

"And I'm telling you no. It's affecting you already, Malcolm."

Suddenly he pulled his Magnum out of his belt. "Don't make me use this on you, Lara. I want that thing, and I'm going to have it!"

"What's happened to you?" she said. "I almost don't recognize you any more!"

"I'll kill you if I have to!" grated Oliver. "Hand it over!"

"Then you'll have to kill me."

If she was counting on his innate decency to overcome the effect the Amulet had on him, she was mistaken. He pointed the gun right at her heart and pulled the trigger—

—and nothing happened.

He frowned and fired twice more. There were two more explosions of sound, and still Lara stood there facing him.

He checked the Magnum, searching for the malfunction.

"It's not the gun, Malcolm," she said. "As long as I'm in possession of the Amulet, you can't kill me."

Something snapped inside Oliver, and with a roar of rage he launched himself at her. The force of his attack knocked her over. Ordinarily she'd have pulled out her Black Demons and dispatched him, or at least defended herself with the Scalpel of Isis, but she knew she couldn't be killed, and she had no desire to kill a friend who'd gone temporarily insane due to his proximity to the Amulet.

She tried to get up, but he threw himself on her and began pummeling her with both hands.

It hurts! she thought, surprised. *I thought I was invulnerable.*

You are immortal, said the voice within her head. *You cannot be killed, but that is all.*

"Great!" she muttered. "So I could spend the next five thousand years in a wheelchair!" *And if Malcolm hadn't aimed those shots at vital areas, I'd have three bullet wounds now.*

She tried to push Oliver off, but he was fighting with an energy born of madness, and he kept smashing his fists into her, right, left, right, left.

And then, suddenly, he was lifted high in the air and hurled against a wall of the tiny church.

Lara got to her feet and saw three of the huge, shambling sand creatures, the same that she had seen in the desert, approaching Oliver. He seemed to come out of his madness as they closed in on him, and began screaming in terror.

Two of the sand creatures grabbed his arms, and the third reached out a huge hand and closed it around his head. They each pulled, and his arms and head came away from his body.

Lara turned away in disgust, then realized that she was alone in the church with three supernatural beings that had just killed her friend. She looked to the door, but one of the creatures stood directly in front of it. There was only one window, and it was too small and too high for her to climb through it before they caught her.

She knew from past experience that bullets wouldn't stop the creatures. Maybe the wind might, but there was no wind inside the church. She had once thought water would be effective against them, but there wasn't any water either.

The three sand creatures approached to within ten feet of her, then eight, then five.

She pulled the Scalpel of Isis out of her boot, prepared to sell her life as dearly as possible.

"Come on!" she grated. "I'm ready for you!"

But instead of attacking her, the three creatures knelt down in front of her.

They are the Servants of the Amulet, said a voice deep

inside her head. *As they did with this man, so will they do with all our enemies.*

"There are a lot of Mahdists the world could do without," she said softly. "Not to mention the Silent Ones." *And then,* she added mentally, *we'll go after the murderers, the rapists, the child molesters. Then the terrorist states. And then . . .*

"Hold everything!" she said aloud. "You've got me thinking like *you* now!"

We are bound together, you and I. My power is your power. My servants are your servants, bound to do your bidding.

"Wait a minute," said Lara slowly. "Are you saying that I could have called these creatures off before they killed poor Malcolm?"

Yes.

"I could have saved him," she said dully. "He didn't bargain on being exposed to your power. He only came along to protect me, and that's what he got for his trouble. And now I'm deciding which thousand of my enemies to kill first! Omar was right—no one can help being corrupted by you!"

She held the Amulet up and began uttering the eight words Omar had given to her.

NO! cried the silent voice.

By the fifth word, the sand creatures were rushing toward her, reaching out for the Amulet, but she dove behind the altar and got the last three words out just as one of the creatures' hand was inches from her face.

And suddenly the creatures were gone, replaced by three piles of sand, and in her hand, instead of the Amulet, was a fistful of ashes—and as she stared at them, even the ashes vanished.

Then came the onerous task of burying what was left of Malcolm Oliver. She dug a shallow grave with her hands, and tried not to retch as she put the various parts into it. After she had covered it up, she took the cross from the back wall of the church and planted it on the fresh mound of earth.

I've had it, she thought wearily as she walked to the car. *No more running, no more killing, no more artifacts that are never what they seem, no more watching people I care for lose their lives or their souls simply because they're somehow connected to me. Just no more—not now, not ever.*

PART V

———— • ————

FRANCE

35

The only direct flight to Europe was the Air France jumbo jet, and Lara soon found herself in Paris.

For months she avoided her usual hangouts. In the past she'd always stayed at the Ritz or the Plaza-Athenee, but she didn't want to run into anyone she knew, anyone from what she considered her former life, the life she wanted nothing to do with ever again.

She lived at the small but charming Hotel Brighton, directly across the street of the Tuileries, those mile-long gardens behind the Louvre. It wasn't quite the luxury she was used to, but it was far from unpleasant. Her suite on the fifth floor—it was the top floor, but she didn't consider it high enough to think of it as a penthouse—possessed a pair of small balconies, and when she stood on either of them, she could not only see the Louvre and its glass pyramidal entrance, but also the d'Orsay, the Orangerie, the Place de la Concorde, and, far off to her right, the Arc de Triomphe. Not for nothing was Paris called the City of Light; at night the museums and government buildings were so bright that she could have read a book on one of the balconies.

It was an empty life, devoid of meaning or excitement. Whenever she saw someone she knew she would turn away and head off in an opposite direction. She never ate at Taillevant or Maxim's or Arpege, those $200-a-plate restaurants that she used to frequent. Instead she went to local bistros like the Bar de l'x or Carr's or Le Sablier.

When she ate she ate alone; when she shopped she shopped alone; even when she went to the opera, she went alone. There would be no more adventure for her, no more world traveling, no more hidden treasures that were never what they seemed—and no more friends dying simply because they had the misfortune to know her. She made no plans for the future. She lived her life one unhappy day at a time. Paris was as good as any other city; when it wasn't, she'd move on.

One afternoon she took the tiny elevator down to the lobby of the Brighton, picked up her daily copy of *Le Figaro* from the desk, went out the door, turned to her right, walked about forty yards up the rue de Rivoli, and entered Angelina's. It had become her daily ritual.

"*Bonjour, mademoiselle,*" the hostess greeted her. "I will take you to your usual table."

"*Merci,*" Lara replied, falling into step behind her.

She sat down, ordered the *espresso* that had replaced tea in her affections, opened *Le Figaro*, and began scanning the various articles.

Then a name caught her eye, and she paused and read more carefully. One of the society columnists mentioned that Von Croy was in town. It was the one bright spot in her months of bitterness and isolation. Maybe she would pay him a visit. If anyone could assuage the pain and disillusionment she felt, could convince her that she was not responsible for her friend's fall from grace, it was Von Croy. Yes, she'd definitely see him tonight.

She was just about to put the paper down when something else attracted her attention and she began reading avidly. It was an interview with Dr. Kevin Mason, the famed archaeologist. Toward the end he was questioned about the strange Circassian who had, for a time at least, masqueraded as his dead son. The man had walked boldly into the Seychelles Airport, claimed to be the reincarnation of the Mahdi, announced that nothing could kill him, demanded that he be supplied with a plane to the Sudan, and had actually wounded two of the guards who tried to subdue him before he was shot and killed. They later determined that he had killed more than a dozen men on Praslin Island that morning. Dr. Mason expressed his astonishment at the story, but knew no more details than the reporter did.

She placed a few euros on the table, folded the paper in

half, and stood up. Suddenly she felt the need to visit with friends, to go to the theater, even to get out in the field again. Somehow the belated news of el-Shakir's death had finally brought closure to her self-doubt, her crisis of faith. Yes, friends had died, and yes, friends would probably die again—but wasn't that what soldiers had been doing for eons, to make the world a better and safer place?

"Pardonez-moi, madamoiselle," said a Frenchman at a nearby table. "If you are through with your newspaper, I wonder if you might consider leaving it with me?"

"Help yourself," she said, handing it to him.

"Is there anything interesting in it?" he asked.

"Not a thing," said Lara, walking out into the humid Paris afternoon with a new spring to her stride.

Yes, she thought, feeling as if a huge weight had been lifted from her shoulders, *it was time to rejoin the world.* Tonight she would take Von Croy out for the best dinner he'd ever had, and later, as he sipped his sherry, she would tell him a tale of intrigue and magic and murder that had begun more than a century ago.

YOU'VE READ THROUGH
ONE ADVENTURE

NOW PLAY ALONG
WITH HER IN ANOTHER

★★★★★
– MAXIM

★ EXECUTE A VARIETY OF
STEALTH AND HAND-TO-
HAND ATTACKS

★ EXPERIENCE A BRAND
NEW ULTRA-REALISTIC
GAME ENGINE &
CONTROL SYSTEM

★ INTERACTION WITH
NON-PLAYER CHARACTERS
WILL LEAD LARA DOWN
DIFFERENT PATHS
THROUGHOUT THE GAME

★ EXPANSIVE URBAN
ENVIRONMENTS TO
EXPLORE INCLUDING
PARIS AND PRAGUE

Blood
Violence

PlayStation.2